B. A. Smith lives in Torquay, Devon and likes to write romantic fiction, regency romance and science fiction.

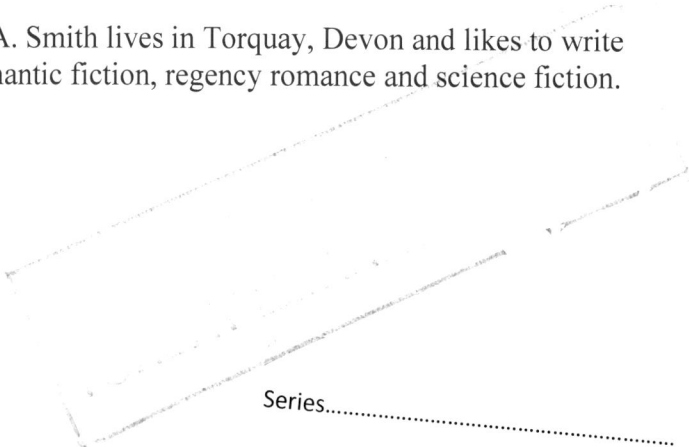

B. A. Smith

HI HAWAII!

AUSTIN MACAULEY
PUBLISHERS LTD.

A CIP catalogue record for this title is available from the British Library.

ISBN 978 184963 540 0

www.austinmacauley.com

First Published (2014)
Austin Macauley Publishers Ltd.
25 Canada Square
Canary Wharf
London
E14 5LB

Printed and bound in Great Britain

Chapter One

Julia saw the man at the end of the corridor, and reminded herself that she was not a stalker. I am a fan and a fellow actor. I admire his acting. I'm crazy about him, I admit it, she said to herself, taking care that her mouth did not. "I am not a stalker," she hissed.

But her mind insisted. You are. You are. Her mind always insisted on the truth. Oh think about it later. This was not the time.

Now she had to deal with the present. The actual, the real experience of seeing him in the flesh.

In the flesh. She had seen him stripped on the seen dozens of times. His real-life appearance did not disappoint. Tall and rangy in a loose young way, his shoulder blades showed through his shirt. He was fashionably thin but the smooth flesh of his body was well muscled and tanned. She knew all this about him before she was close enough to see him for real.

Concentrate on his face. Will him to look her way. She was an actress and must move towards him with all the confidence of an actress, in a normal way, not with out-of-control emotions.

Forget the distasteful stalking thing. Don't be so bowled over that you don't know who you are.

Julia Slater, well known British actress. Well, fairly up and coming anyway. Just rushed from a Dairy Milk ad to meet the most gorgeous man on Earth. Yes, that's better. She was cool. Cool Britannia. And anyway she might not like him in the flesh. The flesh, yes, but the mind, that was a different thing altogether. Slowly the distance shortened. A few seconds seemed like a few hours.

He was casually dressed in a comfortable blue shirt and jeans, standing idly in a curiously indecisive way. In fact, an air of indecision hung over him. Julia picked up on this immediately and she prided herself on her ability to sense vibes in other people. Act casual, she thought. Pounding heart cease to pound. Americans expect Englishwomen to be prissy. Don't be too prissy. Don't act the way Americans expect. That's it. Deep breath. Oh, please don't buckle now that you're looking into his eyes.

"Hi, I'm Julia. Could you tell me, er, is this where the auditions are for *Strangers in the Stars*?"

Julia could tell immediately that something about her face had struck Ellis McCready as peculiar. Delightful amusement crept into his eyes and he half smiled.

"Yes, through this door, but they're not ready yet." He turned slightly as though to move away.

Quickly Julia spoke again. Try a bit of helpless female, she panicked, but not too much. But keep him here.

"I wonder if you could help me? I'm auditioning. My name is …"

Ellis smiled. "I know who you are," he said, in warm drawling tones that set Julia's heart thumping. "You're Julia Slater. I saw you in that Brit TV play about mothers. You were good."

"Thank you. Of course, I know who you are. The star of the *Strangers in the Stars* series himself – Ellis McCready."

He turned away, suddenly sour-faced and stared at the floor. "Yeah, sure. I don't like sequels."

All Julia could say was "Oh." She had never considered that Ellis was not happy about being in the final episode of the series.

He looked up. His blue eyes had begun to register interest. The kind of sexual interest that Julia encountered often. "I don't see why you would want to be in it."

"Oh, I'm a great fan." She hoped she wasn't gushing. "I love science fiction. Everyone's waiting with baited breath for the final episode."

"Everyone's waiting with baited breath," he repeated doubtfully. His gaze lingered on Julia's face. "You might like to, um… fix your face before you go in."

Julia sat down hurriedly on a bench against the wall and whipped out her mirror. "Oh," she wailed, "that stupid make-up girl."

He sat down beside her. "Well we always say that the English have bad teeth, but to have one completely missing at the front…" He laughed at Julia's frantic scrubbing at her tooth.

"I was doing a sort of hick country advert thing, all gingham and jeans, as you see. And hair bunches and a black tooth at the front. And I rushed here…"

Having restored herself to near normality, Julia shook out her hair, and grinned. "My agent assured me that a country cousins advert would get me known over here, but I think he was wrong. I might have known that only a British actress would agree to have her teeth blacked. But then he doesn't think I should do this science fiction either."

Ellis slid along the bench and leaned back against the wall, suddenly more relaxed and friendly. "I don't blame him. I'm in two minds whether to do it myself."

Julia burst out without thinking. "But the fourth episode will be nothing without you. An episode without you would be like fish without chips." She stopped. She really was being too forward. "I'm sorry. It's none of my business."

They sat in silence. Julia wondered if she had offended him. She was acutely conscious of his blue-clad, well-made thigh next to her leg. And his large well-shaped hand on his knee. He really had lovely skin. Blondes often did. Julia thought of her mother. She had been fair and had the same churned butter skin as Ellis.

He turned and regarded her closely. Julia became aware of an optimistic sensation rising within her. He wasn't offended. There was something in his deep blue eyes which told her that he was interested in her. Albeit, an early speculative interest, but it was there. Now she must use all her skills to stop him from seeing that she was so attracted to him as to be completely at his mercy.

"I mean," Julia spoke softly. "I didn't want to seem nosey. I was only speaking on behalf of the nerdish hordes of the

UK." Julia sighed inwardly with pleasure. Here she was, lounging against a wall, face to face with Ellis McCready and he hadn't frozen on her, or run a mile. And he seemed very happy to be in her company as well.

"Well, the nerds of the UK you say. I hadn't considered them."

Amusement made his face so attractive, that Julia could have grabbed him and kissed him right there and then. She felt so happy as to be quite light-headed. She had met Ellis. They had established the beginnings of a friendship.

The auditions door opened. A young man shouted a few words in Spanish at Ellis.

"They're not ready." Ellis thumped his forehead in comic dismay. "We should have known. We're the only people here." He stood up and looked down at her. "Not that I'm sorry. Shall I see you in the canteen for lunch?"

Julia said, "Yes," in what she hoped was a casual way. As she watched his tall figure walk away, out came her breath in a long hiss. She had almost a date with Ellis McCready.

Chapter Two

The cafeteria at the Claremont Studios was a huge, bright, spanking clean, clattering place. Actors taught, of course, to throw their voices, boomed and screeched in a storm of animated chatter.

Julia searched for Barbara and, spotting her sitting alone, looking as usual, sardonic and slightly disgusted, hurried over.

"Now, Barb, no priggishness. Remember this is America. You must look bright, bushy-tailed and eager. And smile, smile and smile." Julia flopped into her chair with a brilliant actorly grin.

"Oh stop it Jules. You look ghastly when you do that. Let's just sit here and look miserable and hope that none of these stupid Yanks join us."

Julia wriggled her bottom on her seat and Barbara opened her eyes wide, questioningly. "You've met him. You've bloody well met him. Lover boy himself. And all I got was the brush off from Mr High and Mighty script editor."

"Mmm, he's as heavenly in the flesh as he is on the screen. And, he's coming to meet me here. I've got that far. A suggestion that we might meet here." Julia began to practice some breathing exercises. No use meeting Ellis in a gasping, schoolgirl state, when one wanted to be so, so, cool Britannia.

"Well, quit the smiling. You're making us look like a pair of lessies." Barbara took out her cigarettes, remembered that there was no smoking and swore softly. "Well, I can tell that you are on cloud nine. But you seem to have sprouted freckles and half of your front tooth is missing. Is that for his benefit? Has he strange tastes in that direction?"

Julia sagged momentarily. "Oh it's that stupid country advert shoot. You know, the only reason they have us over here is to make us look like weirdoes. Imagine J-Lo blacking out a tooth," Julia said crossly, as she got up and hurried to the rest room.

Restored to some normality, and thinking that her tight jeans were good and the check shirt not too unflattering, Julia returned to Barbara. She had brushed out her hair and removed most of the hay. Some hay had fallen down her back and she began to wish that she had taken off her shirt and shaken it. Julia hurriedly swallowed a sandwich and orange juice and forced herself not to keep scanning the room for Ellis.

"I'm sorry the script thing didn't go too well, Barb, but you know you don't give them enough."

"Because, I think that they will steal my ideas," Barbara intoned heavily. "I know. But they will. And they do. All I got was an offer of a part in your baby, Episode Four, *Warlords of the Outer Rim* or some such shit."

"Oh Barb, you know I would kill for a part in that. How did you manage it? I've got to go for an audition this afternoon."

"Well, Mr Donne said my beaky nose was just right for the evil handmaiden who betrays the hero to the whatever."

"The Landlizards, probably the Landlizards. I adore it. I know everything about it. And you get offered a part."

"Yeah, yeah, when your agent thinks a part in this crap film is beneath you but my agent thinks I'm on a roll to get in."

"You're saying that my agent hasn't put me forward. Well, I don't care what he thinks I'm doing it. I'm going to strangle Humphrey when I see him."

"So, you've got the hots for Ellis McCready and your career goes down the tubes. You could get in a top Hollywood film and you're doing crap science fiction for nerds."

"But with Ellis McCready." Julia looked appealingly at her friend. "I can't help that I must have some time with him. I may not like him as a person, I know, the odds are about even. But we've talked. He seems nice. And he's divine."

"A divine God. Not a mucky slob. Not an awkward sod. Not a two-faced dog. Not a nerdy bod or a clever clogs. Divine?" Barbara rattled derisively. "But he may have feet of clay, my poor deluded Julia." She paused and her eyes narrowed, witchlike. "They all have feet of clay."

Julia thought how good Barbara would be for the part of the bad handmaiden, with her dark penetrating eyes, hooked nose and wild black hair. "I shall just be one of the pretty stupid ones twittering in the corner," Julia said despairingly. "If I get in that is. And I do so love Ellis."

Julia knew what her friend was going to say next. Barbara had a soft spot for Gerald.

"And what about Gerald? What's he going to think about this?"

"Gerald and I are finished. As far as I know he's fucking his way around the holy places of Yorkshire, starting with Fountains Abbey and ending up in Ripon Cathedral."

"How is he going to screw someone in a Cathedral?"

Julia jumped at the sound of Ellis' voice. Oh bum, he'd heard her swear. There went sweetness and light. She looked up into his face and tried not to blush. She laughed. "Oh they have a crypt." She was aware that Barbara was grinning, and gave her a dagger look for not warning her of Ellis' approach.

Barbara continued to grin wickedly at Julia and Ellis. Julia sighed inwardly. Her friend could do a lot of damage with her waspish tongue if she decided to be mischievous.

Barb raised her eyebrows comically as Julia introduced Ellis. "Oh, so you're the heart-throb of this sci-fi film I'm in. I'm the wicked handmaiden. I believe we have a rampant sex-scene."

Ellis smiled and sat down. "I'll look forward to it," he said courteously.

Julia's heart jumped. Did this mean that Ellis had decided to be in the film, or was he just being polite?

Barb got up to go for more coffee and Julia said thank you with her eyes for leaving her alone with Ellis. With a provocative wink at Ellis, Barbara sauntered off.

Before Julia could gather her wits and think of something to blot out the unfortunate screwing reference, which had been too far along the way to the final 'farting in bed' debacle of every relationship, Ellis turned electric blue, interested eyes upon her and took up the Gerald story.

"Have you ever made love in a crypt?" he said, amused by Julia's obvious embarrassment. "I mean does it give you a thrill? Is it sacrilege to screw in a crypt? What would happen if you and Gerald got caught?"

The cafeteria seemed to explode around Julia. The noise seemed to well up in her head, particularly the clashing of cutlery from a nearby trolley.

Ellis waited, but his face was kindly teasing, and Julia was able to relax a little. "Oh, no, much too Buffyish, don't you think? Gerald and I are finished, anyway. A long time ago. Quite a long time ago."

"Gerald sounds quite a guy."

"Oh, you know, he's Yorkshire. Very bullish in every sense of the word."

"Sh, sh. The way you say Yorkshire. That's very cute."

"Yes, we get a lot of that from Americans." Julia could not help the faint tinge of boredom in her voice.

Julia's sixth sense began to tremor. She looked at Ellis. There it was in his face. He was teasing her about the *sh*.

"And Fountains Abbey? That sounds a wonderful place. Has it many grand fountains?"

"Well, no, not really. It's a ruin. Thanks to Henry. Though a lot of it is still standing. But it is wonderful, nonetheless."

"Nonetheless," Ellis murmured, his face very close to Julia's. They stared at each other. Where the canteen had been too noisy, the sound had now drifted off somewhere else. It seemed to Julia that Ellis was daring her to explain who Henry the Eighth was. Amusement crinkled his eyes. Julia sensed a trap. Ellis could know more about Henry than she did.

Suddenly Julia began to feel wonderful. If he was teasing her it was affectionate teasing. She felt that they were going to go out, be together. She had thought that a brief chat and professional conduct on the set of the film, would be all that she could realistically have with this man. Now she felt that they were going to be an item. They were going to make love. Oh, why couldn't they fast forward to that right now? Julia caught herself up. Steady on. Men did like a bit of mystery in a woman and women didn't want to be just thrown on the floor and ravished, in spite of that being a general view.

But please let Ellis like me, she prayed. They were both leaning on the table regarding each other. It seemed to Julia that Ellis had moved closer. She could smell his aftershave. A surprisingly sweet and cloying scent. Her surprise at the smell showed on her face. She saw that he had detected it. He was sharp. She must be more careful. The way that her thoughts showed on her face made her good actress but often betrayed her in real life.

Ellis smiled. His over-white teeth were not too regimented and his mouth was now so close that Julia thought for one wild moment that he was going to kiss her.

Thankfully, Julia saw Barbara heading back towards them. Barb would bring everything back to earth with a few pithy remarks.

"Hey, lovebirds," Barbara said provocatively.

Julia felt serene enough to ignore that remark, but Barbara's next comment shook her a little.

"God, what is that pong?" Barbara exclaimed, plonking down her coffee and stubbing out the ciggie she had lit outside. "Don't tell me it's you Ellis? You smell like a French whorehouse."

Ellis sat up straight. "Yeah, I know."

"Don't tell me you're a poofter," Barbara ploughed on regardless.

Julia froze. Ellis was so perfectly handsome, that the fact that he could be gay had sometimes occurred to her, except that, so far, she had never fallen for a gay man. Ellis was twenty-seven years old. Plenty of time to be out.

Ellis regarded Barbara for a moment. "Am I convincing?"

Barbara shrugged. "Well, a good actor, and you're not a bad actor, can almost always convince one. But I think that you're not gay but that you are getting in character. You're thinking of doing that Rock Hudson biopic."

"Well, there's a clever lady. You have your ear to the ground, sure enough. It's Rock Hudson or *Warlords of the Outer Rim*."

Oh do the sci-fi, do the sci-fi, Julia pleaded silently. What if he didn't do the film? If she followed him to another film, he would know that she was a stalker. No, no, she was not a stalker. Oh please, she prayed, let Ellis take the part. The highs and lows of Julia's encounter with Ellis had left her feeling drained, and she was beginning to think that the strange burning and itching tormenting her body was due not so much to Ellis but straw shards from where she had been tumbled in the hay by an enthusiastic cowboy earlier in the day.

"Yes," Barbara considered. "It would be difficult to do Rock. I mean, how could he ever have been gay? But, you know, there was a sign. In his smile. Yes, if you get that smile, you're halfway there. I think you should do it."

Ellis nodded. "I think you are right."

Julia groaned. Did Ellis mean right about Rock's smile or doing the part? Ellis and Barbara turned to Julia in concern.

"Oh," wailed Julia tugging out her shirt to reveal an angry batch of hives on her midriff. "I think I'm allergic to American grass."

Ellis laughed and put his arm round Julia's shoulder. "I have a trailer with a shower and fresh clothes," he said innocently. "Come and freshen up and we will go to the sci-fi auditions together."

It seemed to Julia that she had no choice.

"Don't do anything that I wouldn't do," Barbara called with a leering wink, as Julia left.

Chapter Three

Julia came out of Ellis' shower wrapped in a soft white robe. Ellis was lounging on kind of divan listening to music. Julia gulped. Her throat felt suddenly dry. Her bare toes gripped the green shag pile carpet and she glanced down, amazed at its thickness. Only Americans would have three-inch thick carpet in a caravan. She reminded herself that shag was not a very rude word in America. Julia's heart began to beat faster as she mentally anglicised the word 'shag'. Would she? Certainly not. Even though, incredibly, in the space of a few hours, she had met Ellis McCready and had only to wade a few metres across the carpet to be swept away on a tide of passionate lovemaking.

However, his eyes did not say it. There was no message of desire in his eyes, and surely there was a flicker in hers to ignite a response? Why was he looking merely friendly and uninterested? Her heart plummeted. She could stand here, bare wet feet sinking deeper into the shag pile, wearing nothing but a towelling robe, her dark wet hair swirling around her, her face luminous with showering, and he evinced – zilch!

Julia looked away. "Thanks Ellis," she said heartily, "you've been a brick. Thanks for the – sweats." She seized the tracksuit that Ellis had given her and turned away. Suddenly she stopped in mid-flight. She realised that Ellis was practising for his forthcoming gay role, and that he had been acting the part of a friendly homosexual man. She turned to meet his amused oh so sexy, eyes.

"I'd rather," she said frostily, "that you didn't clutter my downtime with acting."

He had the grace to look sheepish. "I don't usually with my friends. This was too good an opportunity to resist. Julia Slater coming out of my shower. I must have a 'no attractive women' written into the contract – if I do this gay thing, that is. Certainly not you. I wouldn't be able to keep it up." He paused and looked mischievous. "Or down rather."

Julia affected to be only partly mollified. She smiled tightly and then gave in and laughed. "Thanks anyway. You've been very kind." She sat on the edge of a padded bench, a little deflated that he did not consider her a friend.

"Kind!" Ellis laughed, showing his straight, white American teeth. "You just have to tell me that you've really finished with this guy who likes to screw in crypts, and I would describe myself as predatory."

With one swift stride, he was sitting beside her. There was now no mistaking that he was not gay. His kiss was rather sweet and electrifying. Julia was conscious that the robe was slipping off her shoulders, and also that she was fully determined to act like Doris Day. She resisted his tongue and any pressure to lie back. He had removed the poncey perfume and smelt of aftershave. She was full of new sensations – a rosebud opening – a fresh box of Black Magic – a spring meadow in Wales. And him. A little young. A little rough. Honest though, with it. He knew that he was not going to score. Enjoying their first kisses.

When he finally stopped kissing her, Julia tugged the robe collar to her neck. He smiled a smile that said he didn't need that signal.

"Hey," he said tenderly. "I didn't invite you here with any ulterior motive, you know."

"I know. I'm cool. You're cool."

"And a brick!" He pulled her closer.

"I know. I'm sorry. We get afflicted with saying things like that when we're over here. No one says brick anymore."

"And using very big words."

"Yes, that too." Julia snuggled into him with delight.

"OK, I confess. Because we think that you don't know what they mean." Oh God, he's bloody clever, Julia thought as she disentangled herself and kissed him lightly. "We have auditions to go to."

"Umm, the kiss-off." He considered her for a moment. "I like you Julia Slater. He kissed her an end of sexual engagement kiss, light, sweet and full of promise that was somehow one of the most erotic kisses Julia had ever experienced.

As Julia was dressing, she heard Ellis arguing with someone outside the trailer. She could not hear everything that they were saying but it was about Ellis not doing the film.

When Julia came out she found Ellis waiting at the bottom of the trailer steps. "The auditions have been rescheduled for tomorrow," he said, still with an edge of annoyance in his face and voice from his argument. He took her hand. "I'll see you then?"

Julia nodded happily. "If the handmaidens' clothes are as sexy as I think they are, it's better that I get rid of my spotty chest."

"Well?" Barbara demanded of Julia as they left the studios by taxi.

"Well what?" Julia was very tired, and wanted just to look at the blue sky, white buildings and heavy traffic that was Los Angeles in the evening rush hour.

"Oh you poor thing," Barbara said sarcastically. "Up at the crack of dawn cavorting with crazy cowboys in the hay. Meeting the man of your dreams whom you have stalked, no sorry, whose career you have followed for six years. Rampant sex in his trailer. Dumped by himself. Hanging around for auditions that never happen, when you could be getting into the next Dustin Hoffman movie."

Julia yawned. She appreciated her friend's arch sympathy. The trouble was that Barb always liked to know everything and now that Julia had met Ellis, she wanted to hug the enchantment to herself. "We did not have rampant sex."

"So he is a poofter. So you are going to be Julia Slater, third handmaiden, right at the bottom of the credits, below my name, I might add, when you could be Dustin Hoffman with Julia Slater. Julia, darling, is he worth it? Is pretty boy Ellis really worth it?"

"Oh Barb, I find Ellis so desirable. I can hardly hold on to any kind of common sense when I'm with him. I'm exhausted now, just by actually meeting him."

"You do look a bit limp, but it makes you look all sexy when you flop. Ellis noticed it. You definitely melted when he looked at you. You can't analyse sexual attraction. To me, Ellis just looks like a handsome young actor and I suppose I would screw him if he asked me to, but he only has eyes for you, as the song goes."

"And I have to meet him with a blacked-out tooth and spots. And now you're saying I was all swoony as well." Julia groaned. "Oh Barb, one night of passion is all I ask. Just to get him out of my system."

"Well, you should get that at least. You're looking very good. Sort of glowing. So, he must have kissed you in his trailer."

"Yes, he kissed me. But tell me Barb, how do I hide what he does to me?"

Peter Martin was an aspiring Brit actor. He gazed around the poolside of his large Hollywood home, striking a pose very like a young Laurence Olivier. "I may be black, but I've got the Larry look, haven't I, Julia darling?"

Julia smiled and nodded. "Your profile is divine." She fuelled Peter's ego with affection.

Barbara went in for sarcastic ribbing. However, they had both known Peter from childhood.

"Well girls," Peter said, placing his half-naked body between Julia and the last rays of the sun sinking over the Hollywood hills. "Went the day well?"

Julia, seeing Barbara's lip beginning to curl, said hastily "Oh, good, Peter, good."

"Like your cossie." Peter peered at Julia's midriff where the last of the hives lingered between barely-there halves of her snazzy red bikini. "Not sure about the tattoo."

Peter plonked himself down on the next sunbed. "You haven't got a rash have you? Nothing catching, I hope." He peered at Julia's navel again. He was a bit of a hypochondriac.

Julia smiled and held Peter's hand. She loved him unreservedly. He was her dearest friend. She lived at his lovely home in return for a few chores, mutual ego bolstering and gossip. But even if she were penniless in the street, she could still come here. She never had to ask to stay with Peter. "It's only a cowboy rash from down on the farm."

"Oh," Peter minced. "I would definitely like some of that."

"You'd like Ellis McCready then," Barb drawled. "He's a suspect limp wrist."

"No he is not!" Julia felt cross that Barb would malign Ellis without proof, especially to Peter who was bisexual. "I've kissed him and he is not gay."

"He could swing either way," Barb retorted.

"If he's doing any swinging, it's my way," Julia snapped.

"Girls, girls, please. End of round." Peter laughed. "That's what I like about you two. Ding-dong. No PC. Aren't we just such good buddies. I love it. If I couldn't come back here, from that awful place down there, to a decent bitchy conversation with my friends, I would go absolutely stark staring. Now, come on, come on, spill the beans on *Warlords of the Outer Rim*. I'm going for it, you know. I'm going to be Count Something. My costume looks divine."

"Oh you're just as stupid about sci-fi as Julia," Barb moaned. "I've virtually promised to do the wicked handmaiden with a stab at the script as well."

Julia sighed. "I'm trying to get a part too, but my agent's blocking it, I think. If you two are in it and I'm not…"

"Ooh, the wicked handmaiden gets to screw Ellis," Peter crowed. "I wouldn't mind screwing him myself. Cruel isn't it? Barb gets to clinch him, and me and Julia, who really fancy him, will never get any closer than two metres.

"Still I might be able to cop a feel when we fight. He is one hell of a sexy guy. You never know, it might be better than sex. The way his eyes crinkle when he smiles. And when he gives you that long, deep blue look from under his eyelashes. No wonder Julia's smitten. We're going to fight for possession of the Lost City of the Rim, or some such crap. Or whatever storyline they come up with. As long as they don't let Barb write any of the script."

Barb stuck her tongue out at Peter. "I shall try to get some more female leads in it, if I get the chance."

"Precious few female leads in this particular sci-fi. But seriously, dear Barb, any script of yours will be oodles better than that lot can produce." Peter waved his hand in the general direction of the studios, lay back, stretched out his long smooth body and looked smug.

Barbara became immediately irritated and sat up. "God, I hate it when you do that. You're going to tell us some juicy little tit-bit about this film, aren't you, no doubt culled from your rabbity executive bed-hopping?"

"This woman is a witch. Julia, darling, this woman is a positive witch," Peter yelled.

Julia smiled, content to be surrounded by her friends. "Tell us, Peter dear." The hassles of the day were beginning to slip away with the sun, helped by several large gin and tonics. Delicious thoughts of Ellis floated dreamily through her mind. She began to go over what he had said, what she had said. Later she would go over what they had done. The affair had begun quite well.

She heard Barb complaining about not really wanting to be in the film. Then suddenly Barbara gave a loud shout. "Hawaii! Hi Hawaii!"

Peter shushed Barb. Julia, now fully awake, sat up. The three heads bent together. Peter put his finger to the side of his nose. "Yes, my dears, they're going to film it in Hawaii!"

Julia had a small blue room at Peter's that looked out over lush gardens. She had resisted sleeping with Barbara. She needed time to herself. Time to think about Ellis. She knew that Barbara resented any moving away, either mental or physical. They had always shared everything. But Ellis was in Julia's life now and whether it was to be a short or long time, he counted. Barb understood that.

They had often discussed Julia's obsession with Ellis. Sometimes they had treated it as a joke, and Julia herself acknowledged the stupidity of falling for a screen phantom.

"Still," Barb had said considerately. "It's happened before. It's only natural that the film depiction of a male sex symbol will be almost as potent as a fleshly one. Didn't Sir Michael first see his wife rolling cigars on her thighs in a TV advert, or was that someone else?"

Julia had confessed that she would like to marry and have children. Perhaps a soppy idea for an actress. But Barbara often declared that she would never marry, herself.

Peter's house was an ultra-modern haven of blue and white with 1930s glamour thrown in. Julia felt happy and relaxed as she settled down for an early night. But first, it was time to phone mother.

As Julia reached out to the phone, a quick knock heralded the exuberant entrance of Peter.

"Ha, caught you! The Barb said you might be calling your mother. That woman is a mind reader."

Slowly Julia withdrew her hand. With a theatrical air, Peter sank down next to her. He smoothed her hair on the pillow. "Fair Desdemona," he murmured. "It gives me wonder great as my content, to see you here before me. O my soul's joy!..."

Chapter Four

"That was beautiful." Julia caressed the smooth brown arm above her. "A handsome man reciting Shakespeare over my pillow. My own dear Peter."

"Yes, I was great in *Othello*. That's one part I knew I'd get, so I really studied it. A good black actor is almost guaranteed the Moor."

"Oh, darling, do I detect a note of bitterness there? You know it's better now. We've had a black Henry Fifth."

"Not so much this side of the pond. I may look like Larry, talk like Larry and act like Larry but I ain't a new Larry. I'm an oddity. A black man with a cut-glass Brit accent."

"You're more than that. Black American men are more – loose limbed. They move around differently."

"Like this. With a wide grin Peter jumped up and proceeded to lurch and slouch around trying to look like an American. "Yo baby!" He was wearing a vest and shorts which showed off his tightly muscled six-foot frame.

Julia clapped. "But you still don't move like an American. Black American men look as though every bone in their body is made of rubber, while you look like any stiff Brit."

"Yes, I know. That's OK for this stiff-arsed science fiction thing. I mean would they have a Brit if they weren't stiff-arsed. But they're hardly likely to let me smooch Reese Witherspoon, that's for sure. Anyway, would I want to? Would I like a white American actress smooching me and giving out the vibes, 'look at me everyone, I'm actually getting up close and personal with a black guy'?"

Julia laughed at Peter's squeaky voice mimic. "That sounds nothing like any actress I know. Stop wriggling your hips. You're making me feel seasick. You don't look like an American. You look like a Brit with a rocket up his arse."

Peter fell back onto the bed. He was such a fine physical specimen that his breathing was soon almost normal. "That's an unfortunate turn of phrase to use to me."

"I know, I'm sorry. You've waxed your chest." Julia touched Peter lightly.

"Yes, apparently, future humans are all without any body hair at all. Your precious Ellis will be as smooth as the proverbial baby's bum, and so greased up he'll slip right out of your clutches. You'll need a full Brazilian yourself."

"Surely, I won't have to show my fanny?"

"Believe me dear, a mere shadow will be enough."

"And I've got to get my teeth capped," Peter continued gloomily. "Honest, do I need it?" He turned his beautifully sculptured face on the pillow and grimaced, his eyes startlingly blue in his brown face.

"No, you're perfect. You'll end up looking like a shark. Nobody looks good with wrap-round teeth."

"I bet you any money old Barb arrives any minute to see what we're up to."

Julia surfaced from a brief daydream about Ellis and sighed heavily. "Probably."

"If I leave she'll come in, you know. She doesn't like you phoning Mother. Me, it's what makes you happy princess." Peter rose from the bed, placed a gentle kiss on Julia's hand and made a bowing stage exit.

Julia reached for the phone again. "Hello Mother, it's Julia. How are you? I'm fine. I'm in Los Angeles. America. You know, Hollywood land. Everything's OK with us. Yes, Peter's fine. Barbara's fine.

"Do you remember when Granny nearly drowned at Porthtowan in 1952? When she met God. Do you remember telling me? What did Granny say out there in the bay in the grip of that vicious tow? God help me! And He did!

"Granny, who never went to church. Who said she did not know if there was any God. Until she met Him, that day, in 1952 in the Atlantic rollers off Porthtowan Beach. Do you remember it Mother? Of course you do. You told me. You were thirteen at the time. And when you said that Granny had actually met God – well I was knocked all in a heap. And I had to believe you. Though cynics would say that it was just the wondrous machinations of the brain when it realises that the stupid body is about to peg it…"

A light knock on the door brought Julia back to the present. She quickly put down the phone. Barbara opened the door. The ping of the phone hung accusingly in the air.

Julia sat miserably at the edge of the auditions room. Actors talked and laughed all around her. Grimly, she sat up straighter and fixed a determined smile on her face. The people in the room would sense her failure. They would drift away and consolidate it. No, if she had learned anything in show business, it was never slip, never drop your guard.

Oh well, she thought, time to ring Humphrey and grovel. She might have known that her agent would be right about the sci-fi. There would be no Ellis under the Hawaiian moon. She had failed to get a part in the film.

Barbara hurried over. "What's happened? You look sick."

"Oh I was hoping it wouldn't show. I didn't get a part."

Barbara jostled to get the chair next to Julia. "What was that?" she shouted above the din.

"No go," Julia shouted back. "Tits not big enough."

Barbara gawped. "Tits what?"

Julia made a huge loop over her bust and screamed louder. "Tits not big enough."

Unfortunately there was a lull in the sound level at that moment and several actresses, with huge bosoms, turned to look at Julia. They smiled smugly.

"Apparently," Julia explained, forcing herself to stick out her chest, instead of instinctively shrinking into it, "women in the future will have huge breasts, due to genetic experimentation, and will not need implants." Julia gave the large-bosomed ladies one of her best smiles. Well, she was prettier than them.

"Ah, that's just randy little scriptwriters' wet dreams," Barbara sneered. "It's sad, lonely little men who get all the scriptwriting."

A pair of very attractive bare male legs appeared in front of Julia. She looked up to see Ellis smiling down at her, holding out his hand.

Julia rose, unable to stop showing how happy she was to see him. She looked back at Barbara, who flapped her away with a knowing look.

Conscious of Ellis' warm fingers clasping hers, Julia was led away, past the suddenly narrow-eyed, bosomy ladies.

Julia passed into the inner sanctums of the film studios. Here, the hubbub died away as doors closed. The carpet got more difficult to walk on, the smell more expensive.

Ellis stopped and they sat down together, still holding hands. "How are you today?" The warmth in his eyes was quite breathtaking, and although Julia was a film star, of sorts, herself, it was hard not to be bowled over by the full Hollywood glamour of the man beside her. It must be because he wasn't wearing any trousers.

Hurriedly Julia schooled her features into a less soppy mould. "Fine… but I didn't get…" Her voice had become husky, which annoyed her. She lifted up her chin and tried to smile.

"Yes, I know," Ellis interrupted. "It's my fault really. I didn't tell them that you and I… that you and I had something going."

"Have we something going?" Julia was both elated and amazed at the speed at which Ellis was coming on to her.

"Yes," Ellis said emphatically, suiting the word to the deed by suddenly seizing her by the shoulders and kissing her full on the lips.

Embarrassingly, Julia thought, the office staff applauded this display of Ellis' ardour, with enthusiastic clapping and cheers.

Ellis laughed. "You don't like that do you? Look, will you wait here for me for a few minutes?"

Julia nodded and watched Ellis walk away. His bare legs looked just as good from the back. What are you, she thought, some kind of film star groupie sitting around waiting to be kissed, when you should be out getting another job? Another film part, pronto. Was it too late to sweet-talk Dustin Hoffman?

Julia looked down at her jeans. Perhaps that was why she hadn't got a part. Shabby-chic was not a good look for Hollywood. They only understood, glamour, glamour, glamour. Her brown jumper didn't show off her curves either. She should have known that understated elegance had no place here. She should have worn a push-up bra and knocked their eyes out.

Julia's hand was suddenly seized by a very large fat man, who had appeared out of nowhere and was now squeezing his oversize thighs on the chair next to hers, almost as hard as he was squeezing her hand, and breathing out strong garlic fumes. Julia hurriedly changed her moue of affront into a charming smile. It was Bernard Donne, the producer.

"Julia Slater. You remember me," he wheezed, still holding her hand in his large warm paw.

Julia did. He had told her not half an hour before, that she had not the right frontage, as he put it, for the part of a handmaiden in Episode Four.

"Here's your script. Parts aren't finalised yet, but you'll be in it, somewhere. We'll run over your résumé. Work something out. Contact your agent." Bernard released Julia's hand at last.

"You mean I'm in the film?" Julia took the script, surprised and suddenly very happy.

"Sure you are. Got to keep Ellis happy. He's just on the point of committing himself, and he's not going to pass up a sweet little thing like you, is he?"

Julia bridled. Did this Bernard really think that she was so dim that sugary flattery would cut it with her? She primmed up her lips.

Bernard changed tack. "The thing won't work without him. And if you keep him really sweet for the duration, there's a bonus in it for you."

He's tried flattery, now he's trying cash, Julia thought, smiling disdainfully. But part of her desperately wanted to be in the film. But at what price?

Bernard winked, jumped up surprisingly quickly for such a large man, gave a Julia a rather piercing, calculating look and rushed off.

Julia just managed a little puppet-like goodbye. Then her face flamed as the meaning in Bernard's words hit home.

She was Ellis' bit of fluff. Something to keep him warm at night. Something to keep him from upsetting the expensive female leads with his amorous attentions. She would be found a part. Any part. Or worse, have a part made up for her. Probably some batty witch. They were always played by batty Englishwomen. Or perhaps some kind of goddess, when she would brush up her best upper-class English accent until it choked her!

"Well stuff it, Ellis. You're not stuffing me!" Julia hissed to herself and made a graceful exit right.

Julia went back to her small blue room. Luckily the house was deserted. Everyone was out hacking it in Los Angeles. Just like I should be Julia acknowledged gloomily. She was already regretting her abrupt exit and wondering what Ellis would think when he returned and found her gone.

"'Gone, gone, and never called me Mother'!" Julia quoted tragically from the Victorian melodrama to her empty room. She slumped on her bed. Here I am, she thought, talking to myself. I'll be calling Mother next and it's not even six o'clock.

Got to ring Humphrey. She dialled her agent's number and was informed that he was not available. No doubt Humphrey had got the hump. He had been phoning her for days for film auditions. "Look Julia," he had said to her. "You have made a name in Brit TV doing the anguished mother and daughter thing and you have to follow it up over here. You know it makes sense."

Yes, it made sense to Humphrey to be busily lining up meaty, gritty dramas, but it did not make sense to Julia. She knew that no one could understand why she wanted to do a kind of *Kill Bill* meets *Dune* sci-fi. Even Barbara would rather be penning serious drama than getting involved with a hit and miss space epic.

Julia looked round the little blue room. She must get out. Resist the urge to burrow under the bedcovers. Firstly, she scrabbled around for her little sleeping face. There it was secure in its little cloth bag. Pink felt face, sleeping eyes and tiny bead mouth, tucked in its tiny quilted bed. She placed her talisman in the palm of her hand and looked at it. She wondered briefly what kind of person she was who would make such a stupid lucky charm. Just to remind herself that, because she suffered from insomnia, and had an instant flare-up temper, not to break too many balls during the day.

Julia lay by the deserted pool. She had dressed carefully in one of her most attractive swimmers which was turquoise and brought out the colour of her bluey-green eyes. She checked her voicemail again but still no Humphrey. She wanted to phone Ellis but did not know his number.

"Yes, I should think so," Barbara's voice pierced through the sun haze. "You just phone him now. Here's the number. Like your cozzie."

"You are a witch Barb."

"And you are a fool. Bernard's told me all about it. He had no idea you would flounce off like that…"

"I did not flounce. And what's with the Bernard? He must be one of the most…"

"He's standing right behind you Jules dear," Barbara cut in quickly. "You know. The producer of your precious sci-fi."

"It's Ber-nard, not Bernud," Bernard said. "Can you lot not speaka da Engleesh?" He subsided heavily onto a sunbed wheezing slightly.

"Now Nuddy," Barbara said playfully, "or rather Ber-nard, you know you like it. You know you prefer sassy English dames with a touch of the Boudicca menace."

Forgetting her present woes, Julia sat up in amazement. Was she hearing alright? Was Barbara love-rapping Bernard Donne, ace breather of garlic fumes and the reason for her own misery?

Barbara pulled a sunbed close to Bernard's, sat across it and held Bernard's hand with a lover-like zeal. "Yes, Jules, dear, I see your face. And yes, Bernard and I are an item."

Bernard winked at Julia. "She's only doing it because she wants to write some scripts. Ah, here comes Ellis. You're right Barbara, Julia's sure got him going. He looks quite flagrante delicto already."

"Oh it's love's young dream. Both so good-looking. Our Julia, you know, has men falling at her feet all the time. But she's a right picky bitch." Barbara grinned slyly at Julia.

Julia hardly noticed. Her heart had begun to beat faster at the approach of Ellis. He looked a little angry.

Chapter Five

Julia sank back on her sunbed and pulled her wrap over her body. She did not want Ellis to sit next to her and stare at her semi-nakedness. Although she had a slight tan, she was not the sun-bleached, shiny, perfect, Hollywood actress specimen of a woman that he was used to. Well, that was the reason she told herself but she knew that she was seeking protection. From what? As always – loss of control. She put on her sunglasses.

Ellis did sit down next to her but apart from a gentle "Hi" he seemed to be waiting for her to begin.

Julia sat up and turned to face him. Their knees touched. Ellis was wearing shorts. Touching kneecaps became suddenly erotic and she almost forgot what to say. "I must apologise. I shouldn't have left without leaving a message."

"Are we on or not?" Ellis said abruptly. "I'd like to know. I don't mind if you give me the run around as long as I know that you are really interested."

As Julia hesitated he added, "Think about it." He stood up, stripped off to his trunks and dived into the pool.

"Bernard has something to say." Barbara and Bernard were standing, intertwined, obviously intent on finding somewhere more private to continue with even more elaborate intertwining.

"Sure," Bernard muttered hastily. "Put it badly. Ellis not to blame, of course. Sure we want such a good actress as yourself in the film. Er, you'll love Hawaii. Er, sorry if I, er… expressed things badly, er…" Bernard gave up trying to stop Barbara pulling him towards the house.

Allowing for the fact that Barbara was having nooky with Bernard, and therefore Bernard must now be treated by herself with caution, Julia had realised that to receive such an apology from the main producer of the film was no small thing. She would have to brave the garlic fumes and give Bernard an apology herself for acting like a prima donna.

Julia slipped into the pool. Ellis swam towards her. They met, body to body, and kissed. The kiss tasted of chlorine and suntan lotion. An exotic scent from some lavender-type bushes drifted across the water. As they were both out of their depth, they sank and had to part. Julia knew that she would remember the kiss for ever.

"I feel that I have behaved badly." Julia turned to Ellis as he lay on the sunbed next to her. "And I feel that you have not quite forgiven me. I wasn't giving you the run around." Apart from the one kiss in the pool Ellis had shown no signs of wanting to follow Barbara and Bernard to the bedrooms.

Ellis smiled and seemed to relax a little. "I was upset when I found that you had gone. That's why I'm so cross with you, because you have the power to upset me."

Julia pretended to misunderstand Ellis' confession of weakness but her heart jumped a little with joy. "Bernard put it to me that I was in the film purely as your bit on the side."

"Bit on the side? You mean arm-candy? Bernard doesn't have the time to waste soothing bit players in one of his great sci-fi productions."

"I know, I know. I'm going to apologise to him. I should know better. There is no good way to get a part. There is only getting the part."

"And you want to be in this film because you love science fiction, particularly this series."

"Yes, I really do." And because I love you, Julia added mentally.

"And I'm in it because you want to be in it."

"Oh dear, that's quite a responsibility you've saddled me with."

"Well, I was in two minds, and you clinched it."

"I shall feel awful if you don't enjoy it. But really it would not be the same without you. It would not be worth doing the fourth episode without you."

"And not forgetting the massed nerds of England. But I've already done two of them. The character was starting to get to me, you know. And the script is terrible. I rather liked the idea of the Rock Hudson film."

Julia felt rather guilty. Here she was lying on a sunbed in Hollywood next to the most gorgeous man in the world. Going to Hawaii with him. The man of her dreams. And yet she had apparently persuaded him to do a film he didn't want to when she herself had run a mile from Humphrey's attempts to get her to do the mother and daughter thing again.

"Will you move into my house in LA?" Ellis asked abruptly. "We could go over the script together and... get to know each other."

With Ellis leaning over towards her with an intense look in his incredibly attractive blue eyes, a small enticing smile playing over his features, Julia felt like saying yes, yes, yes!

But she did not, of course. She kept the lid on her rising tide of sexual exhilaration. She acted looking doubtful.

"OK. I'm rushing it." Ellis stood up and put his hands on the sides of her sunbed and assumed a semi-mating position. "Your eyes say yes." His soft seductive voice held a note of teasing regret. "Your eyes say yes but... well, shall we have dinner tonight?"

Julia was so entranced by the semi-naked Ellis leaning over her, his arm muscles bulging slightly under the strain, that all of her self-control seemed to be slipping away. But it wasn't just sex, was it? It was all of him. The whole, unknown, devastatingly attractive man.

Her hands rose slightly as though to run them down his chest. But she stopped. Her fingers curled. She knew that if she touched him he would kiss her.

His eyes and mouth said kiss me. The tension between them rose. It was a battle between his arm muscles and her willpower and she won. He looked disappointed.

Then he jumped up, pulled his bed right up to hers, and lay on his side, as close as possible, regarding her, acknowledging her victory, his nostrils flaring slightly as he steadied his breathing.

Julia turned to him. "I'm not playing hard to get," she said softly. "You know I like you, and of course I will have dinner with you tonight. It's just that... I'm not keen on open air sex when people can see you." Julia gestured to some of Peter's male friends sunning themselves around the pool.

"I do it all the time. Open air sex. It's great." Ellis tried to keep a straight face and failed.

"Tease." Julia smiled. Her hand reached out to caress his smooth golden chest. But she didn't. Her eyes suddenly registered a small tattoo running along the top of a faint appendix scar on his right hip. The writing said 'Penny'.

"Who's Penny?" The words were out before Julia could stop them.

Ellis laughed. "Oh she was a bitch, a real bitch. I'll tell you all about it tonight."

After Ellis had gone, Julia stayed out on the sunbed coping with the cold douche of the tattoo 'Penny'. She had no wish to go in anyway and listen to the grunting and groaning no doubt coming from Barbara's room next to hers. Barbara liked noisy sex.

Eventually, Barbara appeared looking smug and rosy. There was no sign of Bernard.

Julia was going to have to wait to apologise to him. "Shagged Bernard senseless then, have you?" she said dryly.

"Ooh hark at you. Just about." Barbara flopped down and began dragging furiously on her fag. "Could ask the same about you, but I know my Miss Prim Knickers. Or did you do it in the pool? I saw you in a clinch in there, when I came up for air. You know, there's more semen in that pool than a sperm bank."

"Only James Bond can screw under water," Julia sniffed.

"Oh a bit flaccid was he?"

"Half-mast. He's annoyed with me for not waiting for him at the audition."

"How sweet. You know that's a good sign. Shows that he had emotional depth. It means that when he really fancies you, boy will he fancy you."

Barbara lit up another cigarette and inhaled deeply. "Smoking is so good after sex. Surfing and sex. Two things you can't beat a good smoke after. It also means that he's not one of those who uses sex to punish types. They can be real sods. I remember…" Barbara stopped and took another drag. "Still, I got my own back. He never did find out who kept putting itching powder in his underpants. I bribed the maid, you know."

Julia sighed. A side effect of Barbara's sex life was that she became even more garrulous. Normally Julia didn't mind. Barbara was always an entertaining talker. But now Julia just wanted to think about Ellis, the mysterious Penny, and their date.

To hurry up the proceedings, Julia cautiously asked her friend about Bernard. "I was surprised to find that you had taken up with Bernard."

"Shagging him, you mean. He shags me. I get to write some scripts. Perfect."

"He's very large."

"Oh yes. It's like fucking a waterbed with a built-in dildo. I like him though. As a person. He's very funny. We're going to a French restaurant tonight. He loves French food."

"And garlic." Julia was determined to be very careful around Bernard in the future, but she couldn't resist asking about his bad breath.

"Oh the garlic. Yes. He reminds me of a French lover of mine I once had. Now, he was worth the stench and I've got a feeling that Bernard will be too."

Barbara gave a 'yummy, yummy' chuckle, and rubbed her hands together. "Talking of shagging, do you remember when we went on that lovely trip on a boat up the River Dart at Dartmouth? That summer you had it away with Garth. I ask you Garth! And we passed Colonel Jones' house on the hill and everyone was very sad when the cheery guide pointed it out. You know, I actually shed a few little tears at the thought that he never saw his beautiful house again. And the next minute the guide was looking sly and asking us to watch out for the shags on the rocks."

"Mother was offended," Julia murmured.

"Isn't that strange?." Barbara carried on ignoring Julia's remark. "From war hero to dirty little joke. Get a bit sad, what do we do, tell a dirty joke. Phone a girl in the fifties and mention the word 'shag' and you got arrested. I got that from your mother. And all those endless jokes about blue tits..."

"Mother didn't ever say 'shag'. She would have spelt it out." Julia's eyes were beginning to glaze slightly.

Barbara rattled on. "Here we lie, by this beautiful pool in this glorious sunshine, two little common girls, talking dirty, when everyone thinks we're two little poshos from England."

Julia's eyes became fixed as she stared into the distance. "Two little common girls from Netherfield. The wrong side of the railway tracks."

Barbara sat up in alarm, a frown of concern on her face. She leaned over to look at Julia. "Julia!" She snapped her fingers. "Julia, wake up!" she shouted louder.

Julia turned, her eyes clear and hard. "What do you mean?" she asked aggressively. "I'm not asleep."

"Jules darling," Barbara said gently. "Your mother came from Netherfield not you. You come from Newton Abbot, remember?"

"So?" Julia was crosser still, as she realised that Barbara had caught her out. "You made me do that bloody TV thing about Mother."

"Perhaps it was a mistake. But it made us Jules." Barbara spoke in a wheedling way and leaned over to put her arm round Julia's shoulders. "Your mother's input was too good to miss out on. It was my big writing break."

"Oh yes." Julia's voice was bitter. "We must allow for artistic writing talent, mustn't we? Everything must give way to the genius writer. Even friendship, even love, even sanity." She threw off Barbara's arm.

"Look Jules, you're an artist too. You understand. You're bound to be sensitive. You'll get over it. You can play a whore but it doesn't mean that you will become one."

"But it was my mother, Barb, my own mother."

"Anyway, you're doing the sci-fi - with Ellis. It's time you got into another film, instead of brooding about the last thing. It's Ellis, Jules. The one you've been gagging for for ages. The man you've crossed the Atlantic for."

"Yes, he's doing it because of me. But he doesn't want to Barb. What if it's the same for him doing the fourth episode as it was for me doing Mother?"

"Oh for God's sake stop whingeing," Barbara exploded.

Julia got up, feeling hurt. She had expected some sympathy from Barbara. But then her friend was obviously quite taken with Ber-nard. "Oh sorry to spoil your post-coital glow, Barb." She stalked off feeling dissatisfied and irritable.

"Oh go and get your own bloody glow," Barbara shouted. "The sooner you screw Ellis the better."

Julia smiled. As usual Barb was right.

Chapter Six

Julia was still smiling when she saw Peter hurrying towards her. Men often had old girlfriends' tattoos on their bodies, she reasoned. Yes, she was going to have a fabulous evening.

"Hi Peter," she began and stopped. Peter looked rather agitated.

"There's some fat guy stuck in the bathroom, on the floor." Peter was sweating. "I tell you Jules, he's like a beached whale. I think he's Bernard Donne, but I'm not sure because he's face down and I can't move him. One of the most influential producers in Hollywood is jammed in my loo."

Barbara was now hurrying over, having caught some of Peter's words. "He's what?" she shouted. "Don't say he can't even take a piss without falling over?"

All three hurried to the aid of the trapped producer.

"You've over-screwed him Barb," Peter admonished. "If anything's happened to him, we're finished in Hollywood."

"Nonsense," Barbara snapped. "He's a duckie. A grossly overweight duckie. He has trouble peeing because he can't see his John Thomas, or the toilet for that matter."

Bernard was indeed in dire straits. Somehow he had slipped and jammed his head between the side of the toilet and the washstand. He lay on his belly, feebly waving his arms.

"Oh, Bernard darling, speak to me!" Barbara screeched, crouching down under the sink.

"Honey." Bernard tried to smile and squint upwards. "Get me out of this goddamn dinky can."

"Right, oil." Barbara sprang up. "We need a lubricant. You should have plenty of that."

Peter scowled but grabbed some massage oil and they both rubbed it into their hands and onto Bernard's head and the rings of fat round his neck.

Then, with Barbara and Peter pulling his shoulders, and Julia his left hand, Bernard was pulled slowly from his prison and turned onto his right side. A pile of towels was placed tenderly under his head by Barbara and he lay there gasping that he needed a stiff drink.

Peter went to get it and Julia whispered to him in the doorway that he had better find some strong men to lift Bernard.

Bernard was now into a bitter critique of English bathrooms and longing for his own which, he said, was thirty feet square and mirrored from floor to ceiling.

The upshot of the incident was that when Bernard was finally lifted up and driven away, he took Barbara with him as nothing would induce him to see her at Peter's house again.

Julia was left to ponder that, amazingly, Barbara, who had known Bernard for only a week, had moved in with him.

And she herself, who had known Ellis in the flesh, for barely two days, had been asked to move in with him.

However, her thoughts came to an abrupt end when she realised that she would now be very late for her date with Ellis that evening. And there would not be time to phone Mother.

The date with Ellis did not start well. Julia had stepped out of the white stretch limo that the Studio had sent, feeling ridiculous at having had to sit alone in such a gas-guzzling monstrosity. Star watchers had rushed forward thinking that some big name was alighting, and had turned away disappointed.

Julia knew that she was not looking her best. The little black dress that she had thrown on looked like it should have been thrown out, compared with what LA women wore. Furthermore, the oil that had been used to winkle Bernard out from under the toilet had a pungent odour and she had not been able to remove the smell from her person. The plush hotel looked a bit like something out of Blackpool and Ellis was looking far from pleased.

Julia was shown to Ellis' table by a less than deferential waiter and sat down with a sigh of relief.

They both spoke together.

"I'm so sorry I am late."

"I waited at the door for you for half an hour."

Julia could have launched into the saga of Bernard but she was feeling too relaxed to bother. She would tell him later.

"I thought that you were not coming," Ellis said evenly, his blue eyes rather hard and bright.

He was wearing a white suit and his dark blond hair was so slicked that Julia longed to ruffle the American out of it. And he looked, well, she was practically speechless with lust. She smiled at the thought of her ever not meeting Ellis.

"I see that you are amused at my…" Ellis paused, "hurt feelings."

Julia's smile of delight lit up the room. She leaned across and took his hand. "No, no, quite the contrary. I smiled because the idea of my not meeting you was too absurd."

Ellis relaxed a little. "You are forgiven, but only because you look sincerely sorry and very beautiful."

Julia hurried on, removing her hand from his suddenly tight grasp, and trying not to blush at the look in his eyes.

"Bernard got stuck under the toilet and we had to pull him out. It took some time. I got covered in some foul-smelling oil, which wouldn't wash off, and…"

Ellis began to laugh. "That has to be true. That man weighs over 300 lbs."

The rest of the dinner began to go well. Julia felt that it didn't matter that she wasn't some buffed, tanned, leggy blonde with perfect teeth and a huge bust. She made Ellis laugh. Ellis liked her. She knew that he liked her.

He told her about his life and she told him about hers. She did not know whether there were any reservations on his part, probably not. But there were certainly some embroidered and hidden secrets on hers.

He liked the outdoor life. He rode horses, of course, most actors did. He assumed that she rode. She smiled thinly. Riding in England was for the rich. They discovered a mutual interest in dinosaurs, and both protested almost at the same moment, that they were just amateurs. Ellis promised to take her to see the tar pits and Yosemite. Julia said, "In my youth, I liked bird watching," which made them both smile. The look that passed between them said, we are still very young. They told each other their birthdays. Julia pretended that she didn't know his birthday but, of course, she did. She knew everything about him that could be known by a stranger. She would be glad when she could cease to pretend. Stalkers walked a crooked path.

Of course, she asked him if he had been to England, Britain, though she was almost certain that he had not, and was not quick enough to prevent herself looking relieved when he said he had not. Oh, he's noticed, she realised, and cringed. She must remember that he was quick to read her facial expressions.

"You look glad that I've never been to England." The teasing look was back in his eyes.

She rode it out. "Well a girl likes to appear mysteriously foreign, you know."

"I don't think of the English as foreign." He looked puzzled.

She knew he expected her to say that she didn't think of Americans as foreign. But she did. However, she answered, that, of course, he wasn't foreign. The fact that she found Ellis exotically fascinating was best kept to herself.

Just when Julia was beginning to feel really happy, she looked up, straight into the eyes of Gerald. There he was, having dinner at a nearby table with Peter.

Julia's eyes returned to her plate. She hoped that Ellis had not noticed her reaction, but somehow, she knew that he had.

Barbara always said that Julia had treated Gerald as a pipe-cleaner. And it was true. Gerald was tall, fair, well made, and well-scrubbed. Useful for cleaning out the tubes, as Barbara had so coarsely put it.

Gerald was amusing, forthright, honest and liked plain speaking. Being a southerner, Julia interpreted northern plain speaking as downright rude. But she had genuinely liked him. She had enjoyed their lovemaking. She had enjoyed his company. He just lacked that something that was Ellis. The excitement, the passion the thrill that was Ellis.

Without thinking Julia's gaze had strayed back to Gerald and she was forced to acknowledge his greeting with a tight smile.

"You're not supposed to be staring at other guys when you're with me." Ellis' words had an edgy tone.

Julia, flustered by Ellis' cool look, floundered. "Oh no, of course. It's just that… he's my ex… Gerald."

"Well, you must introduce me," Ellis turned to look behind him. He turned back. "I'd like to know how many scores he made in the holy places of Yorkshire."

"No you wouldn't," Julia snapped. "That was a private conversation that you overheard… and…" She felt a little choked. Everything had been going so well, and now…

"I'm sorry. That was a crass thing to say."

"Yes, it was."

There was silence for a time. Julia ignored Gerald.

Ellis relaxed again. "Hey, you can't help meeting your ex. Mine could walk in. Thrown you eh?"

Julia looked up at Ellis. A little throb of jealousy bubbled up at the thought of his ex. The 'Penny' tattoo, no doubt. "Sort of. I bet Peter called him, the rat. I'm sorry too." The incredible thought came to her that Ellis might possibly be jealous of Gerald. No, no it could not be true. Could it?

"Now we're grinning at each other like two teenagers." Ellis turned and waved to Gerald and Peter. He turned back. "See I'm totally cool with it."

"A little spat never does any harm," she said. "I think a relationship should start off with a fight."

"And the making-up is usually pretty good too. We can make out and make up at the same time."

Julia wanted nothing more than to run round the table and kiss Ellis when he said those, oh so sexy, words. She hoped that it did not show on her face too much. They both toasted making up.

"I have to go to New York tomorrow. It's something that I have to do." Ellis looked as though he would rather stay. "I won't be back for three weeks. My flight leaves at six. We have barely four hours." He leaned across the table with an intent look. "Shall we go to my house now?"

"You mean for sex?" Julia's awkward reply was mostly down to disappointment that Ellis would be away for three weeks.

Ellis blinked and smiled. "Yes, if you like. We are supposed to be a pair."

"You mean from the Studio's point of view."

"Look, I'll be honest. I saw you in that Brit mother and daughter thing. I thought at the time… forgive me… I actually said 'I sure would like to screw that girl.' I didn't know you then, of course."

Julia's heart leaped. She wasn't a stalker. But he hadn't crossed the Atlantic like she had. But it was the same. She remembered most her words to Barbara when Ellis had appeared in a film. She had been quite drunk. "Oh God, look at him. I wouldn't mind meeting him on a dark night. Who is he? Oh, it's Ellis McCready. Sex on a stick." But she wasn't as honest as Ellis. She could not tell him the truth. She realised that Ellis was a better person than herself. As far as she could tell so far. She was devious, a liar, a sham, a fraud. It would be an honour to sleep with Ellis if he was really as clean cut as he appeared to be. Honour to sleep with Ellis, she scolded herself. Bloody hell, she was crazy for him. But she wouldn't tell him that.

"I suppose we should, sort of, get it out of the way. Become lovers. It's silly to keep wondering about it for three weeks." Julia is speaking throughout. "If we don't expect too much we won't be disappointed. Three weeks is a long time."

"You expect to disappoint me?" Ellis laughed at the thought of it. "Is that shorthand for going easy? Say goodnight to Gerald and Peter and let's go."

Julia was in a quandary all the way back to Ellis' house. Ellis would know when they got down to it just how much she was in love with him. She would have to get him so excited that he would not notice her reaction. She was melting with passion already and she was sitting in a silly stretch limo again.

Due to heavy traffic, it was an hour before they arrived at Ellis' house. It was plain and white and Ellis explained that he rented it. The interior was ultra-modern, all bare boards and no clutter.

Another hour seemed to race away over coffee in the smart kitchen. Julia tried to appear relaxed but it seemed to her that Ellis was taking the going easy thing a bit too far. He kept his distance. Oh God, he is such a tease, Julia thought, trying not to grind her teeth.

They sat on stools at the trendy bar and sipped the steaming mugs.

"Coffee is an aphrodisiac kind of smell, don't you think?" Ellis leaned closer and kissed Julia briefly on her neck.

"Oh yes." But I don't need an aphrodisiac when you're around, she thought to herself. "Do you need one?" she said teasingly. "An aphrodisiac?"

"Not when you're around." He smiled. "I just need the lift."

And that was the difference between them, Julia thought. He wasn't afraid to say it. But then, he was successful. He had more confidence. He was open. Things that she was not. Things that she loved him for.

With only two hours left they finally mounted the stairs. There was, of course, a run-through shower adjacent to the bedroom, and a large Swedish-looking bed with a striped cover on which they finally collapsed, wet and breathless.

Sweet kisses, French kisses, close bodily contact. She was glad that the lights were dim. It was such a relief to hold him close at last, skin on skin. He was warm to touch. She mapped out his body with her hands. Ribs, spine, hip bones, shoulder bones, chin. He smelt of soap, something like Imperial Leather. She was losing the capacity to think straight but she knew that if, when, they broke up, she would never use Imperial Leather again.

"Your skin is so silky," he whispered. "Your shoulders are so smooth." His hands and lips skimmed over them.

At least, she thought, pleased, if I don't have a tanned, buffed skin, it was English weather fine.

Passion flared between them. There was no going back. It was not as awkward as she had feared. But she would not let him see her ecstasy. She buried her head in his shoulder. They had agreed on a condom. They had agreed on conventional sex. Mutual enjoyment was expected. But she ratted out.

Chapter Seven

She climaxed first and struggled not to show it. But he came soon after, so she hoped that he had not noticed. She was filled with exultation. It was all that she had ever hoped for. This was good sex. He would want her again, she knew.

The hours sped away. Eventually he whispered that he had to go soon. He smoothed her hair as he lay half over her. She was pleased that he didn't rake his fingers through it. She hated it when men pulled and tangled her hair. She had a sensitive scalp. She was sensitive everywhere. "You're too highly strung, and you should be" her mother had sometimes shouted with her peculiar mixture of affection and bad taste joke.

"Barbara calls you Jules. Your eyes are like emeralds and your hair is like dark amber. You are a jewel."

Julia rubbed his nose with hers. "Very poetic." She giggled. She felt that he would not be offended.

"That's practically a line from the script when I'm making love to Barbara."

"Is it that bad?"

"It's worse than that, and you have landed us both right in it. We'll never be taken for serious actors again."

"Phooey. Everyone likes a bit of fun. It's escapism. And believe you me, nobody needs to escape more than the Brits. You've never lived through a wet winter in Devon."

"Isn't Devon supposed to be beautiful?" Ellis eased his body away. "I'm sorry, am I crushing you?"

"Yes to the first and no to the second." Considering that this was their first time in bed together, Julia felt almost relaxed and rather playful. She missed the pressure of his body and rolled closer to him. He hadn't drawn his curtains, so they could see each other in the dazzle of the LA lights, which rippled across the bed through the window. She saw that he was pleased that she was willing to show that she liked him close to her.

"Devon is the most beautiful place on earth." She spoke softly. Ellis' mouth caressed her shoulder. It seemed that he liked crooning and cuddling as much as she did. "The land is like a patchwork quilt, all tumbled by a restless soul, or a passionate one." She kissed the hollow of his neck. "And it goes up and down, forward and sideways, until you get quite dizzy and lose all sense of direction. A little like making love to you." She kissed him again.

All too soon it was the last kiss. He began to move away. She was left alone. She longed to call him back but twisted the sheets into hard knots instead.

When he sat on the bed the bedside light shone on his back and there were eight imprints of her fairly short nails in his back. She froze. She was still frozen when he kissed her goodbye. His puzzled look when he lifted his head, melted her and she pulled him down again.

"See you in Hawaii," he whispered.

Julia shimmered in Ellis' bed after he had gone. She could hardly believe that fantasy had become reality. "So far sooo good," she whispered hugging herself. Only the thought of the whoreish stretch limo waiting outside stopped her from slipping into a beautiful sleep.

Was she whoreish, she worried as she hurried to dress and leave? Definitely! Screwing someone on the first date. Even if you had known his image for years. Think of Dame Edna and Warren Beatty. Warren Beatty had had lots and lots of women, as everyone knew. Dame Edna Everidge turned it round. 'Warren Beatty? Everyone's had him!' Yeah, Dame Edna always hit the nail on the head.

Julia awoke to a bright Sunday morning in her little blue room. Every day was bright in LA. Was it beginning to get tedious, she wondered? Was she actually hankering after a bit of Devon sea mist? She could hear Peter and Barbara arguing outside her window but couldn't be bothered to listen.

There were no appointments for today. Was she supposed to go to church? Julia thought it politic to keep quiet that she hardly ever went to church. Some Americans were surprisingly evangelical. There was nothing more boring than an American trying to lead you to the path of righteousness.

She could lie in bed and marvel that she had actually fucked Ellis. She mentally chided herself – made love to Ellis. What the hell, fuck was a good old English word. But then she did not want to be coarse. Ellis was definitely a 'make love to' kind of man. There was empathy between them and romance. Whatever it was it made her full of – only the French had a word for it – joie de vivre. Yeah, she sure was full of that.

And she had a feeling that Ellis was getting serious. There was something about the way he looked at her. True, he was an actor but there was something going on behind his eyes that said 'I've got you and I'm keeping you'. Surely, this could not be true, she thought. How many conversations had they had? Four or five. A few clinches and a night in bed. With all the Hollywood talent to pick from, why would he want her so much? Why be so upset when he thought she had walked out on him?

She hadn't asked him about the Penny tattoo. Would he get a Julia tattoo? Somehow he didn't seem to be a tattoo kind of man.

Whatever kind of man he was, Ellis was in New York doing some film deals she supposed, or was it some kind of preview of his last film? Three weeks seemed like three years. He had promised to call.

Phone Mother. Julia reached out her hand. She always phoned Mother on a fixed line. No use letting fantastical thoughts of Ellis run around in her head. Mother would soon flatten those out.

"I tell you Barb, you are not putting that thing on my wall." Peter tried to seize the object in Barbara's hand.

"Well, this is my room and technically this is my wall." Barbara thumped the listening device viciously onto her adjoining wall with Julia's room. "Bernard loaned me this. He's as worried about Julia as I am."

"You mean you told him!" Peter was enraged. "You told a stranger about Julia and her mother."

Barbara had the grace to look shifty. "Well, he's more than a stranger to me since I'm screwing him senseless every night. Bernard won't tell."

"He could throw her off the film. He could blacklist her."

"He won't do that. Mad actresses are like gold dust. If you can control them."

"Mad? Mad? And you're supposed to be her best friend."

"I am her friend. This is all in her best interests. You know I blame myself for raiding her mother's mind and getting Julia like this."

"I have known her longer than you and if she finds out that you're bugging her, well... you could lose her friendship and mine too." Peter snatched the microphone off the wall and held it high in the air.

Barbara pulled a face. "I'm not jumping up there to get it, you stupid man. Listen, I have this friend, this... expert in human relationships."

"Trickcyclist."

"OK. But he's very good. Very discreet. He will listen to the tapes. He will know what to do."

Peter sat on the bed looking defeated.

Gently, Barb removed the listening device from his hand and began to work out the best place for its suckers on the wall.

Peter grunted disgustedly. "I feel as though we're doing a scene in a bleeding James Bond film."

"It's a good job those twitty English previous owners chopped up these rooms. This wall's quite flimsy."

"I wouldn't mind doing James Bond. It's time they had a black one."

Barbara, having adjusted the microphone and recording device to her satisfaction, turned and stood defiantly. "It's for her own good. Do you want her to be forced to see some crazy

American trickcyclist, which the studio would do once she's signed a contract?. We can help her Peter darling."

"I don't like it, Barb. You're a hard bitch, do you know that?"

"Of course I am. You have to be in this game. We're in the business of prying into people's souls and spilling their guts out on the silver screen all in the name of entertainment. None of the punters really care about actors. They just want their thrills and escapism."

Peter shrugged. 'You writers are far too melodramatic. And don't think that I'm sending the recordings from that thing over to you at Bernard's either."

Barbara purred, satisfied that she had won. "No, no, just keep the door locked and I'll come over and get them."

"Promise me one thing." Peter stood over Barbara, his normally mild face as hard as black rock. "You won't let Bernard hear them and you will discuss them only with me."

Barbara lit up and dragged hungrily. "Sure I know the rules, Peter. We three have a pact. I know what happens if I break it."

The listening device clicked. Barb and Peter jumped.

"Hello Mother. Sorry I didn't phone you last night. I was out with my new boyfriend Ellis. He's an American but he's very nice. Yes, I know you always say that Americans seem to be very sleazy, never draw their curtains leading to much trouble, and have too many guns. That the men appear to go to bed in the underpants that they have worn all day and get up in the morning and wear them again, but Ellis isn't like that. I'm sure he changes his underpants every day and wears something else at night. He's a very clean-cut young man Mother. In fact he's too good for me. He's a gentleman. Yes, Americans can be gentlemen. In fact, you can probably trust an American gentleman more than an English one. An upper-class English gentleman is a robber baron after all. Anyway you've hardly ever met any Americans…"

"So you had him then. At last." Barbara settled herself on her sunbed between Julia and Peter and watched the young men cavorting in the pool. "You know, we seem to be spending most of our life on these bloody sunbeds."

Peter grinned. He and Barbara slapped high hands. "Don't knock it."

"Yes, I know. Back home it would be a wet weekend in Brighton." Barb turned to Julia again. "Well, did you?"

Julia stirred out of a slight doze. She glanced at Barbara and Peter. Their profiles looked decidedly fishy. Too much bonhomie. "Natch."

"And now he's gone to New York and all that you are left with is a yearning passion to have him again."

Julia's crotch fluttered. "Please, I'm trying to keep a lid on it. I'm thinking more moonlight and roses, if you don't mind. Anyway, I thought you had shacked up with Bernard. Why are you back here?"

"Oh I came back to see my friends." Barbara's air of nonchalance was not convincing.

"OK." Julia sat up straight. "What have you two been up to"? If Julia had not been sure that her two friends had secrets, she was now. Their guilty looks said it all.

Barb and Peter exchanged a meaningful glance. "Well," Barbara faltered. "Well, we were wondering if you would like to discuss with us your calls to your mother."

Julia sighed, lay back and closed her eyes. "Why should I?"

"Because it's my fault that you ring her," Barb said gently. "If I hadn't written that play, with your mother's help, and get you to play her, then…"

"I wouldn't have gone potty, and we wouldn't be lying here now," Julia finished forcibly.

Peter broke in. "I don't see how a few innocuous calls from Julia to her mother can possibly be of any import. You girls are making mountains out of…"

"Shut up Peter," Barb snapped.

"OK. I'm just a man, but if Julia's mad then so am I. I think I'm Lawrence Olivier with a good tan."

There was a silence for a time. Julia took her little quilted face in bed from her pocket. The little pink felt face smiled, asleep on its pillow. The little red bead mouth pursed like a rosebud.

"I've never told you why I really carry this around Barb. For luck, you think. This face represents me at night, sweetly asleep. I hold it when I'm about to say or do things that won't let me sleep sweetly at night."

"And you're holding it now." Barbara's deep dark gaze held Julia's flinty green one for a fraught minute.

"Yes, I'm holding it now."

"Right, choke me off. We were only trying to help." Barbara subsided onto her bed seemingly defeated.

Peter and Barbara watched as Julia went for a swim with the cavorting boys. There were always cavorting boys at Peter's place.

"Well, that went well," Peter snorted. "What were you two rabbiting on about sleeping faces for…"

"It doesn't matter. The point is that you can see that I am right. She won't talk about it. The microphone will make her face up to it all. You know, Julia had an office job in the lean times. She had an absolute bitch of a boss. So she wrote down all the insults she could think of like stupid bloody cow, boss-screwing whore bitch, thick, stupid prig of a woman, and put them in a little Indian leather bag round her neck. So when the hell boss was carping she would wave it in front of her face. I thought that she would say all those things when she left but she didn't. That's Julia. She hides herself way. She never lets go. We've got to winkle this mother thing out."

"Lots of people talk to their dead mothers." Peter sounded exasperated. "They go to the graveyard and talk to them. Hell, I even talk to my dead cat."

"They don't phone them and speak to them as though they're still alive." Barb stopped. Julia was coming out of the water.

"She looks good," Peter said. "Five feet, eight inches of perfection. You must admit, Barb, she looks good."

Julia paused and sluiced the water out of her hair. What were Peter and Barb up to, she wondered? They were her best friends but she sometimes wondered if it was she who held them together. She was the jam in the sandwich. If they ganged up against her she would be squeezed until the pips ran.

Barb was making Peter do something he didn't want to. Dear Peter. They had made a vow when they were ten years old that they would always be friends. They loved each other but they had never been lovers.

Julia began to think of her little blue room as a bit of a prison. The sci-fi film was delayed. The film was held up, partly because Ellis had gone to New York and partly because there had been a lot of argument about what to call it.

The fans had not liked the title of episode one *Strangers in the Stars*, or episode two *Love at Minus Sixty*, or episode three *The Sandmen of Ozzibarco*.

"What's wrong with *Warlords of the Outer Rim* exactly?" Julia asked Peter. She nudged him as he lay sprawled across her narrow bed. "Peter. Why have you come in to see me if you are going to be so dull? You've hardly said a word and now you've dropped off."

Peter raised himself up at Julia's annoyed tones. "Who gives a fuck what the bloody thing's called." He spoke with all the bad temper of someone roused from a doze. "Why the bloody hell don't they get on with it?"

"What's wrong with you?" Julia asked a little more patiently.

"Oh I'm fed up with Barb and her mad schemes. Stupid nosey bitch!"

"What mad schemes?" Julia began to feel annoyed again.

Peter hoicked himself up the bed and put his arm round Julia's shoulder. "Never mind princess. I'm going to sort her out. I'm going to tell you what she's up to.

"You know, I was arsed about a lot when I was sixteen." Peter's blue eyes sought Julia's green ones, and he gave her a light kiss on the nose. "Sometimes I wonder if I really am bi-sexual. It was sort of expected you know. Young, poor, black actor schoolboy, playing a schoolboy. They just couldn't resist those grey short trousers and the little black legs. Would I really rather live with you in Bigbury On Sea in a little bungalow on the cliff? Dodge the tides going to the island? Drink in the Pilchard Inn? We have enough money to go in the hotel now."

Julia caressed the chocolate forearm lying across her shoulder. "Were you forced? You never told me you were forced."

"No, not exactly. I was too eager to please. I was always too eager to." Peter paused as the sound of loud footsteps echoed outside the door of the bedroom.

Chapter Eight

A sharp tap on the door broke the mood. Without thinking, Julia called, "Come in."

Ellis came eagerly into the room. His expression of happy expectation dropped from his features. His face closed into tight anger. He shut the door carefully, put down his briefcase, and advanced a few paces towards the bed.

"Hi Ellis." Julia smiled with delight but then her teeth closed over her lower lip in a pensive bite. "You've come back early," she finished rather lamely.

Ellis was wearing a smart dark suit. He looked travel weary and a little dishevelled. He smelt faintly of bad air and spicy food. That crumpled jet plane look.

"I rushed back." Ellis' voice was flat. "To see you."

Peter was completely unfazed. "I believe that I am a little de trop. Don't mind me old chap." He spoke as though he were in a Noel Coward play. He got off the bed and made his usual theatrical exit.

Julia's lip was still trapped between her teeth. She made a comical gesture with her face, and said rather unwisely, she afterwards thought, "Don't tell me you're coming over as the jealous boyfriend?"

Something inside Ellis seemed to snap. "You little slut." He ripped off his jacket and tie and leapt onto the bed. Seizing Julia by the shoulders he kissed her hard on the mouth, forced his arm around her shoulders and dragged her down into the bed where he pinned her with his full body weight.

The bedclothes fell to the floor as Ellis removed his trousers, still holding Julia with his right arm. She took the opportunity to half struggle up.

"Ellis, please, there is no need to…"

She was silenced by another punishing kiss as the now half-naked Ellis forced her vest up to her neck, and, pausing only to rip his shirt open, resumed his demanding kisses, with only a softening of his intense blue eyes to reassure her.

He smelt of airplane food, cigarettes and sweat. Julia had never had sex with a man who ripped his shirt buttons off before. True, Gerald had often been quite boisterous in a Yorkshire he-man kind of way. This fleeting recollection of Gerald was Julia's last coherent thought. Ellis' passion was all-consuming and she could hardly think at all. But she clung to the hope that he would slow down, by some gesture. A light kiss. A pleading look. It became a close-run thing. He was not going to stop. She was not ready but he was not going to wait. One small window in his rage would have melted her. It came with a softer, but no less passionate kiss, a despairing look and a strangled, "Julia."

But he was already inside her. True she relaxed. The penetration and build-up suddenly became intensely pleasurable to her. They both forgot why it had ever started.

Afterwards Ellis was the first to recover. His head was in the pillow. A muffled groan escaped him.

The room was well lit, and Julia reached out and switched off a bright lamp. She turned back to Ellis, whose face was still in the pillow.

She eased towards him and ran her hand reassuringly over his shoulders. "It's OK Ellis," she whispered, kissing him lightly on the neck.

"It's not," he said emphatically in a despairing way. "It is not OK!"

Julia lay back. She had miscalculated the depth of Ellis' feelings for her. She realised that, amazingly, he was as madly in love with her as she was with him. So much so that her apparent sexual relationship with Peter had pushed him over the edge.

She could control her sexual desires and feelings more than Ellis. That was why she loved him – for his strong and open expressions of love for her. So much better than her own mealy-mouthed, scaredy-cat admissions. But could she make him believe that she regarded his lack of control as a compliment to her?

Julia felt quite sanguine. She would explain that Peter was a friend and nothing more. There was always a first time to be forced. English men, on the whole, well the type that Julia liked, didn't usually go in for much forcing, or a lot of passion for that matter, particularly if Leeds United were playing at home.

She saw that inadvertently raising the green-eyed monster in Ellis had not been a good thing in this early stage of their relationship. True, the sex had turned out great, but the beginning of it had left an aura of disquiet not least because he had not used a condom.

Julia turned to Ellis again to re-assure him of her coolness in the matter, but he turned away and got off the bed.

He seemed to be having some difficulty with his breathing. His face was crumpled with self-disgust. "I'm sorry Julia. Oh God, I'm so sorry."

"Ellis, don't go like this. Peter is just a friend. A very dear friend."

Ellis continued to rapidly put on his clothes, ignoring her softly spoken words of healing.

"Ellis, please don't go."

He didn't look at her again as he disappeared smartly, closing the door with a bang.

Julia was left looking at Ellis' shirt buttons lying on the sheet. She wondered if he wanted them back. No, he would throw the shirt away. He was an American. Did he know the meaning of the word recycling? That was unfair. She would ask him – no probably not. She reached for her sleeping pills.

It was time to get out of the blue room. Julia threw herself into a bout of sightseeing. She found LA rather hot and glaring and the constantly surging traffic had an unpleasant smell.

Barbara was talking seriously about setting up house with Bernard who was looking for another property. Not content with his thirty feet square bathroom, Bernard had decided that he wanted a larger house, and the place to go was to an exclusive zip code near Sunset Strip. Julia went with them but soon wearied of bad taste decor and hot streets named after birds.

Julia soon dragged them off to the smart coffee houses along the Strip where the rich and famous played. Julia adored Brad Pitt and was hoping to meet him, not on the Strip of course, that would be too tacky since he might not know who she was, but at a power lunch. Bernard was into power lunches, power brunches and power generally.

Troy was being hotly discussed. Julia maintained that Brad was the best thing in it. "Terrific actor," she proclaimed. "Forget the Aussie, Brad is the one in that flick. I think Aussies enjoy an undeserved rep over here."

Julia paused. Bernard and the other Americans around the table were looking askance. She sighed. Americans just did not understand that the English and Australians slagged each other off as a matter of course and that, in fact, slagging each other off was actually a type of affection. She felt a stab of homesickness.

Barbara plunged into the awkward pause. "You must admit though that Russell Crowe is a really good actor. He was marvellous in *Master and Commander*."

The Devil prompted Julia. "Yes. But they couldn't have a real Englishman in that, could they, any more than the Captain of the starship *Enterprise* could be who he was and not some bogus bleeding Frenchman called Jean Luc!"

Barb stood up. She grabbed Julia's elbow. "Excuse must dash," she cried heartily.

Julia was ready to leave. She felt dispirited and scowled when Barb then stage whispered, "You must excuse Julia, she's had a fight with Ellis."

"Why did you tell them that?" Julia said crossly as they walked past the famous pavement set with film stars' names.

"Everyone knows. Ellis is going around with a face like a wet week and you're blowing off at a power lunch. I said to Ellis, go and see her. Peter is always on her bed. On her bed mark you. Not in her bed."

"He told you?" Julia stopped walking and turned angrily to Barbara.

"No, you ass. Of course, I guessed. He didn't say a word. He just sat there drinking whiskey. Bernard had him over about the film. Ellis is committed on paper but not in his mind. Bernard is worried that if Ellis is turned off the film it will affect everyone else and the whole thing will turn out to be absolute shit, straight to DVD.

"Anyway as I understand it Ellis comes in hot from the airport, not to find his lovely Julia waiting for him all alone and lonely but with a huge black man draped over her. Now, he's entitled to be a bit miffed, you must admit. What did Ellis do?"

"Nothing. As you say he was a bit miffed. He stormed out, sort of."

"But you are going to make it up with him?"

Julia thought about the feelings of angry despair swirling around inside her. Why did she feel this way? Because she would have no peace until she had made her peace with Ellis? Or was it because Ellis had spectacularly lost his rag? Could she forgive him? A wild recollection of the latter part of their encounter ran riot through her. Don't be a priggish fool, she told herself. Of course, she was going back for more of that.

"Julia, Julia! You haven't heard a word I've said for the last ten minutes. Are you going to make it up with Ellis? Bernard wants to know."

"Bernard wants to know." Julia repeated the words and then suddenly smiled at her friend. "Yes, of course."

Barbara gave a whoop of joy. "That's my girl. We've got to do this film and make it work. Any doubt about its brilliance and we're all in the clarts, especially as I'm writing most of the script. Bernard will fix it up for you two to dine together at the most exclusive hotel in this cockamamie city, followed by a night of passion.

"Oh look at that poster of Hawaii. Oh that girl looks just like you. Look at that waterfall. That's where we're going soon. Just think in a few weeks you could be standing under a waterfall in the jungle just like that. Except you probably won't when you've read the guidebook."

"Why's that?" Julia was transfixed by the huge poster in the travel shop, where a svelte dark-haired beauty with very little clothes bathed amid foaming water and tropical blooms. "It looks like paradise on earth."

"Well, the water cascading down is contaminated with goat shit which could give you a nasty disease, and it's not advisable for women to travel about on their own, as they may be attacked by drunken locals."

Julia laughed. "Barbara, you pig."

"And then there are quite a few nasty bugs you can pick up here and there and that's not to mention the mosquitos…"

The dinner with Ellis did not begin very well. Julia had dressed with care in a midnight blue, off-the-shoulder dress. She wore a blue tropical flower over her ear, in defiance of the Hawaiian poster and a subtle French perfume, since perfume had been so sadly lacking during their last encounter.

As usual, the dining area was badly lit. Julia hated eating in a poor light but she hesitated to ask to change their table. The place was so crowded with famous faces that there probably wasn't one anyway and people were queuing. Why rich people would queue for a table was beyond Julia. Bernard had done all this to impress her, she knew. He was saying, play my game and you can have all this.

The silence stretched between them. Below, on the roads beneath their high window, the headlights of the cars made a continuous river of light in the darkness.

Julia felt relaxed. She was in harmony with Barbara and she had absolved Ellis of any wrongdoing when they had last met. True, he had raised some angst in her but she had worked through that. She was ready to proceed as though nothing had happened.

Ellis' face was a little in the shadow but he looked strained. Julia realised that although she had followed his career for a couple of years, gleaned an idea of his character from the tabloids, and seen his physical presence on the screen, she had actually only known him for two weeks.

She suddenly thought that he might well be in the same fit of despondency and anger that had afflicted her earlier that day.

She reached out and held his right hand which lay inertly on the crisp white tablecloth. After a moment he responded and his fingers curled around hers.

This physical contact broke the ice.

"I've got my speech ready, Ellis," Julia said, smiling with a clear look. "Shall I go first? Right, well, Peter is a very old friend and sometimes he comes in to talk to me at night. Barbara monopolises me sometimes, so that becomes his time. I love Peter but not in the way that I would love my lover." Bloody hell, that was clumsy, she thought. "Not in the way that I could love you."

Ellis stirred at last. "I shouldn't have… assaulted you. I am sorry. Did I hurt you?"

"No. And you didn't assault me. I'm cool, honestly I am. I'm annoyed with myself that perhaps I should have changed my ways, told Peter that I was dating and perhaps he should sit in a chair. I did that with Gerald but then Gerald knew the set-up."

"Ah yes, an English set-up. I'm only a foreigner after all. You could sleep six in a bed over there. Weird English sexual practices are the staple of Hollywood gossip."

"That's the aristocracy, Ellis. Not ordinary people. The aristocracy do what they like when they like. They are a breed apart." Julia had begun to feel nervous. Perhaps Ellis was more deeply affected by his loss of control than it was possible to sweep away with a chat over the teacups.

"Look Ellis." Julia spoke forcefully. "You did not hurt me. Perhaps you were a little too rough. Part of it wasn't loving, the first part. But you did not do anything I didn't want you to. I do not have sex with Peter. This bad thing between us is finished."

Ellis leaned forward, suddenly looking as though he had come to life. "I'm ashamed and angry with myself. I love you so much."

Julia felt a heady rush of excitement and wonder. Here I am, she thought, holding hands across an expensive table, with Ellis McCready, and he was looking at her as though he really loved her. Stop. He does love me. He does, you silly fool.

"Oh it's my fault too. I begin a passionate affair with you, and you find me snuggling up to Peter." Julia forgot where they were. She laughed, and exclaimed, "And you did not rape me." Her voice had a carrying quality. She had done theatre. There was one of those sickly hushes made up of pricked ears.

Julia glanced round the restaurant. "Oh bugger!"

But Ellis smiled. At least she had chased his demons away.

Chapter Nine

"We should leave. I have a suite here in this hotel." Ellis rose from his seat, eager to go.

"Wait a minute." Julia sat still whilst Ellis hovered awkwardly over the table.

"We haven't had our first order yet."

"It doesn't matter," Ellis said impatiently.

"Well, what will they do with it?" Julia looked mutinous.

"Throw it away. How do I know?" Ellis sat back in his chair. A hint of amusement crept into his eyes.

"I'm sorry, but we can't have good food thrown away." Julia arranged her cutlery with a determined air, but she looked up and yes, Ellis' look of amusement had changed into a smile. His black mood had lifted.

"I'm glad you're back," she said simply, feeling relaxed and happy again. The first course arrived.

"I know what you are thinking," Ellis spoke in his usual teasing way. "You're thinking that Americans are a set of food wasting morons."

"Something like that."

"What are you thinking, really?"

"Well, I was thinking that but mostly what a moody bastard you are. But that's OK. I'm a moody bitch too."

"When we get upstairs you can slap my face for last night and we'll start again."

"Slap your face? Mmmm I doubt it. It's not wise to do much face slapping in England. English men slap back."

"That's hard to believe."

"Oh yes. They're basically all barbarians. Especially Yorkshire men. They're descended from the Vikings."

"Did Gerald slap you?"

"I don't kiss and tell. I bet you put the toilet seat down when you've finished as well."

"Don't men do that in England?"

"Hardly. You used to see signs sometimes 'gentlemen lift seat' but I think that was to do with them not peeing on the seat."

"Oh I can't stand any more of this." Ellis laughed. "You're pushing me away with your foreign ways. Now that you have eaten your fish, let's go upstairs."

The middle-aged lady at the next table, already tuned in by Julia's cry of rape, now twinkled openly across at them. For one horrible moment Julia thought that she was actually going to speak. Julia supposed that it was romantic for Ellis and herself to be arguing. Ellis was quite well-known as an actor and people were bound to stare at him. Oh no! Julia cursed herself for not leaving – the woman spoke.

"Oh Mr McCready, Ellis, I know you won't mind my saying how wonderful you are in your latest film. We've just seen it at a special viewing. I was so impressed. What a great New York story."

Julia walked away, trying not to look in a hurry. She waited for Ellis in a foyer. The garrulous woman would detain him for quite some time and he, of course, would be too polite to appear bored. She was a fan. At last he appeared.

As Julia headed for the lifts with Ellis, she began to notice that quite a few people glanced his way. He was getting the kind of attention that an actor got who had just starred in a word-of-mouth red hot film. He was congratulated again by the lifts. Of course, Julia thought, that was why he had gone to New York. For a showing. She could not even remember the name of the film. What was it? *New York* something or other.

A flash exploded. Julia was told to cling to Ellis and smile by the cameramen. Another flash, and another. Julia remembered her training. She put on her most flattering smile.

Soon there was quite a crowd of well-wishers. Ellis did his duty. Actors were never really off duty.

Eventually, they escaped to Ellis' suite.

The door shut. Ellis pulled Julia into his arms and kissed her. Not passionately. She noted that. Then he broke away, leaving her puzzled by his coolness.

"Sorry about that. You know what fans are like," he said, flinging off his jacket and tie and leading her to one of the sumptuous sofas.

"No I'm sorry. I completely forgot about your new film. I should have asked you about it at least. But it appears to be a success." Was he annoyed that she had forgotten, she wondered. No, he wasn't like that.

"It looks like it. You'll have to come with me to the premier in a few days. You're my girl." Ellis got himself a drink and made no attempt to get closer.

Julia, who wanted to jump straight into bed with him, forget their last encounters and enjoy their new intimacy, tried to relax. "So, you live here now?"

"Yes, do you like it?"

"Well," Julia looked around with distaste. "It's not to my liking. I feel sorry for you living in a place that's ruched to death."

"Do you want to stay here with me?" he said glancing sideways with a peculiar yearning look.

Julia began languorously to kick off her shoes and lay back on the cushions on the terrible sofa. "I suppose you might be able to persuade me." Her eyes invited him to sit beside her. She was surprised at the gap between them, when he did. "I could stay here, but we fly to Hawaii in two weeks and perhaps we could rent something." She leaned over and ran her hand up his chest. "I still have your shirt buttons."

As soon as the words were out of her mouth, Julia knew that they were a great mistake. A look of pain crossed Ellis' face. Their last sexual encounter was not something that he liked to recall. And it was obviously no joking matter either.

Oh no, Julia thought, surely he's not still traumatised by that silly incident. The only way to cure it was to have immediate sex. This, for some unknown reason, was not going to happen.

The romantic warmth had chilled. "Why have you left your house and come here?" Julia asked after a strained silence.

"Well, it's my new film, *New York Heartline*. I have to do a lot of entertaining, promotion, you know. It's easier in a hotel in town. People can drop in, reporters, magazines, the whole kit and caboodle. And then there's the sci-fi film we're doing. They'll try to drum up interest in that on the back of the *New York* thing."

"So this place will be humming until we fly out?"

"Yeah, morning, noon and night. And we've got photo shoots and publicity for the Hawaiian shoot. You know the kind of thing."

Julia nodded though in reality her fame had mostly been people pointing at her in Sainsburys and saying, 'Isn't she that one from *Eastenders*'. Though she had once made the 'What were you thinking?!' page in *Heat*.

"Is this your bedroom?" Julia got up and crossed to a door which was quite close to the entrance. The room revealed beyond was more like a film-set for *The Sheik of Araby*. "God," she said, "If this room is ruched to death, your bedroom is draped to death."

Julia went back to sit beside Ellis on the sofa. "I'm sorry if I keep saying 'God'," she said, making an effort to break the return of the ice between them. "You might be very religious."

Ellis shrugged. "I have an open mind."

Julia felt relieved. "Good, I'm a 'don't know' too. I suppose we don't really know each other, but…" Julia hesitated, "I want to get to know you. I want to be your girl, as you so quaintly put it."

Ellis moved at last. His kiss was warm. Julia responded, sliding into that state of sweet anticipation which he could arouse in her in an instant.

But they broke apart. "It wouldn't work here would it," Julia whispered. "Not with crowds of people outside the bedroom door."

"No, but we have Hawaii. We can rent a house in the hills. We can have a honeymoon."

For one moment Julia thought that Ellis was asking her to marry him. She dismissed the idea and gave in to the nice feeling of his warm body next to hers.

His voice murmured in her hair. "What do you say? Will you marry me?"

They say that you never forget the moment when some man asks you to marry him. The room seemed to freeze around Julia. The garish flowery wallpaper. The hideous concertinaed curtains which covered every surface, the obscenely thick green carpet. The glitter of mirrors and drinks glasses and huge flashy flower arrangements which oozed a cloying perfume.

Julia felt a little knee-tremblingly weak. "Do you know what you're getting yourself into?," she said with an attempt at a joke.

"I love you." Ellis' blue eyes shone with a deep and wholly mysterious light.

Julia's heart was now beating so rapidly that she began to feel faint. She closed her eyes and lay against Ellis. She must have gone into a kind of trance for several minutes. Then her brain kicked in. Her heart rate gradually dropped to almost normal. She had been paid a great compliment. She must make some kind of reply.

"It might work," she said solemnly as she and Ellis held each other's eyes, now the most precious and wonderful organ in the human body. "I could love, might already… but…"

"Ah, 'but'…" Ellis held her close and began to place small kisses on her forehead, cheeks and chin. She waited for the final kiss, but he didn't do it. His look said that he knew that she wanted him. Then he brushed her lips with his.

She leaned back. "A minute ago, I thought you were being rather cold. I had almost begun to think that you might suggest some kind of trial separation."

Ellis laughed. "Never. I was worried you wouldn't say yes. Have you said yes?"

"You don't know much about me."

"I know that I wanted you from the moment we met."

"You're so sure, Ellis. You're smiling like we can get married and live happily ever after, just like that." Julia said pettishly. She leaned forward impetuously and kissed him.

There was a clatter outside the door. A voice called "Room service." Ellis told them to enter. The waiter came in with a trolley covered with champagne and titbits. He had only advanced three paces when a huge crowd burst in around him shouting "Surprise!" in a deafening chorus. Julia thought that she and Ellis could be at it like rabbits in the bedroom but would this crowd have been deterred by that small thing? No, they would be in the bedroom now grinning like idiots around the bed.

Get a grip, Julia told herself. This partly explained Ellis' stand-offish behaviour. His time was not his own. He was the golden goose laying the Studio's golden egg. And she had promised to marry him!

Before Julia had time to recover from Ellis' proposal and the invasion of the room by a party mood crowd, there was Gerald sitting beside her and kissing her on the mouth with great enthusiasm and familiarity.

Inevitably Ellis was drawn slightly away by the congratulations and general crowing over the huge box-office receipts generated by *New York Heartline*.

"I thought you'd gone back to the UK," Julia said in an unwelcoming way.

"You mean you hoped I'd gone back," Gerald quipped merrily nuzzling Julia's unresponsive neck.

That was the trouble with Gerald, he was always relentlessly flip, Julia thought.

"Thought I'd come and rescue you from these poncy Hollywood types," Gerald continued insultingly, with one eye on Ellis.

Ellis smiled but his eyes were wary.

Weight for weight, the two men were physically similar. Both were six foot two and fair. Facially they differed. Ellis' features were more defined and his mouth was finely cut. Gerald had an aggressive nose which coupled with a general quizzical expression gave him great charm of manner.

Julia began to be aware that Gerald and Ellis, alike in some ways, had been made even more alike by make-up. Gerald's blond hair and been cut and dyed a darker shade to match Ellis' exactly. Julia felt that she must be going mad.

"Yes, dear," Gerald grinned wickedly, "that's right, you've got it. I'm Ellis' double."

"But you can't be in the film," Julia began to feel quite angry with whichever one of her friends had enabled this farcical situation to develop. "You haven't got a card."

"Oh yes I have. I've done a bit of Shakespeare in the past."

Julia rose and sidled to the side of the room which seemed to be filling up more by the minute. Although Ellis glanced at her frequently with a warm look, Julia felt unable to return anything but a wry smile. Ellis was doing the pretty. It was his job. Julia sighed. No privacy. Some job.

Gerald was soon at her side. "Have you seen this film? Bernard had a showing last night. *New York Heartline*. Load of romantic tosh. Ellis travels the underground picking up dumb girls and screwing them until he rapes and accidentally murders one of them. Except he hasn't murdered her and…"

"Will you shut up" Julia groaned. "Why don't you just go back to your acres in Yorkshire and leave me alone."

"Nothing much doing over there. As soon as Peter rang me and said you were in Hollywood, I was over here like a shot."

"Why exactly?" Julia asked wearily.

"For you, of course. OK, you want to punish me for that little fling I had at Fountains Abbey, but that was your fault anyway, saying we should part. And I understand why you might want to fuck Ellis. If I was that way inclined, I'd screw him myself. Anyway, you've made the pact."

"The pact's not everything. Not entirely real…" Julia sighed. Even as she spoke she felt its pull.

"Well, that was the whole point of it wasn't it? It was to make life real." Gerald pulled Julia close. "You're mine," he whispered fiercely in her ear.

Chapter Ten

With the party hotting up, Julia realised that she would not have Ellis to herself any more that evening. She must get away from Gerald who hung by her side and had even taken to putting his arm possessively around her back. Any moment now he would be stroking her bum in the circular motion he, and she, had liked in the past. She would have to question him first and find out who was behind the plot to bring them together again.

With Gerald still in tow, Julia tracked down Barbara and Peter in the kitchenette. Bernard was sitting nearby consuming serious quantities of drink and snacks so Barbara was at liberty to ask Julia how the Gerald and Julia romance was going.

"No Barb, there is no Gerald and Julia. It's Julia and Ellis now." Julia stood her ground in the foursome. She was to blame for the inclusion of Gerald in the original pact of herself, Barb and Peter. She had been too weak to exclude him, particularly as Gerald had displayed a quite touching desire to belong to it. And also because he was very, very rich.

"This isn't the time to discuss pact business," Barb whispered, which was unnecessary as the din was deafening.

"Especially with all these mad Americans braying around," Peter added.

"Julia seems to think that I no longer belong to the pact," Gerald said, unable to keep the genuine hurt out of his voice.

Barb and Peter said, "He does," simultaneously.

A little flutter of fear assailed Julia. This was serious business. The pact was as dear to her heart as the other three but she was too sensible not to see its drawbacks, and her breaking up with Gerald was one of them. Someone else now figured in her thoughts of love, marriage and, perhaps children. Barb and Peter were perhaps the most committed to it. They had never intended to have a conventional married existence. And Gerald, well Gerald, just wanted her.

Julia tried another tack. "But you've got Bernard now Barb. What about him? Can you imagine him incarcerated in Bigbury On Sea in a tiny bungalow. God, he would hardly get through the door."

"I don't view Bernard as a long time arrangement. Look, the poor dear will hardly make forty-five."

The four looked at Bernard happily consuming way beyond his capacity to survive the strain of so much food. Bernard waved back. "What's with the cabal in the corner?," he shouted.

This jerked the four back into a lighter mood.

"This isn't the place." Barb tried to look casual. "Look Jules, we all understand why you have the hots for Ellis. Take your fill of him. Why not? He's a bleeding heart-throb screen idol. But, you're still committed to the pact, the least being two months a year for the rest of your life."

"I know. I am." Julia felt a warm feeling that these two months were guaranteed to herself as well.

"After all," Barb spoke a little spitefully, the pact was dearest of all to her, "it's not as though Ellis is going to ask you to marry him is it? He's been very involved with a model – I forget her name."

"Penny?" Julia asked, with a pang of jealousy.

"No, no, Carmella something."

By mutual telepathy, the four locked in a break-up ritual, with their arms over each other's shoulders.

Gerald was at her side again, suggesting that she come up to his suite. Trust Gerald to point out that he was loaded and quite able to afford a suite of his own

"Oh Jules." He tried to pull her close to him. "You are looking fabulous. You're getting that burnished Hollywood look but..." Gerald refused to let her go. He held her tightly with his right arm and ran his free fingers lightly along her breasts and then her mouth, "...Don't let them touch your breasts or your teeth. They belong to me."

"They don't anymore," Julia faced him down stonily.

"Oh?" Gerald resumed caressing her breasts, "I can feel them perking up already."

"That's a purely physical reaction, Gerald, not a mental one."

"Well," Gerald pushed his crotch into Julia aggressively. "Would you like to feel my physical reaction?"

Julia willed herself not to break, not to feel some sympathy for Gerald's obvious refusal to believe that they were finished.

"Why are you behaving like this Gerald? You seem to have left all your usual charm on the other side of the Atlantic."

"You don't need charm over here," Gerald said surly. "Look at this lot." He glanced around contemptuously at the raucous crowd. "They don't know the meaning of the word. Anyway, I'm drunk. You know how badly behaved I am when I'm drunk. You used to like it."

"Did Barb encourage you to stay in Hollywood and get in this film I'm doing?"

"I don't need encouragement to get close to you Julia." Gerald spoke softly, pressing himself closer and nibbling Julia's earlobe in a familiar, practised way.

"We'll always be friends Gerald," she said calmly, tossing her head and pushing him away. "Now, leave me alone!"

Gerald threw up his hands angrily. "All right," he shouted as she hurried away. "Screw your poncy American actor. But you'll come running back to me." Several guests at the party stopped talking and stared in his direction. Gerald smiled his charming smile at them and shrugged. "Fight like cat and dog. But she loves me really."

Julia found it impossible to get close to Ellis. The party had been thrown by the Studio and everyone was determined to celebrate Ellis' hit film. Julia was not one for getting drunk. Something to do with loss of control, she supposed. She decided to leave.

Julia gained the sanctuary of her little blue room. She called Ellis and explained that she was tired and had decided to leave. She could hear the party going on in the background.

"I understand," Ellis sounded rueful. "But you know how it is. If you get a success everyone wants to know you. I've already been offered some good parts in new films."

"Yes, yes of course, you deserve them."

"Gerald's challenged me to an arm-wrestling match. He's getting very drunk. By the way, did you say yes to my proposal?" Ellis' voice had an anxious note to it.

Julia's eyes misted with tears. What wouldn't she give to get Ellis in her room right now so that she could prove that she loved him. "Well," she teased, "you can take it that I don't see much possibility of saying no."

"I think that I shall have to try to pin you down more on that tomorrow."

"I shall look forward to that…"

"I've got to go, the crowd is…"

The next day Julia signed her contract with the Studio and met her agent, Humphrey St Clare, in the Studio diner.

"This is not a good deal for you," Humphrey was cross and severe. "Though the money's good. Make a hash of this and you could be finished in the States. You only get one chance over here, you know. Any novelty value you may have soon wears off without some backup."

"And this from the man who booked me to do a stupid TV dairy advert." Julia fought back. She was not very fond of Humphrey. In many ways, as an Englishman, he was not really competent in his dealings in America. He neither liked nor trusted Americans. It was his age. He was over sixty and had been brought up to think of Yanks as an inferior breed.

He liked to curl his lip when they mispronounced his surname and he never corrected them.

"It got you noticed. Do you think I could show a wedge of British TV to these idiots? They lose interest at the first word they can't understand. Show them your arse in the dairy advert – then they get interested. By the way, they want your tits done."

"No."

"Very well, I'll plug the push-up bra. I think you're wise. Big false tits don't go down all that well in *Eastenders* which is where you will end up if this all goes fanny up, they like the real thing."

"I'm not going to argue with you about the mother and daughter thing. All I can say is, that I got Dustin very interested and even got a feeler in to Redford. This crap science fiction film had better be worth it. Still, sequels are getting better at the moment, not worse.

"I understand that you're shacked up with Ellis McCready. Milk that, he's hot at the moment. Go around with him and smile, get in the papers, show some cleavage, get some garish clothes, all that bo-ho chic you like falls flat on people who don't appreciate it. Marry him if you can. Now, that would give you a boost over here.

"And remember, no common Brit accent at any price. No, no, no! Pretend you can't do it. Keep to the upper-crust accent. It's expected. You get stuck with your roots and no matter what you do, you will always be a common little thing with no brains."

At last Humphrey heaved his tall, angular, grey-haired figure out of the canteen chair, fixed the English gentleman smile on his face, and sallied forth to do business all sweetness and light.

"I don't know why you put up with him," Barbara slid across from Julia into Humphrey's place. "My agent will take you on like a shot."

"But you write, Barb, and now you're getting wads doing the script for this film."

"Ah, but you're screwing Ellis, Jules, and I must say he seems pretty besotted. Several girls got him quite blatantly by the crotch last night and he said he was taken. Gerald got quite uppity because you wouldn't have him back. He arm-wrestled Ellis. Ellis won. Gerald passed out. It was quite a good party, there was puke everywhere. Even Bernard fetched up his vol-au-vent. He said they were off, but he guzzles so many you'd think that he must surely explode at any moment."

"Do you like Bernard really?" Julia asked quietly.

"Well, he expects me to tell him not to eat so much. But why should I? I tell him if he's got a death wish to die by eating, what can I say that will make him stop? That stops him a bit. But, yes, I like him.

"But you, Julia, what's with you and Ellis? Why aren't you in his suite screwing him silly? No, perhaps the smell of sick is not romantic, but you could relocate to another suite. True the crowd would find you but you might get one night of peace. Of course, Gerald was on about you breaking the pact. But I know you will never do that. You are in it as much as I am."

Julia took a deep breath. "Ellis has asked me to marry him."

Barbara was astonished. "Oh poor Gerald. But bingo! What a boost to your career. He's set to become a Hollywood A-lister. You'd be made."

"That would not be why I would marry him, Barb."

"Of course not. It's love, love, love. That's the story for the press."

"It's the true story, Barb."

"Of course it is. How could he not love you. I love you. Peter loves you. Gerald loves you."

"I sometimes wonder if it was a good idea to let Gerald into the pact."

"And what would we have bought the bungalow at Bigbury on Sea with, might I ask? If not with Gerald's money. How else were we going to spend our twilight years watching the two tides meet before the island. Five years ago we had practically nothing Jules. Gerald had the money. It took him two years to get into your bed, but he still paid for the bungalow. Oh yes we can buy one now. Hell, I can afford three. But he had the money then and we needed it. Anyway, he's as needy as we are. He's into the idea. Insurance for old age. Get three people to swear to honour and keep you in sickness and health for the rest of your life. Find somewhere as breathtakingly beautiful as Bigbury on Sea and the South Hams and stick to it like glue. It's beautiful.

"Anyway, Gerald will always have money. He owns a buggery lot of Yorkshire. We might lose all of ours. Get into a bad lawsuit, or a sour marriage deal, over here and it's gone."

"Where does all this leave Ellis?"

"Nowhere. He's a foreigner. He won't understand."

"What won't I understand?" Ellis was leaning over the table. He sat next to Julia and they exchanged a sweet kiss. "Sorry, I have a habit of doing this. I'll just pretend I didn't hear anything."

"Stupid English ways," Barb said lightly.

"Oh no," Ellis grinned. "You don't say. Well I have a surprise for you. My grandmother is Scottish. McCready is her name. And although the Scots don't like the English, they sure know a lot about them."

Ellis laughed at his companions' barely concealed dismay.

"Ha, caught you there. Now you can't play that mysterious English card quite so well, can you?"

Chapter Eleven

"It's as I always expected." Julia hoped that she sounded casual. "You were always more clued up about us than you let on. Actually we were talking about ways of getting Gerald out of the film."

Julia thought for a moment that Ellis was going to take issue with her lie. Had he heard Barb say 'nowhere' and 'foreigner'?

Ellis had a doubtful look in his eyes. Julia leaned closer to him. "You shouldn't take any notice of us, Ellis. Barb and I talk such rubbish as you'd never believe."

Ellis responded by putting his arm around her. The touch of his brown, masculine hand, which was well-shaped and attractive, though with the inevitable poncy American manicure, was so different from Gerald's forceful attentions of the night before. Where Gerald had elicited an animalistic response from her, Ellis' soft touch engaged Julia's feelings and emotions in a surge of desire that was impossible to conceal. She was glad that she was wearing a bra or her nipples would have been popping up in full view of the curious canteen watchers.

When Ellis kissed the back of her neck, Julia was able to recover a little by engaging in a silent dialogue with Barb, who was mouthing "get a room" and grinning.

This jerked Julia back to the problem of Gerald. Barb was half rising to leave but Julia's shake of the head stopped her.

"I've still got this bone to pick with you Barb." Julia brought herself back to Earth with a deep breath and her latent anger at the inclusion of Gerald in the film. "How come that Gerald is Ellis' double?"

"Well, Bernard thought that Gerald was a good friend of yours, which he is, and noticed that he looks like Ellis, and gave him the job. It's as simple as that."

"Oh no it's not. You know I don't want Gerald here."

"I'm not in control of Bernard, Jules. Remember he's in charge."

Julia looked at Ellis, but he made a gesture of resignation. "She's right," he agreed. "What Bernard says, goes."

"So," Julia began to wearily resign herself to seeing more of Gerald. "the scene is set and I have to engage with Gerald in lieu of Ellis while they do the lighting or make-up. Thank God there are no love scenes."

Barb pulled a comical face and did not appear to be sorry for what she was about to say. "I'm sorry to say, Jules that you have been upgraded to wicked handmaiden which I was doing, and which I have magnanimously let you have because of my writing commitments. You should be pleased. It's a better part. Humphrey will be really pissed off if you don't take it. Remember you're a professional." Barb rose and waved a cheeky goodbye.

"But Gerald isn't. You enjoyed that didn't you?" Julia called after her.

"Well, you get to kiss me," Ellis said with mock offence.

"Kisses on a set with everyone gawping are not the same as kisses in private, as you well know." Julia admonished tenderly.

"I have an answer for that." Ellis was now anxious to leave. He had been causing quite a stir in the canteen. *New York Heartline* was being avidly discussed and at any moment a crowd of wannabe-known actors would descend on their table.

Ellis would be trapped. If he brushed them off there would be tales in the magazines the next day such as 'I thought he was a regular guy, but fame has gone to his head because he wouldn't speak to me at all', and a girl with a large cleavage might very well declare, 'Ellis McCready made me cry!'

Julia was ready to go. She knew that Americans thought that the slightest eye-contact gave them the right to charge at anybody they damn well pleased.

Ellis drove Julia out to the Malibu Hills.

"This really is Hollywood movie style," Julia laughed, and had to shout to be heard above the roar of the engine.

"I have found a house with a view to die for," Ellis shouted back.

Julia looked out over the sun-baked hills and the weirdly shaped trees. She pointed. Ellis obligingly stopped by a view.

"Look at those trees. How can they be real? They are straight out of *The Cat in the Hat*. I always thought they could not possibly be real trees."

"I don't think they are." Ellis smiled at Julia's look of doubt. "They are cactus plants, I think."

Julia was quiet for the rest of the way. She was feeling dizzy with it all. Hollywood, fast car, Ellis McCready, sunshine that shone with no hint of stopping, fantasy trees come to life. Fantasy house with a fantasy view and Barb and Bernard waving from the balcony.

Julia and Ellis came down to earth with a bump.

"Oh damn, damn, damn!" Ellis swore. "Don't tell me that's Bernard."

"He's too big to miss. I take it you were not expecting them here."

Ellis turned and hugged Julia almost in despair. "No, but you know what it's like. I'm their property and although I bribed that secretary not to tell anyone where we were going, I can't expect her to lose her job over me."

Inside, Ellis and Julia were greeted by hairdressers, costumiers, make-up artists, scriptwriters and producers.

"Sorry Ellis," Bernard said, not sorry at all. "But things are moving fast now. The backers want their profit like last week. We've got barely six months to do this thing. Now this is just a little confab to do the basics. Like, what are you going to look like, your costume and your make-up? Should your hair be different than last time or a little bit longer? If we can get this thing thrashed out now it will save time. Great place you got here. It will be days before the press find us.

"Now people. We can do this. Concentrate. Firstly, Ellis' costume. No, no, we must all call him Pawl, that's been his name for the last three episodes. Now, he is a warlord of the outer rim. Why the outer rim? You all know. Because he was cast out in the last episode. Now I don't want any of you scriptwriters here if you don't know those first three films backwards. So anyone who doesn't know had better know by tomorrow. And that goes for any actors here as well. Now, what would a warlord wear? We thought a Japanese or Chinese take on that."

Ellis took his seat in the inner circle and Julia was left on the outside. Barbara was in writing mode which mostly meant arguing fiercely with the other writers.

Julia explored the house which was perched above a wonderful view of sun-baked hills. The absent owner had marvellous taste in decor with polished wooden floors and American Indian-style cushions and rugs in vibrant colours.

Julia found a lovely bedroom with a patchwork quilt on the bed. It was empty and she staked her claim to it. She had to be somewhere whilst Ellis was put through his paces. The meeting was likely to go on all day. Would they all go away eventually and leave Ellis and herself alone? Julia had a bad feeling about that. They had only had sex twice. The first had been awkward and the second a little rushed to say the least. Hell, she wasn't even sure if he was circumcised. A day of making love in this beautiful house, talking over Ellis' proposal of marriage and forgetting the rest of the world, had gone completely down the tubes.

By the time Ellis appeared in the doorway, Julia had explored the garden, studied the cactus plants and changed her cotton top to a glamorous daffodil silk number. She had been served lunch by a houseboy and was now wondering whether to go down and ask Ellis about dinner.

Ellis' appearance was rather a shock. His hair was gone, replaced by a half-inch of stubble. He was wearing an atrocious leather-type jerkin and shorts. He grinned as he entered the room, running his hand over his crop ruefully.

"I take it you don't like it." Ellis walked straight to the bed and lay down next to Julia with a sigh.

Julia turned to him and kissed him as he lay strangely inert. He did not respond with any passion. He looked pale and his forehead was beaded with sweat. Julia ran her hand down the strange leather jerkin towards the equally strange trunks.

Before Julia had time to take in Ellis' apparently sick condition, a large woman dressed in a nurse's uniform briskly entered the room carrying a tray of water, and was soon busy feeling Ellis' pulse. She glanced at Julia. "I'd leave him alone if I were you dearie," she snapped in a Birmingham accent, "he's got to rest. No hanky-panky."

"Of course." Julia leapt off the bed.

Ellis grinned at her confusion. "Caught with your hand in the cookie jar."

"You under contract?" the nurse asked Julia abruptly. "I can do your shots now if you like."

"Shots?"

"Vitamin shots."

Julia shook her head dumbly.

"Thank you but I'll see a doctor first."

The nurse took umbrage. "Well, if I'm not good enough have it your way. It's in the contract. You get sick, you can't sue the studio. They have dengue fever in Hawaii you know. From the mosquitos, so you need to be fit. Pretty nasty fever – sickness, nosebleeds, headaches, muscle cramps, possible fatal haemorrhage."

"Oh thank you so much," Julia said sarcastically, inwardly alarmed.

The nurse laughed. "Pretty hoity-toity aren't we for a groupie? And remember, leave him alone, the poor man needs his rest. And make sure he drinks this water."

The nurse left. Ellis held out his arms. Julia reluctantly climbed back beside him on the bed. "I always react badly," he tried to pull Julia close to him.

Julia didn't usually try to mother her lovers, but she was feeling a surge of tender concern that Ellis was ill. She laid her hand on his hot forehead and regarded him with narrowed eyes.

"I don't see how vitamin shots, which we don't do much of in England, I admit, would cause you to feel so ill."

Ellis looked down at his well-muscled body. "I need to bulk up a little for this part. Remember, he's macho man of the galaxy."

It was a minute or two before Julia realised the meaning of his words.

"I love to see you looking puzzled. Your eyes are like emerald chips and you have a little frown right just there." Ellis caressed Julia's forehead and tried to pull her towards him. "You don't know how sexy you look with your hair falling over your shoulders, and that little frown that needs to be kissed away."

Julia resisted his soft, seductive words. "You mean to tell me that you have taken some muscle-enhancing drug – like steroids?"

Ellis relaxed resignedly. "It's common practice. People are putting millions into this film."

Julia felt unable to say anything. She was not his mother. She was not even sure whether she would be his wife.

She lay down and responded to his embrace. "Next time, you must play someone weedy. Promise."

Julia ran her hand over the leather jerkin. It was tightly tied. "Shall I help you to take this off?"

"Naughty girl," Ellis teased as Julia helped him to ease himself out of the tight jerkin and trunks. He was completely naked under them. He had been circumcised she noticed. Julia pulled the quilt over him.

"Things are rolling along too fast with this film. Still it's a test, isn't it?" Ellis turned his eyes to Julia's with a look of such affection that her breath caught in her throat.

"A test of whether you still love me now that I'm bald and sick?"

"Sickness, yes, but I'm not sure about the baldness." She ran her hand over the coarse stubble.

They lay in companionable silence for a time. Julia handed Ellis the water. He seemed to be feeling better.

It was surprisingly nice to lie platonically together, Julia thought and for the first time she began to consider whether she might actually marry him.

"I shall be OK tomorrow, but," Ellis paused and grimaced, "I have to fly down to Florida to do some jungle scenes for the publicity people. I tried to avoid them but... you know what it's like."

"It doesn't matter." Julia was quick to reassure him. "What we have will survive a few setbacks. Anyway sex isn't the be all and end all of a relationship, is it?"

"Well, couples have usually managed a bit more sex than us before they start talking like that," Ellis complained with a smile.

Julia's mind wandered back to their last sexual encounter. She had been intrigued by Gerald's description of Ellis as a rapist in the film *New York Heartline*.

"What was it like playing a rapist in your last film."

Ellis shifted his weight restlessly. "I was going to talk to you about that. It doesn't explain my behaviour. It doesn't explain that I jumped to the conclusion that you and Peter were laughing at me. It doesn't excuse what I did."

"You didn't do anything wrong Ellis. I had an orgasm. I enjoyed it. I started enjoying it almost immediately."

"Did you? You didn't show it."

"Well, as you said, we are still feeling our way."

Ellis was about to say something. Julia cut him off.

"Look, let's get back to your feelings. When you were in New York at the preview, did you re-shoot – some rape scenes?"

"Yes, but it's not an excuse is it? When we are married am I going to play a wife-beater and come home and beat you up? Am I going to play a homosexual and ignore you physically?"

Julia felt Ellis becoming heated and the sweat formed on his brow again.

"Shh darling," she soothed feeling closer to him than ever before. "It does explain it. You know it does."

"It's the loss of self-control that bugs me the most."

"I understand. Why do you think I fake that I don't have an orgasm with you?" As she said the words Julia felt a sense of shock. She had never given away such an intimate secret about herself before.

Chapter Twelve

Ellis had been looking sleepy before Julia dropped her bombshell. But now his eyes opened wide and darkened with desire. Julia felt the sudden tension in his body as he rolled towards her and kissed her a feather kiss on the mouth.

"Look, I'm not having that nurse coming in here and accusing me of molesting you again," she said quickly, fending him off. "You are sick, Ellis, sick."

"I've recovered." Nevertheless, he did not resist when she pushed him back onto his pillow. He laughed up at her. "Not so cold English miss," He was quite delighted by her confession.

"It was a mistake to tell you that," Julia teased. "If you are a gentleman, you will not take advantage of it."

Ellis just smiled and looked thoroughly content.

"We're just whores where our acting professions are concerned. We do what we are asked to do. Cut our hair, wear ridiculous clothes, go to places we don't want to, see things we don't want to see, conjure up emotions we didn't know we had. Prostitute ourselves in the name of art cinema. Disappear into whatever role it is we have to do."

"Yes," Ellis said softly, his eyes holding hers in rapt attention.

"Sometimes, it's hard to break away."

Ellis nodded again.

"You didn't want to do Pawl again did you? Is it my fault that you are?"

"No. I was already feeling guilty about all those actors relying on a job in it. He's not a very nice man. He's a bit of a mindless macho stud. Someone I used to be."

There was silence for a time. Julia could see that Ellis' fight against falling asleep was beginning to crumble. She eased herself away from his hold.

"Yes," Julia whispered dreamily, "it's hard to break away. It's hard to become your mother and return intact. Hard to become a twenty-first century sexy girl. Girls just didn't do sex in the 1950s. Girls who liked sex were prostitutes. They strutted Long Row in their wedgy shoes. To become one of them was to become a leper who would never get clean."

Ellis fell asleep with a frown of puzzlement still lying gently on his features at her last words.

Julia scolded herself that she shouldn't have kept Ellis awake so long. And why was she going on about her mother? She never talked to anyone except Barb about her mother, and very often then, she wouldn't know that she was.

Was it because she loved Ellis and he loved her? Would she finally manage to extract herself from the shadows of the past when before she had had no will to do so? Was Ellis her prince on his charger come to rescue her?

Ellis flew to Florida to try out his leather tunic, shorts and helmet in the Everglades. He rang Julia. He had recovered from his 'vitamin shots'. He longed to see her. She longed to see him. Their only real chance of meeting again was at Los Angeles airport en route to Honolulu on a 3 a.m. flight.

Julia had several photo shoots lined up where she was dressed like a harem slave and posed with lots of leg and breast on show. The other girls exposed even more flesh. She had got her script and worried at it to try and make some kind of realistic sense out of the plot. She was to entice Ellis, or rather Pawl, away from his intended bride and then betray him to his enemies.

Julia would try to get the ear of Barbara. There was more to luring a man than half exposed breasts and a come-hither smile. Barb had better write some good lines pretty damn quick.

Ellis flew back to Los Angeles to attend a showing of *New York Heartline* and he insisted that Julia go with him. That same night they were to fly out to Hawaii. Julia was to meet Ellis at the movie theatre.

Julia chose a glamorous black full-length evening dress for the premier. She wanted to look good on that red carpet. Black was safe. There was no danger of her clashing horribly with another actress. Some of the fierce competitive spirit that seemed to flow around Hollywood was infecting her, she knew. Barb was going with Bernard, of course. Anyone who was anyone would be there.

It turned out that Ellis was to escort both Julia and his co-star in the film, down that red path of dreams.

Julia didn't care. She was so pleased to see Ellis. The crowd cheered when they met at the entrance to the theatre and kissed. They were not quite sure who she was but she was being kissed by Ellis McCready and that set the flashbulbs popping.

Ellis' blonde co-star, Erica Black, dressed in ruffled orange, forgot to smile for a moment as her face betrayed her annoyance at the appearance of the undoubtedly chic but unknown Julia. Of course, the next day the magazines declared 'Ellis kisses brunette English actress Julia Slater and snubs Erica. Wow does Erica look mad!'

The film was good. It was cleverly shot and obviously going to be a winner. It had a slightly uneven ending when it turned out that Ellis' character had not, in fact, accidentally killed the girl. She was miraculously alive and the audience loved it. Julia reflected that Americans had a lot of trouble with the finality of death. The ending would have been better with the girl dead. Not that she was going to say anything, of course. Films were made for American audiences not British ones, after all.

Ellis, of course, as one of the chief money-spinners was now flavour of the month; until, that is, he made his next bad film.

It's so tedious to be with Ellis and not with Ellis, in this crowded premier thing, Julia sighed to herself. She was tired of smiling, of being asked who she was and what she had done.

"Cor, I have never seen so many bum-lickers in my life," Barb declared when they met. "Some of these Botox smiles are really scary don't you think?"

Julia laughed. What would she do without Barb? Ellis, looking gorgeous in his dicky suit, but frustratingly unobtainable, was talking film deals and offers and receiving congratulations with an easy grace.

Julia eyed Barb's exotic Vivienne Westwood creation with interest.

"Don't say it. I know it looks freakish but that's my handle. Eccentric English writer. Goes down a treat. You look fab. Come on we'll go and change. We fly out in two hours.

Julia was truly in paradise, walking with Ellis up the small path to the most romantic dormer bungalow that she had ever seen. It was called 'Hoonanea'.

There was not a chocolate box cottage in the whole of Devon that could compare with it. Julia felt a small fleeting longing for the smell of Devon violets.

But the sun was beating down, the exotic blooms seemed to explode in the bright light and the deep turquoise sea sparkled on the horizon. Strange birds called to one another.

Lastly, Ellis' hand was holding hers in a 'we are a couple' grasp, palm to palm, pulse to pulse.

"We can get married in an Anglican chapel in Honolulu next week. You only have to say that you are baptised in that faith and I, of course, am American." Ellis seemed to be quite confident that their marriage would take place.

Julia smiled but she did not reply. She knew that Ellis took her silence for agreement but she had never actually said that she would marry him.

Mrs Sanderson was waiting at the door. She was elderly and obviously part Hawaiian with dark eyes and long crinkly greying hair. She wore a too large flowered smock dress. Ellis picked Julia up in his arms, honeymoon style, and followed their host into the house.

"Honeymooners?" Mrs Sanderson nodded her head and led them into the sitting room, which opened out onto a terrace with stunning views of lush tropical Hawaii. "You like it?" she asked, pleased by Julia's expressions of delight.

"You English girl like it. He's American. It doesn't matter what he thinks. I don't usually rent my house to Americans, but the English are always welcome here."

Julia gave Ellis a cheeky smile. "Well, we were here first. Thank you Mrs Sanderson for letting us rent your beautiful home."

"Yes, yes, my dear. Would an American thank me so prettily. I think not."

Faced with Mrs Sanderson's hostility, Ellis wisely retreated to a sofa, made himself comfortable, and left the niceties to Julia.

Mrs Sanderson had now also settled herself in a chair and showed no signs of handing over the keys and departing.

Julia thought that as she was now the mistress of the house, so to speak, she would make herself at home. Groceries had already been delivered. "Would you like a cup of tea, Mrs Sanderson?"

Julia was rewarded with a beaming smile. "I will be delighted. And you can call me Gran, my dear."

Over the teacups, Gran and Julia made polite conversation. Gran pointedly excluded Ellis and although Julia told her their names, she still referred to him as 'the American'.

"Julia, what a pretty name. Tell me, why have you taken up with the American? Is there no fine English boy at home for you?"

Julia was not thrown by anything that Gran Sanderson said. England was full of very similar older women, dictatorial, meddling and rude.

"For an American he is very nice," Julia said contritely.

"Oh I suppose he is OK for nooky-nooky. Quite a big buggah." Gran looked disparagingly at Ellis' reclining form. "But you should marry an English boy."

Gran chatted on. She told how Queen Lilliuokalani was deprived of her royal status in 1893 by American businessmen and then deprived of her liberty until she died. Gran spoke of these events as though they had happened last month and not more than a hundred years ago.

Julia knew all this, of course, from school. In some ways she sympathised with the Hawaiians over their lost independence. As a child, Julia had imagined that Hawaii lay off the coast of America' something like the Scilly Isles did in

Britain. Later, of course, she realised that they were thousands of miles away in the middle of the Pacific. The idea that they were an American state was really rather ludicrous. The correct word was colony.

Julia knew that some Hawaiians resented Americans and here was Gran, living proof. Julia liked Gran. She was grateful that she had rented them her beautiful bungalow but the afternoon was drawing on. She and Ellis had been awake all night at the film theatre and had jetted in late in the morning. How could she get rid of her in a polite way?

A gentle snore from Ellis solved the problem. Gran rose and poked Ellis in the ribs. "See," she said triumphantly. "Your American boyfriend has no stamina. No stamina in the day, no stamina in the bedroom."

Julia watched the sun go down alone. Ellis slept on. She was showered and changed into a strap-less flowered dress and had prepared a meal. She sipped her wine. It was so beautiful on the terrace. Everything was so perfect. Exotic perfume from the flowers drifted across. It was heaven.

A whining noise sounded close to Julia's ear. Mosquitos! She slammed down the shutters to the terrace. Hunted around for the plug-in deterrents. And fell upon Ellis with squeals of alarm.

At first, Ellis was so sleepy that all he wanted to do was kiss. He groaned when Julia tried to wriggle free. "I don't think we're in the area where the dangerous mosquitos live," he protested. And then, noticing that they were alone at last, he refused to let Julia go.

Much as she was enjoying lying full-length on top of a suddenly caveman-type Ellis, Julia could not relax.

They shut all the windows and, lastly, put up the mosquito net over the bed. Ellis stripped off his travel-stained clothes and went towards the adjacent shower room.

Feeling slightly more relaxed about the mosquitoes, Julia turned to leave the bedroom, but the next minute a naked and wet Ellis' arms were around her. He carried her into the shower.

When she protested at her wet dress, he kissed her. "That's for sucking up to that old woman," he said. Another kiss. "And that's for letting me sleep on after she had gone. But then…" Ellis looked at Julia with that peculiar, focused, hunter look, overlaid with love, that signalled overmastering desire. "It has given me the energy to punish you properly." She did not protest, the wet dress was already sliding to the floor.

Chapter Thirteen

Sex in the shower was quick but very nice Julia assured Ellis. They still had to secure the house from the dreaded dengue-carrying mosquitos. Then they had to eat some cold spaghetti and drink some red wine before the white-dressed bed with the white mosquito nets was finally fallen into.

Julia had drunk just enough wine to be relaxed enough to lose some of her inhibitions. She wasn't a lying on the bed, legs open invitingly kind of girl. Sometimes she envied girls who were up for anything. She rarely got really drunk. It was that 'losing control' thing again, she supposed.

Gerald had been her last lover. Gerald had approached sex with great enthusiasm. He was an up for anything type of boy. She had been willing to follow him, mostly, but, because she had never loved Gerald, her approach had been a bit clinical, in a, is it really possible to do it like that? kind of way.

With Ellis was different. She was pretty sure that she loved him, and because her heart was engaged and he would have to do nothing more than look at her, or she see him, for desire, a really rather delicious, all-consuming desire, to run through her body. But it also meant that sex with him was fraught with anxiety. She had no confidence in her sexual allure. She didn't have particularly big breasts, for example, which seemed to be de rigueur this side of the pond. Most Englishmen, sensibly, didn't really mind what size they were. The thing was, did Ellis fancy her as much as she fancied him?

Gerald, of course, was English and they had understood each other in a way that it would take some time to achieve with Ellis.

"What are you thinking about?" Ellis whispered as they settled down in the deep bed.

"The pleasure of our naked bodies pressed together."

"Yes."

"Wondering what you like."

"Yes." Ellis was punctuating his questions with a kiss and making it very hard for Julia to think of anything at all.

"Gerald."

Ellis rolled onto his back. "Not that jerk."

She knew she shouldn't laugh, but she did.

She climbed on top of Ellis. "You're jealous."

He looked up. "No."

"I never loved him. Well, I was fond of him."

"That's better."

She snuggled her face into his neck and gripped him suggestively around his hips with her legs.

"I haven't had a lover since him."

Ellis ran his hands down the curve of her waist as her closeness became too much for him to lie passive any more. He only managed to say, "Good."

Julia would have liked a little more chatty foreplay but then, their sexual relationship was much too new for much of that.

She luxuriated in the pleasure of taking him inside her. It was such a natural thing to do. A natural desire, and Mother Nature always knew best. Her silly feelings of inadequacy fell away and the doubts about their future. There was only now and this man, who was telling her in the best possible way how much he adored her.

Later, with Ellis dozing close to her and the strange Hawaiian moon shining through the window, Julia found it hard to sleep. She could hardly believe that six weeks ago, Ellis had been a fantasy pipe dream. That they would meet and he would be as attracted to her as she was to him, was incredible. And, even more incredible was his proposal of marriage.

That was the trouble. She was going to have to tell him, very soon, whether she was actually going to marry him or not.

Did he love her more than she loved him? He loved her and to him, that meant marriage. She was more cautious, an unattractive trait in the lists of love.

But then, Americans married and divorced more than any other culture on the planet. They seemed to expect perfection in marriage. Take that film, *Mrs Doubtfire*. Robin Williams was soon kicked out of the house by his spouse for being, of all things, silly. And a kind of silliness that would pass quite unnoticed in England and actually thought to be quite endearing.

But then that was a film, as unreal as the Scottish nanny Robin had portrayed.

But what would I do if Ellis divorced me, Julia wondered fretfully. She caressed Ellis' rear. Americans rather crudely called it a butt. But then, there was no good name. Booty, behind, situpon, derriere, bottom... Ellis stirred and Julia hurriedly removed her hand and turned away It was unfair to wake up Ellis and have sex for a, Julia counted sleepily, fifth time. He needed all his strength to wield some kind of sword thing on the slopes of an extinct Hawaiian volcano, and it was all her fault.

Julia walked unsteadily onto the terrace the next morning to find Ellis, dressed in jeans and T-shirt, drinking coffee.

"Oh, you should have woken me," she said with a touch of bad temper. "You look like someone in a bloody breakfast advert, and I look, feel, terrible."

Ellis grinned good humouredly. "If you are trying to put me off marrying you, it isn't working."

"Sorry. I didn't sleep well, and I've just had the most awful nightmare." Julia drank some coffee that Ellis had poured out for her and began to feel better. The view from the terrace was heavenly and the smell of the flowers quite intoxicating.

"Perhaps I will marry you." She rose and sat on Ellis' knee, the better to kiss him. "Any man who can put up with my bad temper in the morning, make me coffee and look so gorgeous, is worth marrying."

Julia was wearing a thin silk robe. Ellis' hold tightened as their kiss deepened.

A sudden coughing noise broke them apart. There was Gran Sanderson, beaming and carrying some Hawaiian fruit.

"I see that my honeymoon house had worked its spell real good." Gran sat down comfortably in a chair and put the fruit on the table.

Ellis was not pleased. Julia could see that he was put out by Gran's appearance. But he had been brought up to be polite, especially to old ladies, and was soon offering Gran some coffee, which he went off to fetch with good grace.

"What's he like?" Gran said without preamble.

Julia grinned. "Now that would be telling."

"Well, you look as flushed as a pink dawn, so I suppose he's not too bad in bed, eh?"

"He is not bad at all," Julia agreed with a smile.

"You're a good girl." Gran nodded. "A good girl to welcome an intrusive old woman."

"It's your home, after all." Julia wondered if Gran was lonely. That might explain her appearance.

"I came here with my husband on honeymoon. A long time ago. We sat here like you and the American. I liked the house so much he bought it for me. They were cheap then. The view is just the same. A few more houses, but the jungle soon hides them from view." Gran rose and went to stand by the rail. "He's dead now, of course. I've come to a stage in my life when I have no future, only memories of the past."

Ellis had returned to the terrace in time to hear the rather sad words. He exerted himself to make Gran feel more welcome by offering her a cup of coffee with one of his charming smiles.

"Best party manners now." Gran spoke a little sharply, but she accepted the coffee and sat down again. "But I understand. A nosey old woman coming between you and your beautiful English girl. Her hair, dark but with the red lights. No Hawaiian hair like that, except, of course, the half-caste, like myself."

Gran stayed a little longer. She talked of the past, and how her grandmother had been part of the uprising against the Americans who had forced their Queen from her throne. Julia was interested and, sympathetic. Ellis was uneasy and not sympathetic.

"You would think that they would have forgotten all about that by now," he said testily when Gran had gone, "it's over a hundred years ago after all."

"And that's where we differ. To Gran and I one hundred years of history is a short time. Remember, she heard those stories at her grandmother's knee. To you, one hundred years is a long time because, I apologise I offend you, the history of your America is very short."

"You know, I had an attractive young schoolteacher once who sounded just like you, but I was never able to do to her what I'm thinking of doing to you right now."

Julia backed away from Ellis' mock aggressive advances. "I'm sorry. Can I at least have some breakfast and a shower?"

"I might consider it – afterwards."

Even the most perfect weekend in paradise has to come to an end and this was the last afternoon. Julia may sigh about it, but she hugged the promise to her of many weekends in paradise to come. Gran Sanderson had called earlier and made the surprising offer of the sale of the house to Ellis and Julia at a quite ridiculous sum. Ellis had been stunned at the figure she mentioned, and Julia had worked out that she could almost cover the cost of her share in the house from her payment for doing the film.

Julia had never felt more relaxed in her whole life as she looked round at the perfect room with the perfect view. She was unable to quite believe that it could all be half hers. She lay on a sofa, and opposite, Ellis lay on its matching twin reading his script with a frown.

"I thought you said Barbara was a good writer," he complained.

"If it's not good, then she didn't write it."

"You are a very loyal friend." Ellis glanced across the space between them, affectionately happy, and not afraid to show it. "And a very beautiful woman."

Julia could have replied that he was a very handsome man but one didn't praise men for their beauty. In her eyes, though, he was the epitome of relaxed male attractiveness, being loose limbed but muscular, and handsome, especially now with his face softened by love.

The rain splattered on the windows and Julia withdrew her gaze. She had learnt all her lines – hers was quite a small part – but Ellis practically carried the film. He felt the weight of that responsibility. He was also wearing reading glasses because the light was poor and looked so studious in them and so desirable, that Julia could hardly stop herself from crossing the short divide between them and taking his glasses off as to prelude to... no, his glasses were not a sex aid but an endearing piece of familiarity and trust on the road to getting to know each other completely. Instead she went to the kitchen to make coffee. Ellis drank a lot of coffee when he was studying his script.

In the kitchen Julia ground the beans. What a shame that they had to go to Honolulu tomorrow on film business. Soon it would be getting up at dawn to catch the sun for the cameras, endless retakes, but worse of all everyone thinking 'is this going to work this time?'

Julia had told Barbara to get the writers to watch *Babylon 5*, her fave sci-fi show. Surely there were enough ideas there to poach for at least half a dozen films? She was thinking fondly of a character in the *Babylon 5* TV series that she had called the 'walking wardrobe' because he was at first very mysterious, but later turned out to be a Vorlon, when her mobile rang.

It was Barb. Barb and Bernard had a house further up the Makiki Valley. "I'm sorry to spoil your weekend, but can I come over?"

"With Bernard?"

"No, no, just me. I must see you."

Fifteen minutes later, Barb was in the kitchen apologising profusely for the interruption. This in itself was not usual Barb behaviour.

"Oh, Ellis doesn't mind," Julia reassured her. "He wants to ask you about the script anyway."

Barb sat down at the kitchen table. "How is life with Ellis?" She lit up and puffed nervously.

"Heavenly, just heavenly."

"Mmm, quite a Barbara Cartland kind of reply."

"Well, we are in paradise."

Barb grimaced. "Even paradise can turn into hell."

Chapter Fourteen

"The worm in the bud." Ellis had come in for more coffee. "Hi, Barb, what's Bernard been up to to make you so cynical?"

"Oh, a small quarrel, nothing serious. I've left him looking like he's caught his dangly bits in a mangle."

"I bet you have," Ellis laughed. He then glanced at the two slightly serious faces. "Well, I'll leave you to talk girl talk. You two go back a long way don't you? Sometimes you even sound the same. Make the same kind of jokes."

"We've been together since juniors." Barbara spoke dully, obviously wishing that Ellis would go.

Julia and Ellis exchanged a surprised smile that made Barb shift uncomfortably in her chair.

"I'll be taking Julia up to see Bernard," Barb said defensively. "You don't mind, do you Ellis?"

"No, no. Has she told you that we are getting married next week?"

"Well, she told me that you had asked her to marry you. I didn't know about next week." Try as she would Barb could not inject any enthusiasm into her reply.

Ellis considered Barbara's words for a moment and directed a hurt look at Julia, who felt quite serene and was looking forward to later when Ellis would be left in no doubt that they would marry exactly when and how he wanted to.

"Well, as I'm obviously in the way. I'll get some more coffee and return to my script, which by the way, needs much more work."

Julia considered following Ellis and reassuring him about the marriage. He was hurt. He was wondering whether she had any doubts about it. She had suffered doubts, but no more. She was going to marry that man. But the quick kiss and assurance she was planning was halted by Barbara's next miserable words.

"Bernard has let me down, badly." Barb came straight to the point as soon as Ellis was out of earshot.

Julia prepared for tales of infidelity and started to make the tea. One always made tea in cases like this.

Barb tried to laugh and failed. "He's like a whale out of water. He is truly sorry, believe me. What he did was more in, more in ignorance really. He had no vicious intentions. He was only trying to help."

Julia struggled to understand what her friend was saying. "Help who, or is it whom?" To Julia, it seemed an odd way to describe an affair.

Barb lit another fag. She stared at the table, and reluctantly raised her eyes to Julia's. "Help a friend."

Julia said slowly. "He tried to help a friend but… somehow it all went wrong?"

Barb nodded. "Yes, that's it. He wanted to help but he made things worse, much worse."

"And what did the friend say?" Julia was now imagining that some buxom wannabe-known actress had flung herself across Bernard's car.

"The friend doesn't know."

Julia was beginning to feel disturbed. It was unusual for Barb to be so dramatic and upset over something that could be sorted out. "Does this involve dead bodies, fatal accidents, stuff like that? I mean serious stuff. Won't some kind of apology fix it?"

Barb took her tea but the teacup rattled in the saucer and she was unable to lift it up. "I'm so sorry Jules." A tear spilled down her face. "That's why I'm here."

Julia's alarm exploded into full-blown fear. Had Barb murdered Bernard because he had screwed some actress? Then she realised what Barb meant. She was here because the friend was here. "What has Bernard done, for Christ's sake, tell me? What has he done to Ellis?" In time, Julia managed to temper her furious shout, conscious that Ellis was a thin wall away.

"It's not Ellis, Jules – at least it is sort of – but the friend… is… you."

"If you give me another 'sort of' I will ring your bloody neck." Julia sat down. Her head was beginning to pound. She took a deep breath. "How dare you come here and frighten me like this," she hissed.

"I'm sorry."

"Stop telling me you're sorry."

"Bernard and I are going to be there for you both, all the way."

"I'd rather you left right now and stopped this silly nonsense."

"I wish I could Julia."

There was a heavy silence. Julia took Barb's hand. "What have you done? What has Bernard done that could be so awful. It is really awful isn't it?"

"Yes, but Bernard's promised to fix it, and I think he will. He's very clever underneath all that flab."

The journey up to Bernard's house was silent. Julia had stopped wondering what on earth the problem was. She would listen to the tale calmly and carefully. There would be no hysterics. She compressed her lips and breathed deeply. She must trust her friend and if Barb vouched for Bernard, maybe she could trust him too.

Bernard's house was big and swanky, naturally. The light was fading a little and a rumble of thunder echoed around as Julia entered the house.

Bernard's greeting was reassuringly calm and he appeared to be suffering from no anxiety whatever. It was obvious that Barb was furious with him, directing angry looks at him from her dark expressive eyes. This was the only thing that discomposed him, a little.

"Barbara's told you then," he asked hopefully.

"No," Julia answered shortly not willing to make anything easy for him.

"Well, since it was her idea in the first place, I think she should begin the explanations."

"If you had kept to my idea," Barb said icily, "we wouldn't be in this mess now."

"OK, OK, we've been over all that. I need a drink. You start, I'll be back in a minute."

Barbara came to sit beside Julia on a startling zebra-skin sofa. "Is this real zebra?" Julia asked dully.

"Yes, terrible bad taste isn't it? The place is full of dead animals. Of course, going on at Bernard about it is like…" Barb paused as Julia's eye's flashed with annoyance.

"Do you remember, when we first came to LA, that I was a little concerned about you phoning your mother?"

"Oh what does that matter? What are you saying? I refuse to talk about it. I have Ellis now. I'm happy."

"I know you are darling. I wish I'd never thought of it."

"Thought of what? What doesn't matter?" Julia snapped. "If you don't tell me I'll walk right out and never speak to you again."

"Well, you are so happy with Ellis. You have him for a shoulder to cry on, so to speak, and you may even marry him."

"I am going to marry him."

Barb gulped a little and doggedly carried on. "My recording your talks with Mother – to help you of course – was, in hindsight, unnecessary."

"You recorded my phone calls to my mother!" Julia shrieked. "How? Why? Why would you do that?" Julia seized Barb by the wrists.

"Believe me." Barb tried to shake free Julia's painful grip. "Please believe me Jules, I did it for you. To help you."

Julia slowly released her hold.

"You do believe me, don't you?" Barb pleaded. "Jules please, when have I ever done anything to hurt you?"

"I believe you," Julia said dully looking into Barbara's anguished face. Barb had never hurt her before. But the sheer horror of being bugged made a small amount of stinging vomit rise to Julia's throat.

Seeing Julia's face pale, Barbara jumped up and fetched a glass of juice.

Slowly Julia recovered. She almost sounded matter-of-fact. "Where was it? In the ceiling? Why did you do it exactly?"

"Peter begged me not to do it but I talked him round. He did agree that it might help."

"Peter knew? My best friends conspire against me and I'm supposed to forgive them? Why did you do it Barb?"

"A very good friend of mine was going to listen to them and suggest ways of helping you."

"A friend? An American psychiatrist, no doubt."

"No, no, silly, an English one, I'm not that mad. And Bernard was never going to listen to the tapes, of course."

"Of course. And what did he say, this friend of yours? And haven't you got your tense wrong. Bernard 'was never going to listen to them'. Isn't that supposed to be 'has never listened to them'?"

"Oh he said it was quite normal behaviour, you know, a self-regulating, semi-delusional adjustment to the stresses inherent in the artistic lifestyle and temperament, something like that."

Barbara had not answered all of Julia's questions. This fact was not lost on either of them.

"Right," Julia stood up, suddenly anxious to get away. "OK, you've told me. I'll go now and we'll go over it again tomorrow." She was thinking fast and furiously. This wasn't so bad. She could cope with this. She believed Barb's vow that the motive for the bugging was only the intention to help. Anyway it would make her own inevitable moving away from her friend on her own marriage to Ellis easier. In her heart she knew that her friendship with Barb had suffered a serious blow, best recovered from alone.

"And Bernard's seen them now, but only because he was forced to."

If Julia had thought that the present situation was just some kind of unhappy experience over her friend's disloyalty, she now knew instinctively that a real nightmare was just beginning. "You said *seen* Barb. You did say *seen*?"

Bernard emerged from the shadows and walked heavily across to his chair and sat down.

Julia was amazed that she was able to notice that the floorboards creaked under his weight.

Bernard spoke as though they were all having a nice cosy chat. "It's not entirely Barbara's fault. She asked me for another machine because the recording wasn't very good. She didn't know it was a camera as well and that it was active when she hid it in your bedroom. I'm sorry. I didn't check."

Julia could do nothing more than lean on a chair, mesmerized by Bernard's large, calm face, his rather piercing eyes behind his glasses and the softly spoken words that she could not halt.

"Barbara told me that no one ever went into your room, except her and Peter, that you never screwed him, and anyway he knew all about it. We never considered other boyfriends."

Ellis, you never considered Ellis, Julia thought as her stomach dropped sickeningly. She closed her eyes as her mind went over Ellis' visit to her room. Her little blue room that had been something of a sanctuary and was now something horrible.

Julia opened her eyes. The long dark shiny floor was still there. Bernard still sat like a Buddha on a stupid cow-skin chair with horns and Barbara still hung worriedly over the arm of the gross zebra-striped sofa.

"You stupid fat beast. You stupid, bloody, fat bastard. I hope you enjoyed your little voyeuristic show. Did it get you going, eh? Can't you get it up without help?" Julia was so angry that further words choked in her throat. She slumped slightly.

Barb got up and steered Julia back to the sofa. She got a brandy and Julia drank it, her trembling hands barely able to hold the glass. Barb treated Julia like something fragile.

Eventually Julia recovered enough to mutter an apology.

"Sorry Bernard. Destroy the tape and we will forget all about it."

There was a silence in the room. Into Julia's pounding brain came the realisation that worse was to come. Why tell her their dirty secret? Why not just destroy the tape?

"Of course, we would have destroyed the tape," Bernard said coldly. "Though, strictly speaking, it's a chip."

Bernard spoke in a mimsy way that made Julia long to smack him. "But you filmed me and Ellis... filmed us making love." Julia bent her head and clawed her hands through her hair.

"We only watched it till Ellis took his trousers off," Barb chipped in, in all seriousness.

Unaccountably, Julia giggled. "How nice of you."

Chapter Fifteen

"We never intended to watch it all but..." Barb faltered.

Julia waited in dread for the 'but'.

Barb was unable to continue and turned to Bernard for help.

"Of course we would never have watched the shots of you and Ellis," Bernard said huffily, "but some mother fucker stole it off my computer and this fucking hacker is demanding a ransom for its destruction... or he puts in on the Internet. Hell, it's not as though I've never seen Ellis fuck a broad before."

Barb jumped up angrily. "You're talking about simulated fucking, you sod, and Julia is not a broad."

Bernard pursed his lips in displeasure and Barbara went behind his stupid cow chair and put her head next to his. They both regarded Julia slumped, white-faced, on the sofa.

This is it, Julia thought. This is the crunch – Ellis and me having sex on the Internet. A thrill of pure horror passed through her. She felt that she could not stand the sight of Barb and Bernard any longer. "I have to think about this," she said slowly, getting up to leave.

"Just a minute." Bernard's voice held a note of command. "You can't tell Ellis. This film is costing millions of dollars. I have to keep good relations with him, you understand, and I don't want him upset. I'll pay the ransom and it may not get out. But if it does, Peter is going to take the blame, at least until the film is finished."

"You've got this all worked out haven't you?" Julia sat back down.

"Sure I'm going to save your asses. I don't know what kind of kinky sex you English like, but that tape ain't no simulated rape, and Ellis is finished in Hollywood if it gets out. That mother fucker hacker knows he's struck gold."

Julia looked at Bernard doubtfully. Could she trust him? She realised that she had no choice. She nodded. "OK."

"And another thing," Bernard said casually. "Barbara told me that you are going to marry Ellis next week. Ordinarily, it would be good publicity for the film, but this situation has to be handled very carefully and it should be postponed. It will be better if you return to LA as soon as your scenes here are finished."

Ellis was lying in bed reading when Julia returned. The bedroom was softly lit so Julia hoped that he would not notice her look of strain. She spent a long time in the shower. Perhaps Ellis would fall asleep. She really could not talk to him. She took a sleeping pill.

Ellis turned to her as she climbed into bed beside him. She hid her head in his shoulder and held him. He seemed to understand that she was holding him more like a child seeking comfort than her usual sensuous wriggling.

"Was it bad?" he asked.

"It was bad!"

"I thought Bernard was really keen on Barbara, you know. I thought he was getting serious. He doesn't usually make much play with the casting couch. Is it really true?"

Here comes fudge number one, Julia thought glumly. "I think Bernard is in love with Barb."

"Have they patched it up?"

"Well, you know, the least said the better, but they're still together." Fudge number two.

"You feel kinda tense." Ellis put his arm over and began to massage Julia's spine. Quickly she turned her back on him. As his hands caressed her neck Julia began to relax. He moved his hands down her body but avoided her erogenous zones. A little tear slipped down Julia's cheek. Ellis was so understanding. He was the perfect lover. He knew instinctively that sex would not make her feel better.

Julia willed the sleeping pill to work. TV and Internet screens began to dance in front of her eyes. She and Ellis were making love on a luridly lit bed. They were kissing. They were making love in a succession of kinky ways that they had never actually performed. All the people from every TV advert she had ever seen were watching – eating chocolates, quarrelling. Dogs and cats were watching. What would the Royle family say? As she fell asleep even Denise was sitting bolt upright on the sofa, usually animated, eyes riveted on the TV screen. Then Julia's usual thought tattoo, when falling asleep, that's not right, that's all wrong, released her into oblivion.

Julia awoke with a feeling of doom. Last night, her mind had not completely accepted that this thing had happened. Now, she played back the scene in her little blue bedroom, from the hidden camera's point of view, like a DVD loop. The urge to wake Ellis up and confess everything, was very strong.

Ellis was sleeping heavily. How did you wake up your lover in your perfect house, in its perfect setting, in the beginnings of your perfect love affair, and tell him that… No, Bernard had condemned her to fudge, ad infinitum.

After the stormy night, the day was more beautiful than ever. Julia stood by the bedroom window. Ellis slept on. He had been building up a lot of muscle for his part and needed his sleep. She went to the bed and kissed him lightly.

He looked and smelt so nice that she had a fierce desire to keep him, whatever the cost. She could not tell him – yet.

Julia had a real sense of something ending as she waited for Ellis to join her on the terrace. They had to go down to Honolulu on film business. She had to meet Bernard and Barb again. She had to continue to not quite lie, to Ellis.

Julia sat with her knees hugged up to her. Perhaps he will think that I have my period, she thought. It will buy me some time.

True, things did not seem quite so bad in the morning light but she and Ellis did not have nine-to-five jobs. They made their living being paid very highly to produce fantasy. Ellis would make millions of dollars if the film did well. The studio would make even more. There were fans avid for every last detail of his life and news editors waiting to print every triumph and disaster. It was all the same to them, and overall, the disasters probably sold more copies.

"You are looking very solemn this morning Julia," Gran came puffing up the steps to the terrace.

Julia smiled welcomingly. "Hi Gran."

"But I bring good news. The legal details are settled and you can have the house next week." Gran sat facing the view and looked out over the hills.

"But Gran, are you sure? Ellis tells me that the house is worth a great deal more than we are paying."

Gran did not answer immediately. She sat looking at the view with a small smile on her face.

Julia went to get the tea. She met Ellis. "Gran is here."

He pulled a face, but Julia put her fingers to his lips, then kissed him, and then told him to be nice for Gran had come to sell the house to them.

When Julia returned to the terrace, Ellis and Gran had already finalised all the money matters and shaken hands.

Julia shook Gran's hand. The deal was done.

The pleasure of owning, part owning, the beautiful bungalow made Julia feel more optimistic about her other worries. If the worst came to the worst, she and Ellis could live here like hermits. But she knew as she thought it, it wouldn't work, but it was a nice fantasy anyway.

Gran went for a last wander around the house and take any keepsakes that she liked.

Ellis was grinning happily. "What a deal," he said.

"This place is worth six times what we are paying for it."

"But we won't sell it."

"No, we won't sell it. We can pass it on to our kids."

Julia smiled. A lump rose in her throat but she forced it down. "I was thinking about I was thinking about our marriage next week, and perhaps it's not a very good idea."

Ellis was silent for a time. The hurt and disappointment on his face was evident. "OK, I was rushing you a bit. You will have to let you know when you are ready."

Julia went to him and put her arms around his neck as he sat in his chair. She was glad that he could not see her face properly. "I will marry you Ellis. I will. I promise." If you still want to marry me she added to herself, silently.

Ellis cheered up. Well, he appeared to cheer up, but Julia knew that he was deeply upset.

"Why do you want to marry me anyway?" she said playfully. "I'm a terribly moody bitch."

"I decided a few days after we met. She's the girl for me, popped into my head, and I realised that it was true. Because of the way you think, because of the way you talk and because of the way you look."

"I'm glad that 'the way I think' came before 'the way I look'."

Ellis smiled but it was not a particularly happy smile. "Look, let's stop messing around. What's going on? What happened last night? Why have you changed your mind? Tell me?"

"I can't."

"Why not?"

"Because I don't want to lie to you."

Ellis began to look exasperated. His mobile rang. "I have to go down to Honolulu, the car's coming."

"I'll stay with Gran." Julia hoped that Ellis had not noticed her look of relief at his going, but she rather thought that he had.

Gran sat for a long time on the terrace. Julia supposed that the old lady had a lot of memories to go through. But it suited Julia to sit quietly at the terrace table drinking coffee thinking over her own problems.

"You must think me a nuisance staying here like this," Gran said at last. "But it's the last time."

"You can always come and sit here Gran. Don't you have a house just down the road as well?"

"I've given that to my friend. No I won't be coming back here, except perhaps as a spirit."

Julia took her chair over to Gran. There could be only one meaning to her sad words. Julia didn't try to say anything cheerful. She held Gran's hand.

"I have to go into hospital in LA. The doctors there say I shall be back on my feet in no time. But I know. My Hawaiian doctor has more sense. I have no living relatives, so I am happy to die. It's just this lovely view. It's hard never to see it again."

"I'm going back to LA soon, I can come and see you in hospital."

Gran was surprised out of her reverie. "Leave your American?"

"I thought you didn't care for him." Julia smiled cheerfully. Only an utter sod would ruin a dying woman's swansong with their own problems. "It's only temporary."

"He's not so bad. Anyone can see that you are made for each other, as they say. You should stay here, with him, in this house. This is a very lucky house." After a gentle silence Gran squeezed Julia's hand. "Do not worry. 'Hoonanea' will call you back, you'll see. Unlike me, you will have many children. Daughters I hope."

Julia tried to look happy. She wondered if Gran was a silver surfer. Thankfully, there was no Internet connection in the bungalow. But Gran had another bungalow. It would be too embarrassing if Gran ever logged onto the Ellis and Julia sex show. But then, Hawaiians, supposedly, had a very relaxed attitude to uninhibited group sex, something that had delighted the first visiting sailors and horrified the English missionaries.

"Yes, you will have daughters I am sure. And bring them up as loyal subjects of your great Queen. The Americans do not understand these things like you and I."

"No, no, they certainly don't. What is your Christian name, Gran?"

Gran's face lit up with a huge smile. "Would you call one of your girls after me? My name is Victoria."

"Yes, yes, of course. If it ever happens." Julia had been expecting an unpronounceable Hawaiian name, which she would have to write down.

The morning was advancing. Julia was expected in Honolulu. Even now Ellis would be waiting for her. She had switched off her mobile at Gran's first sad words. What was ordinary life anyway when someone you knew was preparing to die?

Gran was sitting quietly again so Julia went into the house and called Barbara.

Barb was delighted. "I'm glad you called. Bernard's choppered Ellis over to the Big Island for some location specs. I'll come down for you right now and we'll go to Honolulu together."

Julia tried not to look downcast as she took out Gran's tea. Ellis wasn't waiting for her. Bernard had spirited him away.

Barb soon arrived looking determinedly cheerful. Neither Julia nor Gran were very welcoming, and Julia could not be bothered to enlighten Barb as to the nature of the rather solemn occasion that was the old lady's last visit to her beloved 'Hoonanea'.

Barb asked immediately what 'Hoonanea' meant and Gran told her that it was Hawaiian for passing the time in ease and pleasure.

Barb raised her eyebrows at Julia at the word *pleasure*, but soon schooled her features to match her two companions' rather solemn expressions.

"What's with the old bird?" Barb asked as soon as Julia had seen Gran to the gate and waved goodbye.

"She's not well," Julia answered shortly.

"Not potty is she? Her relatives can challenge the sale of this place to you, you know, if she's do-lally."

Julia sighed. "Why has Bernard choppered Ellis to the Big Island exactly?"

Chapter Sixteen

Barb's veneer of cheerfulness began to slip. "Are you still mad with me? Life's too short for you to keep up this righteous indignation act, Jules. Anyway, Bernard's going to fix it."

"By separating me and Ellis."

"That's part of his plan, I admit. He doesn't tell me everything, you know."

"You've got a good imagination Barb. Can't you see it all over the *Sunday Mirror*, or whatever they have in the States: Ellis McCready, the rapist from the hit film *Heartline*, rapes Brit actress Julia Slater in real life. And then the grainy, dirty pictures from the Internet. Everyone peering. Is he really? Pausing, playing back, wanking. How is Ellis going to feel about that? It was our personal, private life. We sorted it out, privately. Privately Barb. Tell me the pictures are grainy, Barb, please. How is Ellis going to feel about it? How is he going to feel about me?

"And you. You waltz in here saying 'Are you still mad with me'? My best friend. My so-called best friend. Bugging me. Secretly bugging me."

Julia stalked back to the terrace, conscious that she was stamping through paradise in a foul mood, and knowing that Barb's comment on life being too short was all too true.

"Oh I know you," Barb sneered when they were sitting at the table. "And you may insultingly offer me cold tea with that imperious wave of yours, but at heart you haven't got the guts to ditch me. You'll just rack it up – Barb's betrayed me. But consider this, I was trying to help you. I was only trying to help you."

"I know," Julia said quietly. She sat back and regarded her friend. "You're different Barb. Do you know that? The LA glitz is showing. New hairstyle, new clothes. You'll be having your nose and tits done next."

"Well, why not?" Barb said airily. "You look terrible. Hollywood men expect one to vamp to keep them"

"Why not?" Julia was shocked out of her misery for a second. "You'd have surgery? And whose fault is it if I look terrible." A little taste of normality made Julia return to feeling even more miserable. "What am I going to do about Ellis? How can I keep on lying to him? He will keep asking me what's going on."

Julia felt the hot tears on her face. Unable to look at Barbara, and suddenly tired of the relentless sun, she went into the kitchen and began to grind the coffee beans. Toast, coffee and pills. Anything that would make the pressure inside her head go away.

Barb followed. "You could come up and see the film. It's not so bad. Shocking, erotic…"

"Entertaining?" Julia cut in bitterly. "Why would I want to see it? I know it off by heart already. Man enters room. Discovers lover in bed with another man, who is black and beautiful. Black man leaves. Man rips off clothes and forces woman to have sex. Man leaves."

Barb took the mill from Julia's lifeless fingers. Nothing more was said until the coffee was drunk and the pills swallowed.

Barb said carefully. "Ironically, the… thing was done for sound but the sound on this piece is crap. Those buggery hackers will try all they like but they will only ever get the timbre of the speech, not the words. And lip-reading, you and Ellis speak too quickly for that. In one way, it's bad, because no speech means that the nastiest interpretations can be attributed to the words."

"Would you like me and Ellis to dub it?"

"Now, sarky. Listen. In another way it's good because it makes the piece mysterious. Mystery means confusion and confusion leads naturally to fantasy."

"What the bloody hell are you talking about?" Julia was jerked out of her doldrums by annoyance. "And why aren't you smoking?"

"That's better," Barb smiled. "What's a fuck between friends anyway? You won't be the first to have your amours beamed around the world."

"Easily said when it isn't you Barb. I shall be on sleeping pills for weeks over this."

"Bernard is going to fix it. I've given up smoking and he's given up eating too much. We're getting married next week. Your wedding gave him the idea."

"My wedding is off, if you remember. By Bernard's order. It's bloody cheeky to steal my wedding day. And what about the pact?"

"Oh that won't suffer. Filming makes grass widows and widowers of us all. There will be plenty of time for Bigbury, you'll see. The pact works. This thing could have ruined our friendship but it won't – the pact won't let it. That's what the pact is for."

Julia felt a little annoyed that Barb assumed that they would be friends again. The bleak prospect of losing both Ellis and Barb kept her from saying anything really hurtful. The pills had done their job. They had to go down to Honolulu to work. "You didn't say what the pictures were like."

Barb made a helpless gesture. "Sharp as a pin, but," she added quickly on Julia's dismayed expression, "that's good. It's good Jules. It fits Bernard's plan."

Julia didn't like the look of Waikiki very much. The high-rise hotels were crowded far too close to the splendid beach. *Warlords* was getting well under way. The studio had hired a hotel for the duration of the filming in Hawaii. It was buzzing with costumiers, artists, writers, script editors and sundry hangers-on. It was hot and noisy. Everyone looked purposeful and committed.

Barb led the way to Bernard's suite on the top floor where she had a writing room. They went over Julia's script. Julia was to be choppered over to the big island that afternoon to do some scenes with Ellis and other cast members.

Barb exerted herself to improve Julia's lines but there was an air of hurry about it all. Julia knew that Bernard was anxious to get rid of Ellis' troublesome girlfriend.

"Has Bernard forgiven me for calling him a fat bastard?"

Barb paused, glasses suspended on her nose. "'Stupid, bloody, fat bastard' I think it was. I don't think he's seen that Mike Myers' film, Austin Powers something."

Barb and Julia grinned at each other like the naughty schoolgirls they once were. Transplanted from Nottingham to Devon at a young age, both had struggled to adapt to the more prosaic surroundings of Newton Abbot.

"I thought that you would never smile at me like that again, you daft 'apoth." Barb's eyes had a suspect mistiness as the two girls enjoyed a brief forgiving embrace.

Julia cheered up, or was it the pills? She didn't care. "Let's do it. We love sci-fi!" she shouted. She and Barb began to jig and sing. "It's sex Jim, but not as we know it, not as we know it, it's sex Jim, but not as we know it, not as we know it, not!"

"We never did find out how the Vorlons had sex, did we Barb? Bolts of lightning, we supposed."

"Is it bolts of lightning with Ellis, Jules?" Barb cradled Julia against her.

"Yeah Barb, bolts of lightning."

"You'll get him, you'll see. He won't give you up over this. He's not such a fool."

Julia didn't like the helicopter much. The happy pills were wearing off very quickly as they dipped and circled towards the Big Island. It all looked so unreal. Unreal blue sea. Unreal tropical islands falling away dizzily on either side. Julia only just managed to locate the sick bag in time.

Ellis was not there to see her ashen face. He was up the mountainside setting up for a trial take.

Gerald was there looking quite stunning in some kind of glam rock meets *Celebrity Come Dancing* get-up.

"You look like shit!" Gerald said comfortingly. He got some coffee and sandwiches, found a sunshade and was generally helpful.

"Thanks Gerald." Julia began to feel better. Her head had cleared in the mountain air and she was looking forward to seeing Ellis. Also, she was friends with Barb again and willing to believe, like Barb, that things would turn out right in the end.

"Can't have my girl feeling icky."

Julia smiled a tight smile at Gerald. Then she saw Ellis striding towards them wearing the same extraordinary costume as Gerald. Fixed gaze, on her, muscles bulging, sweat glazed skin. Julia began to feel a little dizzy again.

Ellis was hot, sweaty and not pleased to see Julia and Gerald enjoying a mutual flirtation. He cast them such a filthy look that the canny director, realising that the backdrop was OK and that Ellis was in the right state of glistening, sweaty menace, ordered Gerald into the planned fight.

Gerald didn't have to be told twice. He jammed his helmet on his head, strode towards Ellis, and raised his sword to meet the aimed blow. They paused, sword to sword, while the lighting people tinkered about.

The sound was to be dubbed in later so Gerald felt free to needle Ellis to his heart's content. They were supposed to be deadly enemies in the film. Gerald had landed this small part and he was determined that it would not end up on the cutting-room floor.

"I hear she's called the wedding off. I should think so. Nottingham girls marry Yorkshire boys. Nottingham is the Queen of the Midlands and it is also known as the city of beautiful girls. Now Julia is beautiful, I'm sure you will agree. I don't mind her having her little fling with you, she has to sow her wild oats after all, but…"

The instructions came to begin the choreographed fight. The bystanders were amazed at its energy. Hope began to blossom that perhaps *Warlords* would not end up a turkey after all.

At the second break, Gerald began again. He was short of breath but he persevered. "And then there's the pact. No, you've never heard of it, have you? Ask Julia who's in the pact. Not you, for sure."

The fight began again. At the third break, Gerald was gasping. Ellis was all tight-lipped silence but his eyes betrayed his real anger.

"And then there's Barb," Gerald continued to drip his poison. "They're a pair of lessies, you know. I don't mind sharing, but you might not. Do you, Ellis, do you – mind?"

Julia watched the scene with something akin to terror. It looked so real. It looked like Gerald might actually pierce Ellis with his sword. Gerald was talking; but she could not hear what he was saying. Something that Ellis did not like. She was glad when the scene finished.

Ellis came straight to her. He was dressed in an uncomfortable scratchy costume, he was hot, exhausted and sweaty, but Julia was glad to hold him, to kiss him.

Erica Black, the leading lady was not pleased although the rest of the cast and onlookers liked it. It seemed that Pawl, Warlord of the Outer Rim, really did have the hots for the lowly handmaiden.

With the afternoon light gone, the cast and crew reassembled on the Kohala Coast. Julia was shown to Ellis' bungalow which was right next to beach. Julia unpacked her bags feeling quite excited. Viva happy pills!

The accommodation was basic by American standards but it looked exotically jungly to Julia with its bright colours and view of the sea and palm trees.

There might be a hook-up to the Internet lurking somewhere round about but it was easy to forget that for a moment.

Julia dressed carefully in a green sheath dress and decided it would be polite to put on the lei of yellow hibiscus hanging by the bed.

Julia joined the film people at the beach party which was to celebrate the beginning of the Hawaiian shoot. It was understood that tonight they would all drink, stay up late, and get to know each other. Afterwards, until the final wrap on the island, it would be strictly early nights and dawn risings.

Gerald was already well on the way to being one over the eight. Barb was there keeping a place for her and Ellis. Julia wished that they were further away from Gerald, who was sitting opposite, but the beach cafe was too crowded for a move.

"Never mind him," Barb hissed, giving Julia a kiss.

Julia saw Gerald wink at Ellis, who was moving close to her along the bench. Ellis ignored Gerald and kissed her chin and smiled into her eyes in his own delightful way.

A tropical night under the stars with the man she loved. Julia was almost happy, her first drink and Ellis' kisses, already spreading a delicious warmth through her body.

Yes, a perfect tropical night on one of the most beautiful islands in the world – and Gerald. A rapidly getting drunk, Gerald.

"Do you know how many words there are for the word 'drunk' in the English language?" Gerald was enquiring loudly. "Does anybody know? Well, there's pissed, smashed, blotto, soused, stinking, legless, pickled, inebriated…"

Peter appeared, wearing a staggering Hawaiian shirt, covered in pineapples, for which he was duly insultingly ribbed. He kissed Julia briefly. "You look fabulous, princess. Hi Ellis."

As Peter gave Barb a hug, Julia wondered when Bernard was going to tell him that he was being set up as the patsy for the bugging. Peter's appearance in the scene would be brief. He would get off the bed, say a few words and leave. The viewers would be left to draw their own tawdry conclusions. They could also use the part where he had spouted Shakespeare but it wouldn't be Shakespeare. She did not think that Peter would be unduly worried about his appearance on the Internet. He had been in loads of porno flicks, after all.

Julia shuddered. She had always undressed in the bathroom, thank God. She couldn't remember walking about naked or doing anything too embarrassing, except phoning Mother.

She wished she could feel more optimistic about Bernard being able to buy the hacker off. She hardly noticed Ellis asking her if she was cold and although she knew that he was offended by her lack of response, still she could not stop staring blankly ahead.

Julia reached for more alcohol. This thing is going to turn me into a pill-popping lush, she thought in a stricken way, suddenly realising that she had a pain in her chest and was holding her breath.

"Well, here's my favourite black bugger, dressed as only a fairy knows how," was Gerald's cheery greeting to Peter.

Chapter Seventeen

Luckily for Gerald the word *bugger*, derived from buggery and often used in England as vulgar affectionate abuse, sounded almost like *buggah*, a Hawaiian word for 'guy'.

Julia had learned this from Gran who called Ellis, 'your buggah'.

Everyone was getting steadily drunker and even Ellis was knocking it back. The general feeling was that *Warlords* was off to a cracking start. The vibes were good. The tables were all placed close together and the general tone of the conversation was one of high spirits.

Bernard was in evidence, tucking into an enormous barbecue meal with some executives. "Those Brits are getting a bit loud," one of them said. "Do you really need all of them?"

"I don't know," Bernard answered looking over to where Barb was cheekily giving him the backward V-sign. "But they've got something we don't have, centuries."

Safe in the circle of his Ellis' arms, Julia felt secure; but soon he would be asking questions that she did not want to answer.

Gerald was getting louder. "This is my best mate, Peter. Or as you lot say – Peda. It's Pe-ter, you berks. Pe-ter."

Gerald waved his glass. "To my best mate, Pe-ter. The pact's all here. To the pact. God, this beer tastes about as good as my piss. I'd sell my soul, right now, to whatever God you've got over here, for a decent glass of Yorkshire bitter. We like our beer warm and our women cold. Here's to warming up cold women." Gerald gave Julia a knowing wink.

Barb laughed. "Stop stirring it Gerald." She liked Gerald and in some ways they were very alike. They both liked to mouth off in an outrageous fashion.

"Oh, Barb, what wouldn't we give to be – you know where. I mean, this place is alright, but we know, we know,"

Gerald wagged his finger, then paused to belch. "Better in than out no, no, that's not right. Better out than in. Where paradise truly is."

"He's getting too drunk, Barb. I shall have to throw him in the sea if he doesn't stop," Peter drawled. He was drinking steadily through umpteen glasses of cocktails and was actually in danger of sliding under the table, himself.

Barbara and Julia exchanged glances. "You and Ellis had better go before Gerald says anything else," Barb whispered in Julia's ear. Barb was too drunk to judge her whisper's carrying potential and Julia felt Ellis stiffen as he heard the words of warning.

"I'd like to hear about this place Gerald," Ellis said affably. But his expression was wary and cold. "This paradise."

Gerald stood up unsteadily. "Well, there's this little island, you see, in the sea, uh, uh, with this Art Deco hotel. A bit like all that shit in LA but better, much, mucho better. And these two tides come in like this." Gerald made a coming together motion with his hands falling sideways onto Peter, who propped him up again. "It's lovely. Much better than this." Gerald waved his arms around again. "Well, Julia and I stayed at this hotel, because I'm bloody rich, you see. Full of Yanks all rabbiting on about Agatha Christie – but no matter. She's such a good screw Ellis. Well, you know that. Not very adventurous but wheeeee when she gets going, hang on to your..."

Barb reached across the table and slapped Gerald across the face. "Shut up Gerald!"

Gerald's face turned an ugly red. "I've started so I'll finish." He sat down suddenly, seemingly incapable of any more speech.

There was an awkward silence. People sitting by began to drift away. "If the Brits want to drink and fight, let them. I don't understand what they are saying anyway," said one.

"What a plonker you are Gerald." Barb lit up and inhaled deeply.

Peter laughed, quite merry. "He can be a really awkward sod when he wants to, especially when he's smashed out of his skull. Got a constitution like an ox, though. Apologise to Jules, you wanker."

Ellis got up and walked off down the beach.

Gerald suddenly turned and yelled at Ellis. "Your sanity, Ellis, your sanity! Hang on to your sanity. On dodgy ground."

Julia looked after Ellis. What did he think? And this wasn't the worst of it. Things were going to get much, much worse. She turned to Barb. "You're smoking again."

"We quarrelled. Bernard's eating and I'm smoking. Mind you, we manufactured the quarrel so that we could indulge for a bit. We'll make up tomorrow."

"Well, that's OK then because I want you to tell Bernard to rein Gerald in. He's getting way out of line."

"I will, of course. But Gerald's hurting Jules. He really loves you." Barb grabbed Gerald's hair as his head lay on the table. "You've got to stop this, Gerald. You really have."

Gerald raised his eyes. "I know, I know." Gerald screwed up his face in pain and not just because he was having his hair pulled. "But it's hard, Barb, it's hard."

Gerald stretched out his hands, one to Julia and one to Peter. Barb completed the circle. "We're still the pact. We're still bound. Julia will never get rid of me. And when her Hollywood fancy man's finished with her, she'll come running back to Burgh Island."

Gerald stood up unsteadily and Peter helped him. "I'm not that kind of a boy," Gerald minced to Peter in a high voice. "Backs to the wall boys," Gerald roared as they staggered off. "Bum shaggers are wild on the beach."

Ellis was standing moodily looking out to sea. He didn't hear Julia coming over the soft sand. She wound her arms around him and felt his response.

"I've been longing to do this all day," she whispered, before they kissed. The sand shelved a little so they were able to lie down and kiss comfortably. Julia's head was spinning a little and Ellis wasn't entirely sober.

It was warm in the last rays of the sun and there was no cool breeze whipping up the Channel. By the sea in England, except on rare occasions, there was always a cool breeze whipping up from somewhere.

"I'm sorry about Gerald. He's always shooting his mouth off."

"It's not your fault. He's a grown man. He knows what he's doing."

"He's trying to split us up."

Ellis' kisses were warm and sweet. Perhaps a little languid. "I ache all over," he said teasingly. "For you, of course, but mostly from waving that damn stupid sword about."

Julia sighed with pleasure. When Ellis teased everything was alright in her world. "You're tired. You've been fighting the hero's fight all day on that hot mountain. Is it going well? You're not sorry you're doing it?"

"Not now. Not here, with you, like this. Not to mention that house on Makiki Heights which is worth a small fortune and belongs to us. Bernard practically had an apoplexy when I told him."

They walked back to their bungalow. It was quite magical. Julia prayed that nothing would spoil it, not now, not tonight.

"What was he talking about? Your ex Yorkshire he-man."

"Who? Oh look at those palm trees. I must take some photos tomorrow…"

"Gerald, of course."

"Oh just drunken talk."

"It sounded like more than that to me. What does he mean by the pact?" Ellis' voice was falsely casual.

Julia dropped Ellis' hand and swept the hair from her eyes. Here she was walking along a romantic beach with the man she loved and they were talking about Gerald. "It's just a holiday time-share thing."

"At this place? This place with the island and the two tides?"

"Yes!" Julia's voice held a touch of annoyance.

Julia knew that she should tell Ellis more. He wanted more. The silence stretched uncomfortably on.

Ellis stopped abruptly and pulled her to him. He held her tight, his eyes were on hers. Trying to see any lies in her green eyes, reflecting the light off the sea.

"You, Julia Slater, are a very secretive woman."

"I know. I know. I wish I wasn't." She tried to break free.

"Something's changed between us. I felt it the other night when Barbara called. I felt it right there in the kitchen. And the next day it was even worse. And you won't tell me why."

"No," Julia whispered.

Ellis let her go with something like disgust and resumed walking. His gesture cut Julia through and through.

"Nothing's really changed between us," Julia pleaded as she followed him. "I won't let it change."

Ellis turned. "Will you ever tell me?"

"One day. One day, you will know."

"Goddamnit Julia, what kind of answer is that? That's why you won't marry me isn't it? Secrets and lies. You'll fuck me. You'll say you love me as though you mean it. But you won't tell me what's making you so – unhappy."

"You must trust me. You, we, have to do this film. Our lives are not our own. You know that. We'll survive this."

"You have a husband already?."

"No."

"You have children?."

"No."

"You're dying of some incurable disease?"

"No."

"You're being blackmailed?"

"Er, no."

"You're sworn to secrecy?"

"Um, sort of."

Ellis began to relax. "OK, I'll play it your way." He kissed her a deep loving kiss. "But I wish it was the same as the last time we made love."

"So do I." Julia could not prevent a few tears from falling.

"Don't cry." He kissed the tears away.

They both looked down. The sea was washing around their knees. Julia laughed and cast her lei into the water. "The mossies are gathering."

Ellis picked her up. "Mossies," he said disgustedly. "You know what I don't like about you Brits? It's your misuse of the English language. All that slang you were spouting tonight between you made my teeth ache."

"That's one of ours."

They walked back to the bungalow without speaking as though they both realised that more conversation was too difficult. There was nothing more to say. The only way to really express their feelings was in the bedroom.

Julia knew that the silence between them was eating away at their happiness. Julia wished again that she could tell him everything. Could it be worse than this? Would they get back their former happiness or would it all be worse?

She would have to tell him about Mother. She shrank from that.

About the pact. That was more than time-share. It would sound a little queer. As queer as her little felt and quilted sleeping faces which she had started making again.

About the Internet thing. Her nerve failed completely. Would he forgive Barb and Bernard? Would he forgive her? Worst of all, would he forgive himself?

Ellis had been the aggressor. He hadn't come into the bedroom and said 'Hi honey, I'm back.' He had been aggressive. She had been passive. It was all far, far worse for Ellis.

Sex under the bedclothes would have raised only a few bored titters from guilty peeping Toms. She and Ellis would both be cast as hapless victims of a cruel hoax. But Ellis could be cast as the villain of the piece, because she hadn't appeared to welcome his advances. The watchers would transfer their guilt onto him.

She had disguised her pleasure. People expected some signs of pleasure from the woman. Her screwed-up control would be seen as unwilling submission.

"Stupid, stupid, stupid!" Julia stopped. "I am so stupid."

"What?" Ellis pulled her close.

"Oh, I'm so stupid. I'm a sexually repressed, stupid woman."

He laughed. "We're working on that. I'm not complaining. Come on, don't cry. Maybe I've been a little rough on you."

"No, no. But whatever happens, it's not my fault Ellis. And if we keep faith with each other, it won't matter anyway. We know the truth."

"Come on. Come on, snap out of this. It's OK. We will keep faith with each other. I trust you. It will be alright."

Julia tried to stop her mind from thinking. She must believe it would be alright. But right there, at the back of her mind, in that little bit of merciless processing, she knew that Ellis would never forgive her.

Chapter Eighteen

Julia waited for Ellis in a bed with a blue striped counterpane. She thought that the white mosquito nets looked romantic with the subdued lighting shining through them. Perhaps she would get similar nets when she returned to England. Returned to England. Was she already thinking that her love affair with Ellis was doomed?

She could hear the sea faintly. A nice soothing whoosh, whoosh. And the slight rustling of the palm trees on the beach. She had a glass of red wine by the bed. She took a large sip. Red wine always made her feel deliciously loopy. She was allergic to it. It made her cheeks go pink. She didn't care if all that she and Ellis had left was sex, it had better be good.

Her spirits dipped a little. Nothing would ever be like their first weekend at 'Hoonanea' such a short time ago. That first weekend honeymoon. The love and trust between them had been right there in her hands, and it had slipped away.

Ellis flipped back the nets. "What are you thinking?"

Julia smiled. Here was the most gorgeous naked man in the world, getting into her bed, and asking what she was thinking.

"That you must be the most gorgeous naked man in the world."

Ellis was not to be swayed by flattery and he leaned over her, and kissed her lightly. "Truly?"

"Truly? Does anyone ever tell what they think – truly?"

Ellis withdrew his intense gaze with a sigh of disappointment, and lay back. "You don't believe then that a couple engaged to be married, as we are…" He put his hand under the pillow and produced a ring box, which he handed to her. "Should be completely honest with each other?"

Julia took the box feeling delighted and trying not to let her feelings of despair at the direction his questions were going, surface.

"Will you marry me?"

Julia put on the diamond solitaire. "Yes, oh yes."

"Do you mean that? You know I love you."

"I love you."

The space between them narrowed and closed. Ellis made love slowly. Agonisingly slowly for Julia. "You beast," she whispered between long kisses.

Julia felt that they had both aged in some mysterious way and that part of their youthful exuberance and delight in each other sexually had disappeared, replaced by what?

For the first time since she had played her mother, Julia did not hold her reactions down. She could not be honest with Ellis out of bed, but she was damn well going to be honest with him in it. That is, if only he would... come closer. She didn't want to think any more.

So she gave more, let slip more of her intense pleasure at their climax, than ever before. She even opened her eyes and looked at him.

The dawn came too soon. Julia didn't want to get out of bed but the transport would soon be arriving.

She twirled the perfect engagement ring round and round her finger. Bernard wasn't going to like it.

Ellis came out of the bathroom shower in a rush. He was smiling, he was happy. He was going to throw himself onto the bed.

"I think we had better keep our engagement secret, Ellis." Julia said it quickly before her nerve failed.

Ellis stopped as his knees hit the bed. His smile faded and changed to wary disappointment followed by a frown of displeasure.

He turned away. "OK, have it your way."

"It's difficult. On set. The gossip. Barb's marrying Bernard and that's caused some trouble. Favouritism and all that. And now you and me."

"OK," Ellis said again irritatingly, Julia thought. "You have your hidden agenda," he continued in the same hard, careless vein. "Whatever it is. I asked you last night Julia, if you thought that engaged couples should be completely honest with each other. I'm still waiting for your reply."

"Of course, if they can. Well, actually if you want me to be really honest, no, I don't think so – not completely. It isn't possible."

Julia got out of bed and went to sit next to Ellis on the bed. "This is pointless," she pleaded. She put her arms round him. "Please darling, please, just this one last little secret. "

"And you are saying that it is pointless for me to wonder why Barbara and Bernard can get engaged – hell, they're even throwing a party get married, almost the same time as we were going to get married, but not us. Why not us Julia?"

"Yes." Julia answered so quietly that Ellis shook her by the shoulders until she said, "Yes" again.

Ellis was late for his pick-up. Julia was going up the next day. She put on a robe and followed him out to the truck, unwilling to be apart from him without some reconciliation.

"Aren't you going to kiss me goodbye?" she said with a nice mixture of aggression and seduction.

"No. I've decided you only want me for my body." Ellis kept his face straight.

Julia looked up at him not sure if he was joking or not. "You know that's not true."

"Do I?"

Julia slapped him quite forcefully across the chest. "You can give as good as you get and I was feeling sorry for you."

They were so engrossed in each other that they did not notice the jeep arriving over the soft sand.

"Ha," Gerald, looking pasty, but raring to go, was jumping out. "That's what I like to see, aggro at dawn. Hi sweetheart. Hi Ellis."

"I swear," Ellis spoke softly, clenching his fists, "I'm going to deck that guy."

"It's what he wants."

"Well, you know him better than I do."

"Yes, I do, but it's not something I can help, is it?."

Their parting kiss was almost a peck.

Julia began to feel depressed as Ellis was driven away in a swirl of sand. They had parted badly and she was not even sure when she would see him again.

The light and the weather were good for filming. Ellis was going to stay in the hills shooting the outdoor scenes, until the director was satisfied.

The director wanted black volcanic rock and the smoking active Kilauea. He wanted Ellis and crew menaced by red-hot lava, real or fake.

Julia sniffed the air. Sure, here there was the smell of the flowers in the garden, the sea and the warm breeze, but also the faint pervasive stench of sulphur dioxide.

On the whole, she preferred Oahu and 'Hoonanea'. It had seemed a good idea to stay at the bungalow on the beach until filming finished on the Big Island. But perhaps the real reason was that they were both unwilling to go back to 'Hoonanea'. It would only remind them how much their relationship had deteriorated.

"It's the lies, lies, lies," Julia cried aloud to herself and a solitary cat crouched on the windowsill of the bedroom.

"Every day, more lies, more fudge, more deceit."

Julia dressed carefully for Barb's engagement bash. She wore a pale lavender cotton suit, with a mandarin collar, with matching strappy sandals.

Erica Black would be there and Julia refused to compete in the breast stakes by baring all. A mandarin collar was classy.

She was meeting Barb a bit earlier than the others so that they could have a cosy The beach-side restaurant was lovely and it felt good to walk into it feeling smart, tanned and loved. It would be early spring in England. The best time of the year. But this was good, this was not to be sniffed at, even if it did smell of hell. Julia always felt optimistic in the late morning.

Barb was waiting at one of the rattan tables, looking swanky.

"Oo look at us," Julia crowed. "Who would have thought it a year ago."

"You look fab, Jules. I take it life is sweet with Ellis?"

"So, so, you know, a bit up and down, no pun intended. He doesn't understand why you and Bernard and getting engaged and married and he and I can't."

Barb lost her smile immediately. "He would, wouldn't he?"

"And why I have to keep my engagement ring in my handbag and you are flashing your rock like the bleeding Berry Head lighthouse?."

"It's because I know that you're woman enough to take it."

"Yeah, OK. I have vented my spleen as they say."

"You need a drink. Are you feeling ratty with me again? Spit it all out, why don't you."

"No, no, there's no point. Who's coming?"

"Oh Erica, of course, she's after more dialogue, together with sundry handmaidens, wardrobe girls and whoever else is free to pop in for a lunchtime drink and snack."

"And bring you presents. Well I haven't got one."

"Actually, Erica not only wants more dialogue, she wants to cut you out altogether, in every sense of the word. She had quite a thing going with Ellis on the last picture. He's hers, so she thinks. Yes, you had better watch out for Queen Titania."

"You can't call her that. She's hardly Queen of the Fairies. Oh, I don't know though, Peter's found quite a few new friends."

"That's her covert name. She's got titanium tits."

"What in the film?"

"No, in real life. You know, a titanium mesh uplift. Welded in, can't take it out. Did you see that film *Eyes Wide Shut*? Did you see those girls' profiles? Not the faces. Who was looking at their faces. Were you amazed how they stayed up like that? I wonder if she sets off airport scanners. I could put that in the script. Spaceship scanners, there's got to be something like that."

"Poor woman."

"Poor woman, my foot. She loves it, especially when she strips off, which she does, frequently, too frequently for Bernard. He wants a classy space movie, not porn. You know, serious, thought provoking, and then he goes and hires Queen Titania."

Much as she was enjoying her catty chat with Barb, Julia felt she was not into it as much as she used to be. Her parting with Ellis had been strained and it was hard to watch Barb showing off her ring and being congratulated by the girls arriving, when she and Ellis must be secretive. Julia sighed. No wonder Ellis was narked.

Julia exerted herself to get on good terms with the other handmaidens. They all agreed that handmaiden was a terrible description of their duties but none could think of a better one, except Julia who suggested 'retainers'.

Barb chipped in. "No, no, that suggests old and look at you all, luscious eye-candy. My idea is marquise, a woman who holds the rank of marquis in her own right. Classy eh?"

"Well, yes." Julia agreed. "I suppose people who don't know what it means will just think that it's a made-up space name."

"Yes, especially if we spell it like it sounds 'markeez'." Barb spelled out the word.

The rest of the girls were suitably impressed. It was much better than endless sly jokes about hands from their boyfriends.

Erica was not convinced. "Well, I'm the Queen. Aren't they supposed to be lowly or something?"

"Of course you're still the Queen," Barb soothed. "But Queens have high-class ladies to serve them."

"But then." Erica gave a sigh of satisfaction and flipped back her long blonde hair. "Ellis thinks I ought to be a princess. A princess is always so much more romantic than a queen. He still thinks of me as his princess from the last movie, when we were younger and so in love."

"Umm, I think the key word here is younger, Erica darling," Barb purred. "You rule that part of the galaxy, you have to be Queen Ti… Theodora. Your costumes will be much more elaborate and revealing."

Erica stared at Barb for a long minute. "I suppose so."

Julia had no difficulty in keeping her face straight. Erica was not so dumb as she looked and she certainly was very attractive in a smooth blonde kind of way and, no matter how they were arrived at, she certainly had the best pair of bra-less tits on this side of the planet.

Chapter Nineteen

When everyone had drunk enough for the middle of the day and eaten enough sushi and snacks, and Erica had earwigged Barb about the script and pointedly ignored Julia, there was just time to round off the gossip and a final hug and kiss.

"I can't believe that you're actually going to get married Barb." Julia spoke softly so that the intrusive Erica could not hear. "You always said you would never get married."

"Well, Bernard's rich. I get to live in a big house with my own writing suite and secretary. People will notice me more, and my writing, if I'm Mrs Bernard Donne and not that homely, peculiar, English Ms Bark."

"We like peculiar English Ms Bark. Anyway you're not homey. Horrible American word. You look fab. This climate suits your Italian looks. And you're not smoking."

"Thanks Jules. Er, Bernard's paid the ransom… but, he thinks that the hacker will sell it anyway, bound to."

"I know. Of course he will. Everyone wants as much money as they can get."

The girls were leaving. Julia sat, smiling fixedly and saying, "See you," but dreading when she and Barb were finally alone. Barb would tell her more of Bernard's plan.

Julia felt that she was beginning to hate Bernard's plan. She was beginning to hate Bernard. He was like a spider spinning a web and she was caught helplessly in it. She looked at Barb with a small cynical smile curving her lips and slightly raised eyebrows.

Barb sipped her drink, eying Julia steadily over it. She didn't try to pretend that they were just two light-hearted friends gossiping over lunch.

"You know Bernard's sorry. It was careless of him to give me that advanced little gizmo that has landed us all in this mess. You know I'm sorry that I thought up such a stupid idea in the first place."

"Yes, yes," Julia said impatiently. "But he wants me to leave as soon as possible. One minute he wants me to come on to Ellis to drag him into the film, and now he's got that, I'm to be sent away before I ruin Ellis' career."

"Now you're sounding bitter and losing focus. Bernard wants you to spend a week here with Ellis. Hit the beach. See the sights. Canoodle at your house, Hoono something. A week for Ellis to remember. To tide you both over for – the bad times."

"What is this – some kind of film script? Have you written out the parts?"

"There is no point in your getting angry."

"I am angry."

"Jules, darling, do you think that I really want to marry Bernard? I would much rather live with him. But he can get us all out of this mess. You must trust him – and me."

Julia felt the cafe spin a little. There was Barb, same old Barb, but not the same old Barb. She looked wealthy. Her dark hair was longer, less frizzy, her face smooth, her lips made up with expensive lip-gloss. The white dress with pink flower splashes screamed high society. And her white bag with the big DG. And her pink spikey shoes. When had Barb ever worn pink spikey shoes? Julia stared down, transfixed by the shoes.

Barb was speaking again. "I'm sorry, I shouldn't have laid that on you, Jules. What's the matter?"

Slowly Julia raised her head. "Do you expect me to say thank you for sacrificing yourself on the altar of Bernard's flatulent grossness?"

"He is not flatulent. You know, Jules, you read too many books. You have a cruel streak." Barb turned away.

Julia and Barbara stared moodily at the lovely beach, waving palms and sparkling sea. A dull robotic feeling settled in Julia's chest. She reached out her hand to Barb.

"You won't have your nose done, will you Barb? You really won't be the same old Barb if you do."

Julia spent the rest of the afternoon in the company of the small striped cat that had taken up residence on her windowsill. She was glad of its company. She didn't handle the cat so she didn't know its sex. Like most British people she had been brought up to be frightened of rabies.

Later in the afternoon, she fed it in the kitchen and saw that it was female. "Well, Mrs Pussy, where have you come from?"

Julia's mobile rang and the cat fled back to the windowsill. Ellis' voice sounded far away. "I'm not able to come back down so I shall see you tomorrow up here. Julia, can you hear me?"

"Yes, Ellis, I can just hear you. Have you got that sexy outfit on?"

"What?"

"I'm going out with Peter tonight."

"Yes, good idea. Not safe for you to go out alone."

"See you tomorrow."

"I didn't catch that. I have to go. I love you."

The line was dead but Julia said, "I love you." Was it good practice for saying it to Ellis' photo when he dumped her? When he couldn't or wouldn't listen? Would she be saying 'I loved you' to empty rooms for years to come?

"Now I'm getting maudlin," Julia said to the cat. "Well they didn't like me talking to Mother, Mrs Pussy, but they're damn well not going to stop me talking to you."

Peter was so bouncy and happy when he arrived that Julia knew that he had been told nothing about the 'problem'.

They went to dinner in a cafe and then walked by the beach.

"How's my princess, really? You look a little – I don't know – preoccupied, sad. You're missing Ellis." Peter lifted up Julia's left hand to look at the ring winking in the beach lights. "You're missing your Prince Charming. Well, he's not having much fun up there. It's hot, smelly and rough."

Julia nodded. What could she say? 'Because you and Barb bugged me, I'm the most miserable that I have ever been.'

Peter was one of her oldest and closest friends but could she confide in him? He had secrets from her and she had secrets from him. Could she tell him that he might be called upon to play the kind of perv who set up bedroom sex scenes without the occupants of the bed knowing, when he was only the kind of perv who listened to them? No, that was unfair. Barb could be very persuasive. Peter had never been able to resist Barb.

"Do you like it here, Peter? Are you having a good time?"

"Oh, best time of my life, and with my two girls, and Gerald. What could be better? But I miss England. But we may be back in time for the football season. No, I'm only joking, or am I? I may have to spend more time in America if my two girls marry these yanks. But I'll put up with it. In the name of friendship. But, seriously, I am glad that the mother thing, you know, that Barb was worried about, has been cleared up. She told me that it had all worked out just fine."

"Did she? Well she must be right then."

If Peter detected a note of sarcasm in Julia's voice, he didn't mention it. "You know I'm no good with this sensitive girl stuff. Supportive arm and all that, that's my role." He hugged Julia to him as they walked.

"Where's Ellis from?" Peter continued.

"Vermont. It's all sort of Englishy type country. They wear bean boots and have lots of loud check sofas. I think I've got that right. Ellis never says much about his family. We had a row about shooting harmless furry creatures in the woods."

"Well, most American action actors have to be able to ride and shoot. Still it's one of the things I never talk about over here. You know, religion, politics, cosmetic surgery, abortion and guns. Best steered clear of."

"Ellis doesn't see his family much. His father wanted him to be a surgeon."

"Don't they all? We just buggered off to Minehead. Hey, do you remember when we were all redcoats at Minehead? You, me and Barb. What daft prats we were. It's getting a long time ago, Jules. We're cracking on thirty. Ineligible for Club Med. I shall change into an old black queen or become some well-preserved rich actress' toyboy, before I know it."

"There's always the pact."

Peter brightened up. "There's always that."

Julia returned to the bungalow by the beach feeling slightly tipsy. She was going to take two sleeping pills and forget about her problems until the next day when she hoped to see Ellis.

The first thing she noticed when she entered the large living-cum-sleeping room was that Mrs Pussy, sitting on the windowsill as usual, had her hackles up.

"What's wrong with you?" Julia whispered, staring into the cat's dilated eyes. Was it snakes, burglars? Julia froze.

Overlaying the usual lap of the waves on the beach and the rustle of the palm trees came the unmistakable sound of a human snore.

Someone was sleeping in the curtained bed. At first Julia thought that it must be Ellis but as she drew back the drapes and snapped on the overhead light, her flutter of hope died.

Lying fully dressed, in grubby jeans and T-shirt, including dirty trainers, was an angelic-looking, muscular young man with thick dark hair. He was unshaven with the most revolting patch of lower lip fuzz that Julia had ever seen.

He looked familiar. Julia placed him. Zack Michaels. Young, hot, sex-symbol actor. Drunkard, hell-raiser, druggie, enthusiastic continuous sex addict, womaniser.

Zack opened his brilliant dark eyes. His gaze wandered appreciatively over Julia's face and low cut dress. "Now you know," he drawled easily with a faint Irish accent, "some girls would be pleased to see me lying on their bed."

Julia smiled thinly, noticing that the gross lower lip fuzz was shaped like a heart.

"Oh yes." Zack swung himself up with easy grace and stood looking at Julia with something like contempt. "Ellis told me he was shacked up with some hot bird."

Before Julia could do anything, Zack pulled her to him with one swift motion, obviously intending to place his revolting bit of facial decoration on her mouth.

He was very strong. He smelt of drink and sweat. Julia resisted with all her strength. He let her go and she staggered back.

"Sorry," he said, not sorry at all. "I always check out Ellis' bits of fluff, especially those who snog hunky black men on the beach while he's away."

With what he obviously thought was an irresistible smile, Zack settled himself in an easy chair by the window, and stretched out his legs. His hand reached out and caressed Mrs Pussy, who hissed.

Zack withdrew his hand. "Ellis said you were a witch. You've even got a cat. I have a way with pussies. She'll come round."

To Julia, Zack's smile seemed to say, 'and so will you'. She nearly said 'Don't you think it's a bit pathetic going around expecting every woman, and cat, to swoon at your feet?' But she didn't. She was thinking rapidly. She must keep her cool. Nothing would please this obnoxious bighead more than for her to lose it. He was needling her on purpose. It was the old story. The battle of the girlfriend versus the male friend, with Ellis the prize in the middle.

"Would you like some tea?" Julia put on her best hostess voice.

Zack laughed. He looked more attractive now that he was genuinely amused. "Do I look like a man who drinks tea?"

"Yes."

"You're right, I do. Can't fool you. We're both loyal subjects of the Crown. You just have to tell me that the big black bloke on the beach is your brother, and I might actually start to like you."

Making the tea, Julia had time to review Zack's career. Good actor, sought after. Hell raiser. Irresistible to women. Voted sexiest male actor of 2004. Nominated for an Oscar. Drank too much. Went in for wild sex parties. Boasted about his many, many conquests. Broken up at least two Hollywood marriages. The thing was, Julia wondered, how could he possibly be Ellis' close friend?

"Feels sort of primitive, doesn't it?" Ellis paused to view the range of volcanic mountains stretching before them. A pall of evil-smelling smog, or vog, hung heavily in the air.

Julia wrinkled her nose. "I suppose the island is still growing. It's like the beginning of time."

Ellis, who was wearing the sexy silver and black trousers and little else, flexed his muscles. "Me Tarzan, you Jane."

Julia had to kiss him. The kiss was long, satisfying and sweet, but nothing further could come of it as they were standing in full view of the cast and crew.

Julia was tired. She had spent most of the morning standing either alone or with Gerald, or running, or falling as directed, doing her outdoor scenes. She knew that she was finished up in the mountains and on Hawaii altogether. The rest of her scenes would be done at the studios in LA.

But they had the week promised by Bernard. It would end with Bernard and Barb's wedding. Then she would return to LA. and the process of separation from Ellis would begin.

Ellis pulled Julia to him. "One more take and we're going down. Tonight we are going to make love on the beach." His last words were whispered, "With no audience."

Ellis' beach was truly the stuff of dreams. Golden sand, blue sea, white rolling surf, palm trees and warm afternoon sun. Of course, the rest of the cast and the crew thought so too, so it wasn't an Adam and Eve kind of paradise especially as Gerald was there trying to surf.

Gerald had no chance of outdoing Ellis at surfing. Ellis had been in a surfing movie. Julia had seen it. Ellis had looked fantastic in it, she had thought. He had been younger and boyish-looking. Now he was much more muscled. Julia hoped that he wasn't overdoing the steroids. Why did every American seem to think that their bodies needed improvement?

Julia knew that she should be out there in the sea with the others. Erica Black was posing at the edge of the surf for a magazine and Ellis had been dragged into the picture. It would make a good spread. Bernard would approve. Julia stretched languidly on her sunbed. She looked good in a bikini but she was no longer going to be able to compete with the beauties frolicking with Ellis in the surf. She would become fat and whale-like. She had missed one period, but this had happened before when stressed out on a film.

No one knew except herself. She always retreated into herself when unsettling things threatened her. She would have told Ellis, of course, if the 'problem' had never happened. Because they would have been happy about it, wouldn't they? They had been in love in a simple boy-meets-girl kind of way. Now the 'problem' had created another problem. A poor innocent baby was a problem.

But she had England, the NHS, and abortion on demand. Better not to say anything while she was still in America. They could be a bit funny about abortions, to say the least. But she must get back to the UK before eight weeks.

Apart from a little sickness and dizziness, she felt well. Her skin glowed with all the fresh air and sunshine. She was young and healthy. Her much desired Ellis was waving to her from the sea. She was keeping another secret from him now. What the heck would that matter, she thought: secrets bred secrets.

Would she have an abortion? Here on an island that was itself giving birth with every spew of lava, it was unthinkable. But, back in the UK rejected by Ellis, perhaps.

Julia didn't want to think any more. She rose and walked down to the sea.

Gerald looked tanned and handsome, and didn't he know it Although he had an attractive girl on each arm, Julia knew that he was still expecting her to go back to him.

At least the obnoxious Zack had not turned up. Julia had mentioned him to Ellis. Ellis had looked pleased that Zack had come to visit him, but not overly so. She knew that the pair of them planned to spend some time together.

"Why so pensive?" Ellis ran up, panting a little.

"Oh I was just thinking that when I told you that a man, who has been voted the sexiest actor in Hollywood, had spent the night on a chair in my bedroom, you showed not one sign of jealousy."

"I'm very trusting." Ellis picked her up and carried her into the sea. "And I can wait until you can completely trust me.

Anyway, Zack said he didn't fancy you himself. Too tight arsed, he said."

Julia struggled in his arms as Ellis waded deeper into the water. "He didn't! You're making it all up." Julia laughed. She could forget for a time. This was primitive and exiting and there was still the night to come. The sea was warm but the surf too rough but Ellis was there to pick her up.

He looked as innocent as his unborn child, and for a week she would pretend that she was too.

Chapter Twenty

They made love on the tropical beach, defying the insects with citron oil. Surely the most intoxicating smell ever, Julia thought, together with the smell of salt drying on Ellis' skin, sun cream and her own 'Quadrille'.

Julia had been a little hesitant at first. She was sure that Gerald was snooping jealously around, or the handmaidens were frolicking nearby. They were still called handmaidens, the male writers having refused point blank to change it.

"I missed you," Ellis pulled her close as they lay in the dunes. "There's no one around. They're all at the barbecue. Nobody can see us."

Ellis could not understand why Julia burst into helpless laughter at his words. "What's so funny?" He broke away and looked down at her. "What's the joke? You need a lesson in loving."

Julia looked up at him. She was not going to resist. She was incapable of resisting him. Terrible secret jokes could be funny. She was worried about people seeing them have sex on the beach when, soon, everyone in the world who wanted to could see them have sex over and over again in the comfort of their own homes.

Julia laughed again, though it sounded to her more like 'on with the motley'.

"Girls don't usually laugh when I'm trying to fuck them," Ellis grumbled affectionately.

"You could try harder."

"I am hard, you witch." Ellis began to kiss her again.

"Seriously Ellis, there could be paparazzi in the bushes. What would you do if a compromising photo of us appeared in print, and you saw it all over a newspaper shop?"

"I wouldn't give it a thought."

"Really?"

"Really. Julia, I love you. I want you, now."

Julia's heart gave a happy little leap. He wouldn't care. Perhaps there was hope for them after all. But now it was nice not to think any more. To receive Ellis, to feel that little lurch inside when his chest touched hers. To feel him, completely. Under the stars. It must be all a dream. A delicious exciting dream.

Julia had never felt so sexy. She knew why. All her inhibitions had melted away. There was only the urgent need to get as close to him as possible, to make love, passionately, tenderly and finally breathlessly.

"That was amazing. You really are going to have to marry me after that. I don't know about the earth moving but the stars are certainly spinning." Ellis lay back a little breathless. "I love you. I just mentioned marriage, fool that I am, but your face still closes over."

Julia was already feeling that she wanted him again. She could only look at him, put out her hands and touch him to soothe the look of bafflement from his eyes, replace it with desire, and joke.

"I know, I'm amazing but I've got a stone sticking in my bum." Julia wriggled suggestively and laughed softly.

Ellis hauled her back onto the blanket and on top of him and began to stroke the afflicted place. "Bum. That's an awful word for this delicious ass. You're spoiling the romance of the moment."

Julia settled comfortably on him. It seemed to her that nothing would ever come between them. "An ass is a donkey."

Julia was already bearing down teasingly onto him so that he could no longer think about marriage.

Ellis had finished most of his scenes on the Big Island and they choppered over to Honolulu. They signed the papers for 'Hoonanea'. They went shopping in Waikiki. Julia looked pensively in a baby shop window. She almost turned to Ellis and blurted out her secret. But it seemed a bit lame to say that there might be a baby.

They went on a nature trail, and a safari-type trail. They went to pay their respects at Pearl Harbor. They stayed at the hotel on Waikiki beachfront for a few nights but two days before Barb's wedding they went to 'Hoonanea'.

Julia knew what Ellis was thinking as they re-discovered their house. They went up to the dormer bedroom, which had a marvellous view. Ellis said it would make a nice child's room.

Julia turned away and went down the stairs. Oh why had they come back here? Ellis was thinking that they should be married by now. And he didn't know why they were not.

They decided to keep all of the old bamboo furniture and have it re-covered. Ellis wanted to rip out the kitchen but Julia said no. It was cottagey, she said. To Ellis cottagey was crappy, but…

They sat on the terrace. Julia wanted to say that perhaps it hadn't been a good idea to come to 'Hoonanea' until they were actually married, but she didn't.

Ellis had his glasses on again. He was checking some American newspapers. He looked a little remote.

As soon as Ellis asked where Gran was, she knew that she was in deep trouble.

"I would have thought that she would have come round by now." He held up his hands. "No, no I really like her."

"Well… she had to go to Los Angeles."

"Why?"

"For medical treatment. I should have told you."

"It doesn't matter. I know you don't tell me everything."

Like the day after tomorrow, after the wedding, I shall be flying off to LA myself, Julia thought

"Is it serious?"

"It might be."

Ellis looked up. "Might be?"

"Is."

"And you didn't tell me?"

Julia stood up suddenly tired of it all and her longing for it to be all over. "Look, Ellis. I don't tell you everything because – I'm not like that. I was very upset when Gran told me that she was seriously ill. She actually stood at this rail and told me that she thought that she would never come back. It upset me and I – buried it – inside. I'm sorry."

"And what else are you, burying?"

"Do you think I am?"

"Don't give me these smartass evasions, tell me."

Julia flayed around desperately for a few seconds. She would tell him, but not here. "Let's go back to the Big Island. To that beach, where it's natural and awesome and nothing seems to matter but us."

As Julia had thought, Ellis seemed to recover some of his equilibrium as they strolled, half naked and carefree along the shoreline. Had 'Hoonanea' become a white elephant, she wondered? Was their wonderful house too wonderful? Had the Hawaiian gods cast them out?

"Now you," Ellis turned to her with a teasing smile, Miss Julia Slater, are going to tell me exactly what you were thinking, right just then, a few seconds ago." Ellis threw his surfboard down with a smack on the sand, and drew her to him for a salty kiss. The slap of a wave parted them.

"There was a French film. In the sixties I think, where a group of young French boys and girls played a game where everyone had to answer absolutely truthfully, any question that they were asked."

"So?"

"As far as I can remember, things didn't turn out all that well."

"You're hopeless, Julia. I give up. Have it your way. I'm finished. Kaput." Ellis picked up his board and ran into the sea.

Julia sat on the beach. She decided that she would just tell Ellis everything. Sod Bernard. After all, it wasn't her fault. Peter and Gerald appeared, heading her way. She had forgotten that they were still staying in the cabins.

Ellis was dipping up and down in the waves. Sometimes skimming, sometimes falling off. There were other surfers in the water. Two of them were Gerald and Peter. Gerald was coming out of the water and so was Ellis. Gerald threw down his board, went purposefully over to Ellis and hit him full on the jaw with his fist.

Ellis went down, his shock and surprise obvious. Gerald stood by menacingly. Before Ellis could get up properly, Gerald hit him again on the side of the face. But this time Ellis was prepared and he struck back. Gerald went down. To Julia's horror the two men, well matched and furious, began slugging it out on the shoreline. She got up and ran towards them. They were both on the sand rolling about in the small waves.

Peter grabbed Gerald. Peter used all of his powerful frame to hold Gerald off Ellis.

"You wanker," Gerald was shouting. "You Hollywood pervert! If you ever come near Julia again, I'll kill you. I'll bloody kill you."

Ellis stood wiping the blood from his face with his hands. "What are you talking about you limey madman?" he shouted.

"About you Ellis. Do you think you can treat Julia like that and get away with it?" Gerald tried to attack Ellis again but Peter began to pull him away. "I'm talking about you putting pictures of you and Julia on the Internet," Gerald shouted. "You dirty swine!"

Ellis walked slowly towards Julia, blood pouring from his nose. He was holding his jaw in pain. "What is he talking about?" he said with difficulty.

Julia began to feel a little sick and dizzy. "I was going to tell you… but I think you had better go and see Bernard. He knows all about it. He's the one who swore me to secrecy."

Ellis flicked the blood from his nose. He stared at Julia for a long minute. "Go and see Bernard? Are you crazy?"

Peter had dumped a groggy Gerald on the beach, and come back for Julia. "I'd better take her back," he said directly to Ellis, taking Julia's arm.

"What, are you going to start hitting me too? You crazy English…" Ellis had the look of a man who could not believe what was happening to him.

Julia stood still. "I'll go with Peter, Ellis. You must see Bernard straight away."

It was a body blow for Ellis. Julia saw it but was helpless to change anything.

Ellis gave Julia a long hard, cold, look. Get used to it, she thought, it's the first but not the last time.

"OK, you've made your choice." He shrugged and turned away.

"I don't have a choice." Julia started forward and took Ellis' arm and placed her cheek on it lovingly. He remained frozen.

"Barb bugged us making love at Peter's place. A hacker stole it and it looks like it's on the Web. I know I should have told you. I wanted to. I was going to…"

"Barbara filmed us? Why?" Ellis turned to look into Julia's pleading eyes.

The ghastly moment was imprinting itself upon Julia's mind. The sun was beginning to sink over the sea. The beach was deserted apart from Peter standing a few metres away and Gerald sitting limply on the sand. And a runner racing towards them along the shore. It looked like Zack.

"That time! She filmed us!" Ellis' face was etched in shocked lines in the slanting light. His voice was disbelieving. He shivered with cold or horror, and Julia clung to him in despair, longing to warm him with her body.

"And you didn't tell me? You've known since Barbara came round that night. You deceived me!" Ellis was talking to himself. He shook off Julia's arms and began to walk away.

A small hurricane hurtled up to Julia as she stood devastated by the way things had turned out. It almost knocked her over. She stared into the angry dark eyes of Zack.

Zack went to Ellis and examined his injuries, exclaiming in surprise. "Someone told me two limeys were beating you up," he said, grinning. "And they bloody well have!"

Zack turned to face Julia and Peter as Ellis continued to walk away. He put up his fists. "Come on then, take me on too."

"It's over," Julia said shortly. She and Peter left Zack torn between forcing a good punch-up or helping his friend.

Julia waited in the bungalow on the beach. Ellis did not return. Peter and Gerald kept her company. Julia refused to talk to Gerald and, eventually, he left to get some treatment for his injuries, vowing that he was going to force them to tell him what was going on, the very next day.

Peter gently confirmed what she already knew. The sex scene had appeared on the Internet. People were entranced by such a wonderful piece of juicy gossip about a famous actor.

"It wasn't as it appeared," Julia tearfully told Peter as he tucked her into bed.

"No, no," Peter soothed. "But you know Gerald. He loves you. He'll do anything to get you back. Come on, take your pills, we'll sort it out in the morning."

Julia heard no word from Ellis. He didn't ring. She felt languid but strangely calm. At last it was out in the open. It could be dealt with, one way or another.

She stayed at the bungalow by the beach. She had a key to 'Hoonanea' but she was too dispirited to go there alone.

She wore the suit with the mandarin collar for the wedding, and packed the rest of her things for the flight to LA. She didn't really want to go to the wedding at all. Not unless Ellis came to her and said that all was forgiven.

Ellis would most likely be there. She didn't know whether he would refuse to view the 'scene', as she had, or manfully face up to it. He wouldn't like it, she knew. He didn't call. She could not bring herself to call him.

There was only Barb on her mobile, chattering irritatingly and not saying what was happening, as though she did not know what to say. All that Julia could get out of her was that Ellis was recovering from his injuries and was bearing up well.

Julia still refused to speak to Gerald and maintained a tight-lipped silence towards him as they travelled to the wedding in Honolulu. Peter was supportive, as always. He kept Gerald at bay and patted her hand comfortingly now and then.

Barb was dressed in a voluminous white dress, which surprised Julia for in the past Barb had been quite scathing about meringue wedding gowns. Bernard had poured himself into a grey suit and, Julia suspected, may have been wearing a corset. Bernard looked unusually flustered.

The wedding was held in the hotel on Waikiki Beach. No expense had been spared as to flowers, which overflowed everywhere. Amid the powerful aroma of garlands and over two hundred very wealthy people, Barb and Bernard exchanged vows, promising to love, honour and cherish.

At the reception Julia was getting butterflies at the thought of seeing Ellis. What would he do? What would he say? Would he speak to her at all?

She was seated with Gerald, Peter and other British members of the cast at a table far away from the top table. At last she saw Ellis sitting quietly, looking purposefully at nothing. He had a black eye.

He didn't look across. He didn't smile. Julia's heart beat painfully and she ate little of the delicious food.

Julia acted out the role of the happy wedding guest. She had done it many times before in films. It was bad manners to spoil a wedding with your own problems. As the afternoon wore on she knew that Ellis was not going to approach her.

Gerald had a cut lip. He glowered a bit but he was much too well brought up to look really angry, and made an effort to dance with, and smile at, the pretty young actresses.

Julia spent a lot of time in the ladies' room. Cowardly, she knew, but anything was better than staring at Ellis' back.

Barb sailed in. "Ah, there you are. What do you think?" She posed before the mirrors. "I look like Cinderella's run off with Buttons and let the ugly sister marry the prince."

"You look lovely Barb. Congratulations."

"You look terrible. Come on, let's fix your make-up. You must look beautiful and without a care in the world. Ellis is playing his part. He's ignoring you. It's just whispers now. They won't grow much. I mean, who wants to admit that they watch porn websites? Have you said anything to anyone?"

"No."

"Good. Keep it up. What did you think of the ceremony? Mercifully free of soppy personal vows, don't you think? Just think what a twat I would feel later, if Bernard and I divorced…"

Julia's mind was fixed on what Barb had said about Ellis. She broke in crossly. "Shut up! Are you saying that Ellis has been told to ignore me?"

"Do you think he's doing it because he wants to, or because he was told to?"

Barb looked serious. She gave Julia a hug. "I honestly don't know, Jules. I'm sorry but he's clammed up. As soon as Bernard told him that it was all true, he went quite white with shock. They got the doctor in. He's been fighting with someone. Two of his teeth needed fixing. He's got them in a brace. And that black eye. The director is furious. But I'm going to write it into the script. Everyone will think it's fake when they watch the film. They won't guess it's a real shiner. Of course, the people at the wedding will know, but he's been going around with Zack Michaels, the dust-up king…"

"Will you try to stop babbling Barb, and concentrate on the important issues?" Julia was so annoyed that she seized Barb by her shoulder puffs and practically tore them off her shoulders.

"I'm sorry." Julia patted the puffs back into place. "I don't know what I'm doing, or saying. What happens now?"

Chapter Twenty-One

Barb hitched up her skirts and sat on the sinks. "I need a smoke. Bernard's eating too much wedding breakfast anyway." There was a small silence as Barb puffed, her dress billowing around her reflected in the many well lit mirrors. "Who was Ellis doing the John Wayne's with?"

"Gerald. They were fighting on the beach."

"Mmm, two hunky men fighting over you on a beach. Primitive. Can't be bad."

"You weren't there."

"So, was it jealousy – or the other thing?"

"Gerald had logged on and seen it. Perhaps he heard a rumour. He thought Ellis had put it on himself, and attacked him without warning. God knows what would have happened if Peter hadn't pulled Gerald off." Julia closed her eyes, seeing again Ellis' shrug and his stony face as he turned away.

"Right. I've got to get Gerald and tell him to keep his mouth shut."

Julia went to a sink and dabbed her hot face with cool water. Her reflection looked blotchy. She began to repair her make-up carefully. Make-up was always so comforting.

"I'm, glad Ellis knows," she whispered to her reflection. "He will forgive me. He must!" A future without him seemed very bleak.

"Was Ellis very shocked when you told him, Barb? Will he forgive Bernard, you, me?"

Barb's solemn gaze met Julia's in the mirror. "It was a blow for him. It's all coiled inside him. Anger and disgust with himself. The horror of people knowing, seeing. Anger at me and Bernard, especially me. Anger at you. He watched it alone. It was a long time before he came out. Perhaps we should have told him straight away, when the hacker got it, especially as it was on the website sooner than we thought it would be. We thought we had a month or two to prepare."

"What do you think Ellis will do?"

"Nothing. He'll keep it all there inside. He's got to do the shooting in LA next week. He'll concentrate on that. He'll drink Irish whiskey, brood, and he says he's going down to Mexico when the filming is over with some friends."

"So you think he's finished with me, really, not because he's been told to?"

"I don't know."

"And Bernard hasn't thought up any plan at all."

"Oh yes, Jules, of course. He is going to keep his promise." Barb jumped off the sinks and held Julia close.

Julia turned into the embrace. "What do I do now?" Her mind and words felt heavy with a dull ache.

"You carry on as though nothing has happened," Barb crooned.

"The crew will gossip. Gerald fighting with Ellis. That's expected. Gerald's been needling Ellis in public for some time. You had a fling with Ellis. Happens all the time on set. No one will think anything of it. You can't be Ellis' permanent girlfriend. You see that. You can't be a couple. A couple who would…"

Julia raised her head, her green eyes lit with a look that Barb had seen many times before. "Behave as in the scene," she finished. "As in real life."

Barb stepped back her face beaming in admiration. "You see it. I told Bernard I wouldn't tell you. He wouldn't believe that you would catch on. Why do clever men have so much trouble believing that a beautiful woman can possibly be as smart as they are? He's a terrible big-head. Of course, he's rated practically a genius over here."

"I see it, but I don't see how Bernard can magic it up."

"Oh he will. He'll pull in all his favours."

"Does Ellis know all of it?"

"Not all. He's got to work through the betrayal first. The humiliation. The self-disgust. Your duplicity."

Barb pulled Julia close again at the look of pain that crossed Julia's face. "There, there, darling. He'll be a fool if he lets you go."

Erica Black and several actresses entered the powder room. "Are we interrupting anything?" Erica smiled a sugary smile.

They all retreated to the other end of the room but made little effort to disguise the fact that they had found the tender scene quite titillating.

"The lessie rumours will be flying. But that's a good thing. Smoke, Jules, smoke. But, brace up, Ellis is to cosy up to Erica a bit more. Now, don't be cross, she hasn't a heart to break. Erica really thinks that she's seduced Ellis away from you. That's more good gossip. Anything, rather than – the problem."

Julia left for the airport without seeing Ellis again. She got into the large car provided and sank down into the back seats. The car hummed but did not move. Julia didn't notice.

After a few minutes, she did notice that they were not moving. The back door opened. Ellis jumped in. The car sped off.

Julia wanted to say something but the words dried in her throat. She waited.

He was still in his dark grey wedding suit. She could smell his aftershave. Men always wore too much aftershave at weddings.

The tension inside the close confines of the car began to eat away at Julia. He had got into the car. He must want to say something to her. If he had got something to say, why didn't he say it? Say it, say it, she pleaded silently.

She turned to look at him. He turned slightly. She was glad it wasn't the side of his face with the black eye.

"I'm sorry," she said at last, painfully aware that his expression was carefully hiding his true feelings.

He nodded.

She felt a little annoyed. "You could say something."

He opened his mouth to show the metal brace holding his damaged side teeth in place. "Difficult."

"Oh Ellis, I'm so sorry. Gerald shouldn't have…"

She was ready to touch him, to kiss him, to make up. But, she could see in his eyes a look that said 'We're through'.

His wary blue eyes were as hard as glass in the light from the windows. The planes of his face that had once smiled so lovingly in their mutual delight in each other, were set in stony rejection of her. She had never seen him as he looked now.

Why had he got into the car? "Why did you get in the car?" she asked almost angrily.

He held his jaw and carefully enunciated "Barbara."

He turned away.

"Oh, I see. I'm sorry." She felt a fool for saying sorry again. "Barbara's a writer. She never really feels anything. She just examines situations and turns them into imaginary happy endings. She thinks she can rearrange people's lives like stories. That's why she did it. That's why she bugged me. So that she could rearrange my life."

Ellis shifted in his seat. "Damn these teeth!" he said holding his jaw in pain. "That still – does not explain – why she did it. You are still lying to me." He groaned.

Julia wanted to tell him everything, although she still shied away from explaining about her mother. This wasn't the time. Ellis was too badly injured to speak properly.

She could do nothing except sit and wonder that this could have been their wedding day. They could be driving, should have been driving, away on their honeymoon right now, when Ellis' groans of pain would have been sighs of delight and pleasure. Now she doubted that they would ever recapture their delight in being together, if indeed Ellis ever thawed out enough to give her another chance.

Somehow, things had all gone horribly wrong. Ellis must wonder why she was still friends with Barb. She could not think of any way to get him back again. "Sorry" she said again. The airport was passing by the windows. The car stopped.

Any moment the door would open. Julia half rose, suddenly desperate to get away.

"Julia. I'm sorry too." It was softly, painfully and regretfully spoken.

It was too late for Julia to turn back. She had to get out. The driver was back in the car. As it drove off, she heaved a big breath of air to stop the tears. They had both said they were sorry. She was sorry for keeping secrets from him. He was sorry because it was over.

Julia went to Bernard's house in LA. Or rather Bernard and Barb's house. She was picked up at the airport. The house was as large and depressingly mausoleum-like as she remembered. Bernard thought the style was grand old English, but then he had probably never heard of the word snug. And that the most commonly used expression that ordinary Britons used, when visiting the grand mansions of Britain, was, 'not very snug'.

Mercedes, the housekeeper, made Julia very welcome. Everything was provided for her comfort. Julia didn't know what instructions Barb had given to Mercedes, but one of them was definitely that Julia was to be cosseted.

Julia went to bed early and slept late. She swam in the pool. Her mind might be all to pieces but she was going to get her body back into shape. Shake off the tiredness, stiffness and lethargy. Her face and body made her fortune after all.

Barb rang as Julia was taking a sleeping pill and looking forward to the oblivion of sleep. Barb babbled on for a time. About the honeymoon, about how was Julia getting on, about film shooting. Finally she said, "Aren't you going to ask me about Ellis?"

"How is Ellis?" Julia asked dully.

"He's better. Physically and mentally better."

"Did he ask about me?"

There was a pause. "Not in so many words. But I think he was fishing to find out where you were settled in LA."

"I have to go to sleep, Barb."

"There's something else, Julia."

"Tell me tomorrow."

The next day Julia realised what Barb was going to tell her the night before, when she received a call from Dr John Fitzgerald.

He told her who he was.

"I know who you are," Julia said frostily.

"Can I see you?"

"I don't see that there's much point."

"It's only for a chat. No office room, no couch, no pressure. Just a coffee in an LA restaurant."

Julia hesitated. She could wear her new clothes from Hawaii. She was an actress. She couldn't hide away. He was English. He was upper class. She was tired of being cooped up in a house where everyone spoke Spanish and she didn't.

Julia was shown to a table on a balcony overlooking a hazy LA. There were flowers. The sun, of course, was shining. She had dressed carefully in a blue, long-sleeved creation that revealed little of her body. Her hair was swept back into a severe plait. She wore sunglasses and she didn't take them off.

They made the formal greeting and then sat and looked at each other under the sunshade.

He was smooth, almost oily. Julia was prepared.to dislike him on sight, but she found that she didn't. She took off her sunglasses. He looked a bit like Roger Moore. Who could dislike someone who looked like Roger Moore?

"Barbara, Mrs Donne, now of course, asked me to see you. Just once, that's all. It's no big deal."

"Barbara is too interfering."

"Yes, but it's nice to have friends who really care about you isn't it."

"If you say so, Dr Fitzgerald."

"Call me John. This is only a friendly chat, you know, we don't have to fence with each other. In fact, I'm really here because you can help me."

"Look I don't know what Barb's told you but… about the tapes, you told her…"

"Barbara and I first got together in a literary way," John cut in. "She was doing *Mothers and Daughters* and I was writing about the repression of young working-class girls after the War. Working-class boys were affected too, of course, but the clever ones were always helped. Yes, they would send the clever working-class boys to the grammar school, to be bullied, but the girls, now the girls could stay in the kitchen and like it. Drink your coffee. It's getting cold.

"Your mother was one of those lost clever working-class girls. Victims of the War, bankrupt economy, at the mercy of blinkered County Council education policy, and the general unpleasantness of the period from 1946 up to the early sixties.

"That element in English society that had always resisted the education of the masses, was still very much alive. Many doctors and teachers belonged to the middle or lower middle class or above. They were mostly taught to despise the working classes."

Julia broke in feeling irritated. "What are you on about? Your own research?"

"Yes. Girls were turned out at fourteen, fifteen, no O-levels because they weren't set any, no French, no science, but lots of needlework, cooking and house cleaning.

"And, probably, worst of all, presumed to be not intelligent. How could they be, their fathers worked down the mines and on the railways. Any show of real intelligence met with accusations of cheating. A most bitter and bewildering pill to swallow. And even if they went on to night school and got some O-levels, some could never catch up. And when they took their triumphs home, dropped their accents, their families would often turn against them. They had jobs, they had boyfriends, they got married, they had children."

"My mother got two Os at night school. The Peoples' College, Nottingham. She would work all day and go to night school in the evening. She did algebra for the first time and really liked it. The maths course was so long she had to give it up. My grandfather called her 'Miss Snob'."

Chapter Twenty-Two

For a moment Julia stared sightlessly over the view of LA. What was she doing here, what was she saying? That her mother would have got down on her knees before The Peoples' College and salaamed if she hadn't feared the embarrassment of it?

That Julia's grandfather had called his daughter 'Miss Snob'. No, she hadn't said any of that. But she had. It was time to stop before she was tricked into telling any more secrets.

"Look Dr Fitzgerald, I know what you're doing. You're trying to unsettle me. Make me break. Well you have unsettled me. I'm going." Julia began to rise.

"May I use the bit about your mother doing O-levels at night school after work, in my book? About being called Miss Snob by her own family?"

Julia sat down again, slowly.

"Look, I'm an historian. Your mother's not the only one."

"I thought you were a psychiatrist."

"I'm that as well. Your mother won't be mentioned by name. She's one of thousands. Barbara contacted me when she was doing research for her play *Mothers and Daughters*, as I said. Later, she contacted me again about her worry that in her excitement at getting her first big writing break, she had failed to realise that she had… betrayed a friend… you. She described the psychological damage that she thought she had caused you.

"The main thrust of the play was that daughters are deeply influenced by having a mother who, in some way, has been a victim of a society that should have helped her.

"As you know, Barbara drew the analogy of the bombed greenhouse roof and the exotic roses escaping wildly out of the top. Your mother was an exotic rose who only partially escaped in a wild fashion from the abandoned greenhouse when it was too late."

"I suppose you are saying that my mother spent her life trying to climb out of a jagged glass greenhouse, when she should have been carefully transplanted outside as a treasured cultivated rose, rather than a trapped wild one.

"And now I'm trapped in there too, along with all her other 1950s inhibitions!" Julia tried to sound derisive but failed miserably. She had nearly said 'sexual inhibitions'."

Dr Fitzgerald smiled, nodding his head in sympathy. Julia felt that he knew very well that she had been slipping into being her mother and then denying it. Never in a million years was she going to admit this to him.

Julia sighed. "All I did was phone my mother to let her know how things were going."

"It's natural to do a little self-help therapy. Your mother died last year, soon after the play was finished, didn't she?

"You were glad there was no Channel Five where she lived so she never saw it. Things only became tricky because you were an actress playing your own mother in a play written by a close friend.

"Call your mother Julia. You're still in mourning. Tell her the things you want to. Believe me when I say there is nothing saner."

Julia jumped up. "I don't need you to tell me that! I must go." She began to walk away, but turned and looked back at her tormentor.

"I'll write down some things. That my mother started work before she started her periods. That her father came home from the War a stranger and stayed one.

"That she slept in the same old bed with her younger sister until she married. That there was only one sink in the house. That one pair of navy knickers had to last the week and do for gym as well.

"You wouldn't know such things unless someone like me told you, would you? Barb can send them to you."

"That's a good start."

"I'm doing it for history, Dr Fitzgerald. To set the record straight. You never know, some people might read your book and actually care. Now, I'm sure that you are eager to get back to your hysterical LA divorcees."

Julia went to the ladies and threw up the very nice little salad and coffee that she had just mindlessly consumed. When she had recovered, she sat in the sun feeling drained but not unpleasantly so. Perhaps there were people who really did give a thought, now and again, about the lives of clever 1950s working-class girls?

On the way home she bought a pregnancy testing kit. Still rattled by Dr Fitzgerald, her fingers trembled as she looked at the test in one of Bernard's oversize bathrooms. She threw it on the floor and ground it viciously with her foot. She didn't want to know.

Julia lay in the pool feeling more relaxed. She had been rude to Fitzgerald and she regretted that. He had been kind in his own self-seeking way. He had read most of his book to her. She had thought that he would never stop.

She supposed he had been using her as some kind of sounding block. She wished that both he and Barb had left her and her mother severely alone.

She was not sure that she would ever ring Mother again. And it wasn't because that stupid doctor had told her that she could.

She had to take stock. She had missed one period. That had happened before. She had been sick and dizzy. But she was feeling fine now, physically anyway. Perhaps not eating as much as she should but, hey, this was a place where people hardly ate anything at all, and if they did, they threw it up.

Like me, Julia confessed as she floated, mesmerised by the shifting shadows of the water on the ceiling. She heard a splash. Ellis had once jumped in a pool and swum towards her. No, it was Peter, black, shiny and grinning.

"Oh, am I glad to see you." Contact at last with the world of films, shoots and locations. All the gossip She became suddenly very anxious to get back to work.

"How's my princess?"

"Fine, Peter, fine. Never felt better. How's Gerald?"

"Um, a bit silent. Unusual for him. Barb's been giving him an earful."

"And you? My darling black knight."

"Worried about you."

"He didn't rape me, you know, Peter. Ellis did not force me. It might look a bit that way, but it wasn't like that at all."

"I know. If I'd thought that, I'd have smashed his face in myself."

"And anyway, you have no right to criticise Ellis when you helped Barb to do such a stupid thing in the first place."

"I know, I'm sorry about that, but you know what Barb's like. She clucks over you like a mother hen. And I thought it was only sound."

"I've seen the trickcyclist. The one Barb knows. The one who listened to the tapes, without the pictures, of course. God knows what he would think of those! He told me that there was nothing abnormal about my phoning Mother. I suppose it was nice to get that in person."

"I told Barb the very same thing, right at the beginning, but would she listen to me? No. And I was right all along."

"He's writing a book about the working-class girls and their lives after the War. You know, all Oxford and Cambridge."

"Does he look as though he knows anything about it, really?"

"No, he's a toff. I suppose that's why he's latched onto Barbara and me."

"Well, you know what they're like in their little cosy world. They only write books and articles for each other. It's nothing to do with the rest of us. We don't read them."

Julia got out of the water. "When's the next shoots? I want to get this sci-fi under my belt. I'm raring to go. The only cure for heartache is work."

"Ellis is back – in LA." Peter grinned knowingly.

"Well, we're finished, I think."

"Barb's sent you some photos. Beach things, you know. The wedding. Ellis with a shiner. Ellis on the beach with something strange written on the soles of his feet."

Peter began to laugh. "Do you know what Barb's written on his feet? What has she written on his feet?"

"Where's the packet? Where's the packet?" Julia could hardly wait.

Peter indicated his coat. Julia grabbed it and removed the envelope. She sat in a pool-side chair and after carefully wiping her wet hands, she began to leaf through the photos.

Barb and Bernard cutting the cake. Ellis sitting at the top table with a black eye. Ellis sneaking a look at her. Julia smiled. Gerald and Peter eating the wedding breakfast. Barb as the happy, radiant bride. Barb dancing on the table. Ellis sucking champagne through a straw and grimacing. Barb hitting Gerald over the head with the sink plunger he had given her for a wedding present. Ellis getting out of a big car in his wedding suit looking grim. Ellis on the beach in his swimming trunks looking happy. Ellis and Erica posing on the beach for photographers in their swimwear, with Erica's hand on Ellis' chest. Ellis lying, face down, on a sunbed on the beach. On the soles of both of his feet, in bright red lipstick, were the words 'CLAY'.

Julia laughed. "Oh, I'll ring Barb's neck when I see her."

"What's it all about then? At least it's made you laugh." Peter sat down and looked at the photo again.

"She once said that all men have feet of clay. Well, Barb sent Ellis out to the car to make up with me when I left for the airport. He didn't, so she's mad at him."

"It would be difficult. He had a mouth full of metal. Gerald packs quite a punch."

Julia sighed. "How is Ellis, really, Peter? I think he takes steroids or something like it. I know you took them once."

"Mmm a lot of them do. This science fiction film is not about reality. It's about big tits and bulging masculine muscles." Peter flexed his own arms. "The pressures are tremendous."

"What are the side effects?"

"They vary. But mood swings definitely. I became paranoid about germs. Still am. But I was changing my clothes every few hours for the smallest stain. Gerald helped me.

Mostly because I kept pinching his clothes but mostly because he's not a bad chap."

"Can you help Ellis get off them?"

"I don't know. I don't speak his language. I'm the black chap lounging on your bed, remember. By the way, that reminds me. Some people have been up to my place asking my permission to film my pad. They seemed particularly interested in your little blue bedroom."

"Oh Peter. That's good news. It's means it's beginning." Julia clasped her arms to her and smiled her delight.

"What's beginning? I take it I should give them permission then? Well, I have. The money was too good to turn down."

Julia fulfilled her promise to Gran and went to visit her in hospital. Gran looked very much the same. She did not look particularly ill and was sitting in bed looking quite glamorous in a pink, frilly bedjacket.

"Ah Julia, my dear."

Julia kissed her. "How's my favourite lady?" She laid a bunch of pink roses on the bed. "I've even brought the right colour flowers. Your bedjacket is divine." At this point in time Julia felt poised, attractive and confident.

"Yes, Ellis brought it me yesterday."

Julia sat down with a thump. Immediately she was hot, nervous and disorientated, and torn between surprise that Gran had called Ellis by his name and the fact that he had visited her.

"Oh yes," Julia stammered. "Er, yes. He was sorry when I told him that you were ill. In fact, he was a bit cross that I didn't tell him straight away."

"Yes, I know. He told me all about it. And his poor face. He said that he had had a fight on a beach with one of your old boyfriends – over you."

"Oh, did he? That was all a misunderstanding."

"Oh no, I don't think so. You must have made him very jealous, you naughty girl. But you are back together again. So, when is the wedding? I am invited, Ellis says."

"Did he mention – a wedding?"

"Of course he did." Gran clucked impishly.

Julia sat by the bed trying to take in what Gran was saying. Her heart was beating fast and her head was starting to spin. Perhaps it was the hospital smells. She fished in her bag for her perfumed handkerchief, taking longer than was necessary so that she had time to think.

When she raised her head, Ellis was sitting on the other side of the bed, holding Gran's hand and kissing her on the cheek.

"Hi, darling," he said to Julia with a charming smile. "Gran is looking better don't you think?"

"Yes, yes, she is." Julia smiled back. Ellis was smiling but – the smile did not reach his eyes. They were a hard bright blue. He had not forgiven her or himself.

He still had some metal braces on his teeth and his bad eye had turned a peculiar shade of green.

Julia began to giggle. She always giggled when she was nervous, often at the most inappropriate times.

Gran took Ellis' hand and then Julia's hand. Julia froze. Surely she wasn't going to join them across the narrow bed? She was. Slowly Julia's right hand was drawn toward Ellis' right hand. His knuckles still bore the new scars from the fight.

Gran joined their hands together and patted them. "There, there, my dears, soon you can go back to 'Hoonanea'. You will be happy there, as I was." Gran began to fall asleep, comforted by their hands all clasped together.

Ellis' hand moved slightly and his fingers caressed Julia's palm. Julia's lips parted. The sensation was electric. She was filled with an almost unbearable physical longing for him. Then she realised that Ellis was not caressing her hand – he was withdrawing his.

Gran opened her eyes. Ellis stopped. Julia lowered her head to the green bedspread She thought that Ellis must surely feel the pulse beating rapidly in her fingers.

Gran stirred and moved her hands to her arms in preparation for falling deeply asleep, and closed her eyes.

Julia looked up. They were still holding hands across the bed. Ellis was looking at her considerately. She met his gaze.

She could not read his expression. Her own was one of transfixed stupefaction, she knew.

Ellis' hand tightened before he released hers. He rose abruptly and left.

Chapter Twenty-Three

Relieved that Ellis had gone, Julia stood for a moment looking down at the peaceful sleeping face on the pillow.

"Well, I'm glad he's gone," she whispered. "It was painful for me to see him, Gran. He's so unapproachable."

Thinking that she had given Ellis enough time to leave, and feeling much more in control of herself, Julia left Gran's room with brisk determination. The corridor bent. She turned the corner. Ellis was waiting at the other end, for her.

The purposeful walk, the returning control of her feelings, all disappeared. Her mind went back to the first time she had seen him, in the flesh. He was wearing similar blue jeans and shirt now. Then she had moved towards him with delicious anticipation. Now, she hesitated. Then she had been dressed like a country bumpkin, now she was more Hollywood glamour and she was wishing that her green dress wasn't quite so waist nipping, for it was resisting the deep diaphragm breaths that she needed to survive another bruising encounter with Ellis.

Thankfully, the dress had pockets. She put her hands in them and walked casually on. She paused politely before him.

Ellis smiled thinly. "I thought we had better get our stories right for Gran. I thought it better to pretend that our relationship was still the same. There's not much time. She's very ill. Stomach cancer. There's nothing they can do."

Julia was shaken out of her own miseries. "Yes, of course, I agree. I'm glad you asked the doctors. I was afraid to. She shouldn't spend her last hours… worrying about us."

"OK. It's no hardship for us to pretend is it? We're both actors."

They stood awkwardly. Julia longed to say, 'Are we really finished?'

As she tried to think of something that she could say, Julia realised that Ellis seemed to be having some trouble standing next to her. He gave her quick looks, but mostly he leaned back on a rail by the window and looked down the corridor, up the corridor or over his shoulder out of the window. She suddenly knew that he could not bear to be alone with her.

"After all." He looked down at the floor. "Tomorrow we shall be making love." He looked up at her with almost a malicious gleam in his eyes. "On set, pretending that we love each other. And I shall be saying 'my dearest Shoala, I can't live without you', and kissing you, like this."

Julia wanted to walk away but he was already pulling her roughly to him. He placed his mouth over hers. It was hard, flat and cold. She could feel the slight pressure of his braces against her own tightly shut lips. She closed her eyes. The hateful pressure ceased. The stage kiss was over. When she opened her eyes, he was already walking away.

He was hurting, she knew. He must believe that because she had known for weeks, she was not hurting. Or that she had never felt as he was feeling now, for otherwise she would have told him straight away.

She had put Barbara and Bernard before him. She had been disloyal and untrustworthy. Perhaps he didn't know about Bernard's plan or he believed it would not work. Either way, he was wrapped in the horror of having his private love life, kinky private love life, beamed into millions of homes. The whispers and innuendos that would fly around the set. Always thinking that anyone he met who gave him a mischievous or knowing look, knew, had seen, everything. And here on the mainland, as the Americans so quaintly called America, everything was so much worse than in Hawaii. There were more papers, more magazines, more paparazzi, more gossip. Hollywood thrived on gossip. Logging onto porn channels, tittle-tattle websites and malicious bloggers, was all part of after-dinner entertainment.

Next day, on the set, Julia stood around with Gerald while they fixed the lighting. She was dreading the coming love scene with Ellis. Gerald was trying not to look pleased. "So, Nancy Boy has high-tailed it."

"I thought you slugged him because he is obviously not a Nancy Boy."

Gerald's face darkened. "I'm prepared to forget it – if you are."

"Right. We'll forget it."

"After all, you are coming back to England – with me."

"Am I?"

"You know you are." Gerald's face held a mixture of love, frustration and triumph.

Julia felt the floor sink a little. Barb would stay with Bernard. Peter was doing Shakespeare in New York. What other choices did she have but to go back to England with Gerald?

"I suppose I might do. But it doesn't mean that we are back together."

Ellis came on set in time to see Gerald's smile of delight and the real kiss he gave Julia for the lighting man.

The director appeared. Julia, as a rather lowly member of the cast with few lines, had not had any dealings with him, as yet. The filming on the mountain had been without sound. She had mouthed the lines, which would be dubbed in later.

The director was charismatic, artistic and according to Gerald and Peter, a real tight-arse Indian. He was the well-known Depak Choti.

Shoala was wearing a strapless chocolate brown cheesecloth ensemble that exposed her smooth shoulders and the top half of her breasts. Her hair was loose and windblown and a necklace of sparkling green stones encircled her lovely neck.

She took up her position in the boudoir-like room on the spaceship and waited anxiously for Pawl to appear through the silver sliding doors.

"Action."

Pawl appeared in the doorway. The doors closed, trapping him. He was wearing the sexy silver and black trousers and nothing else.

"Cut."

"Action."

Pawl got through the doors but tripped on a rug.

Shoala laughed and reached out to steady him.

"Cut."

"Action."

This time Pawl got through the doors into Shoala's outstretched arms and kissed her.

"Cut."

"Again. Action."

Pawl came through the doors into Shoala's outstretched arms and kissed her.

"Cut!"

Depak Choti stalked into the lights. "What are you doing?" he demanded of Pawl in angry bawling voice. "Kiss the bloody woman, why don't you? Is this Stratford? Has she been eating onions? Is she ugly?" The director turned to look closely at Shoala. He put his large brown hand over one of her breasts while his brown eyes roamed over her body. He gave her an unmistakable 'come on' wink. "She is a beautiful woman and you are crazy in love with her. Crazy with lust, do you understand?"

Julia and Ellis stared at each other. Their eyes said that they were crazy in love with each other. Julia wasn't acting, but she wondered, was Ellis?

The director looked at them and turned away. "That's better. That's more like it. Action."

Pawl came through the sliding doors into Shoala's waiting arms and kissed her.

Shoala's mouth was already open as Pawl, at first tentatively, brushed her mouth with his. And then, as his arms tightened around her, slowly, then more deeply he began to kiss her. Their tongues met and caressed. Shoala began to feel the heat rising inside her, Pawl's chest pressed against hers and his erection through his thin space trousers.

"Cut. Cut!"

It was said twice because neither heeded the first call. They broke apart and remained looking at each other.

"More action," the director shouted. "I want that shot. There. I want that shot of their faces. Got it? Cut."

Pawl screwed up his face and turned away from the cameras, but he was too late.

The director's eyesight was very sharp and his voice loud. "Get that man a better jockstrap. One minute he's like a block and the next he's taking off like bloody Concorde. Do you think I want a film I cannot show my aunties? Break for twenty!"

Julia began to giggle as Ellis' face took on mulish look. She teased him mercilessly. "Are you blushing? Laugh, everyone else is."

Ellis threw up his hands with a gesture of comic resignation to the sniggering crew, who immediately broke out into loud guffaws. "OK, you heard what the man said. Get me the boa-constrictor. I told you we needed a Superman undercarriage for this costume." Ellis turned to Julia. "You may laugh, when any moment now you could be falling out of that dress."

Julia laughed even more and collapsed on the satin divan. "I've never heard it called that before!'

Ellis sat down on the bed edge.

"Come on," Julia wheedled, "things have changed since Cliff Richard shocked our mothers by gyrating on the telly." She moved her head along the bolster to better look up at him.

He looked down. "Cliff who?"

"A sort of Brit Elvis."

He nodded his head. He frowned. "I don't like being cast as some monstrous sexual pervert, especially now."

Julia smiled. She pulled his arm so that he had to look at her again. "You're just normal Ellis, you know, a normal man." She knew he was thinking about the 'problem'.

He turned away. The make-up girl came up and began to repair his green eye and give him his brace which he was supposed to wear between takes. She helped Ellis fix it into his mouth before hurrying away.

Ellis turned and grimaced at Julia. "Nice huh."

To divert his mind away from it and his other embarrassments, Julia sat up. "In England, you know, we have seaside dirty postcards. Have you ever heard of them? Well, they are at every seaside town in the country. On twirly racks outside the shops. There are not so many now as there used to be. Some were not PC. But they are quite shockingly vulgar. You wouldn't believe how many jokes can be made out of a male erection. All artistically illustrated in colour."

Ellis abandoned his uncomfortable twisting position on the edge of the divan and sat next to Julia.

"So?"

"Well, the British can be both strait-laced and vulgar all at the same time. And then there's the Morris men."

"Morris men?"

"Yes, go to Sidmouth in August and you will see the Morris men dancing. They wear cricket whites, tie bells to their calves, hang feathers on their hats, carry big sticks, which they crash quite violently together, and dance to an accordion. Another Morris dancer, the fool, runs around doing quite naughty things with a balloon on a stick, depending on the audience and the time of day or whether he fancies anyone watching.

"And the cricket flannels themselves are very sexy. The bowlers, the pitchers, rub their balls, the cricket balls, on the front of them, you see, to make one side smoother so that they will swing. Girls don't go to cricket matches just for the cricket. They go to get all goosey over googlies."

"Enough." Ellis had so far forgotten his problems that he put his arm over Julia's shoulder and shook her affectionately. "You're making my teeth ache again. I've heard of Morris dancers. It's a fertility dance."

"Yes, but you've never seen them. The Morris men I have lusted over on Sidmouth seafront, you would not believe."

Slowly Ellis withdrew his arm. "English guys... like Gerald. He spoke to me before the take. He said Nottingham lasses marry Yorkshire lads. He said that when this is over you're going back to England with him."

"I did say that, but not in so many words."

Ellis became suddenly annoyed. "'Not in so many words.' What the hell does that mean? Excuse me I have to go and get fitted up."

Julia caught his arm and said quickly, "It means that I said that I might do."

Ellis' flight was arrested and he looked down at Julia's hand tightly holding his upper arm. He shrugged as though to rid himself of her touch. "It's none of my business."

"Well," Julia lay back again. "At least we're having an ordinary conversation."

"Yes, we need to work together. And I appreciate you trying to help me feel less of a jerk by telling me tales of merry old England. Though I wouldn't call our conversation ordinary the way you rattle on."

"Oh, Barb and I used to write for lad and chick mags, you know. Barb was quite outrageous sometimes when describing her sexual exploits. Which had never happened, obviously. I wrote about lusting after Morris men, and fast bowlers.

"You know, the ancient Celts in Britain worshipped some kind of magic erect winged penis, a sort of flying fuck, which the Victorians, of course, restricted to locked dusty books."

"That's enough Julia."

Julia stopped. "I'm sorry. I always talk too much when I'm nervous."

Ellis smiled, suddenly seeming like his old self. "I've never heard another girl talk like you do."

"I'm trying to get through to you. To make up." Julia spoke softly.

Ellis would not meet her eyes. Finally he stopped staring at the ceiling and got off the bed. His face was solemn, and not encouraging, when he finally looked at her.

Julia's heart sank. She had come very close to begging him to forgive her, and it looked like she had failed.

"I still like you Julia. But I'm concentrating on finishing this film. It's better that we don't... We..." Ellis stopped.

"We what?" Julia could not bear the suspense, and she knew that her words were too emphatic. "We just end it? The bugging doesn't matter. What happened doesn't really matter."

"It does to me! Hell! It matters to me Julia."

Julia cursed herself for forcing the issue, when Ellis was so obviously struggling to come to terms with what had happened to them.

Ellis was looking down at her with that peculiar, hard, speculating look that he had adopted since their split. A look that said, 'I don't trust you'.

Chapter Twenty-Four

"Cut!"

Julia and Ellis turned surprised faces to where the director was standing just beyond the subdued light, behind the cameras.

"Ha, caught you, haven't I?" Depak Choti laughed a little snickering laugh. He stepped up to the divan where Julia lay and stood with his hands in a picture position focused on Julia's body. "Much better than acting, real life, you know. You two," the director waved his hands expansively over Ellis and Julia, "have a certain sexual tension between you which can't be manufactured. And look at her. What a seductress. How she has been seducing you with soft words, with her eyes, with her body. A real little prick teaser, isn't she?" Depak Choti looked at Ellis and held his hands up. "OK, I'm sorry. I see by your face that you don't like me saying that about your... lovely lady."

Ellis looked like a man rapidly losing his rag. He stared intently at the director and then at the camera. "You've been filming us?"

"Oh yes. I'm going to put this in the film, as the seduction scene, suitably edited and dubbed, of course. I'm sick of those bloody handmaidens, markeez, sirens, or whatever they are, with their titties in and their titties out. It changes every day, you know. I'm having this little seductress, seducing you like she should with her soft talk, the body language, no touching. But then she doesn't need to touch, does she? No wonder you need a stronger jockstrap when you actually get to kiss her. I'd need one too." Depak Choti bent over Julia. He gave her his 'come on' wink again.

"Anyway, it is decided. I am the great director, Depak Choti. The best scenes are always the one's taken when the subject is unaware, don't you agree?" Depak Choti walked off with a wave very like that of the Queen.

Julia and Ellis stared helplessly at each other.

Ellis recovered first. "He's a peculiar sort of jerk, isn't he? You know, he likes it when the girls work their cleavage, he's all over them, but he won't have tit shots in this film. He's screwed at least two handmaidens. Keep your guard up."

Julia began to get off the divan, noting that even this ordinary leaning forward movement showed quite a lot of her own under-wired breasts and wondering if she really had just seen a flash of jealousy in Ellis' eyes, or imagined it. "Oh, I've been groped by directors before."

"What are we going to do about this Julia?"

"What can we do? He's got us on film. We're actors."

Ellis frowned. "He does have a reputation for surprising actors like this. It was that film *Alien* that started a trend. When the monster broke out of the actor's chest and the others didn't know it was coming."

"Anyway… we weren't doing anything." Julia got up and walked towards Ellis. Her eyes were fixed on his and his on hers and neither could break away.

"Not this time," he muttered.

It ran through her mind that they seemed fated to be filmed together in intimate situations without their knowledge. She didn't voice it, but she could tell by the widening of his eyes and the way he looked at her, that he was thinking it too.

Only Erica Black, coming in with loud complaints about the loss of her handmaidens could break the spell.

Ellis ignored Erica. "When this is all over, we can still be friends. I'd like that Julia."

"Yes, me too." As they parted and Julia went to get her make-up fixed, she screamed inside 'I don't want to be friends!' She didn't think that she could ever be just 'friends' with Ellis. But at least he wasn't walking away from her, with a dismissive flick of his hand, as though he could not bear her company. The frozen man was thawing.

Things were easier on set when they did their scenes together. Barb had written some good lines. The final betrayal of Pawl by Shoala was most convincingly acted by Ellis. "You have betrayed my trust in you. But I will forgive you. You were manipulated by other people, I understand that. Your punishment is death. The child that you carry will be removed before you die, of course. And I shall bring him up to think well of you."

Shoala bowed her head slightly and remained impassive. Later, the silent and proud Shoala was dragged off and thrown down a volcano; however, this had been filmed on Hawaii, so that was the end of Shoala's involvement in *Warlords of the Outer Rim*. She was dead!

"Does Barbara always base her scripts on real life?" Ellis said bad-temperedly as he and Julia got a coffee from a machine. "I mean, those words, I could have said them to you. Goddamnit, Julia, that was nothing like the first script."

"She's quite an opportunist when it comes to her writing," Julia agreed uncomfortably. She was mad with Barb herself for including the bit about the baby which had never been in the original story. And Shoala's sick expression when Pawl told her that he was taking the foetus had not been acting at all.

How had Barb found out, Julia wondered? Could it be that Mercedes had found the used pregnancy kit in Bernard's bathroom and emailed her employer about it? Barb was like a sniffer bitch. Nothing would throw her off the scent, now.

"She might change it when she sees the rushes tomorrow," Julia managed to say. "If she's satisfied, I'm free to do Bernard's other film."

"Yeah, what's that about? Bernard's trying to force me to be in it too. Just a small part. He's up to something. And Barbara. Do you know what those two are planning?"

"Yes. It's a bog standard, child tug-of-love story between a divorced couple. The divorced husband thinks that his ex-wife is an unfit mother. You know, drugs, drinking, evil new boyfriend. You and I would just have a cameo in it really." Julia held her breath. Had Ellis noticed that she had not actually answered his question?

"Not me. I'm doing some more *Warlords* shooting on location in Southern California and I'm out of here." Ellis leaned on the coffee machine, looking at her with his deep blue speculating look. "You know, Julia, I'm glad we're finished, since you seem quite incapable of ever giving me a straight answer to any important question I ask you."

Julia looked down quickly to hide her dismay. With a great effort she managed to look up again.

"I should send you back the ring."

"You keep it – as a memento of Hawaii."

"Oh I've missed you." Barb hugged Julia mercilessly. "We got back late last night, and this morning you had already gone to the studios."

"It's only been a week and you've been on honeymoon."

"Yes, but I've been with Bernard all the time. He is so solemn. Now, what's with this piece of you and Ellis on a bed? I didn't write this. Depak's told me he's put it in. Mind you, it's not bad. In fact, it's quite good."

The scene on the divan was played again and Julia settled back into her seat in the studio cinema with Barb. Instead of telling Pawl about Morris men, Shoala was relating her desire for men from her own planet. It was shot in soft focus and not all the dialogue could be distinguished. And yes, there was seduction in every line of Shoala's body and determined resistance to her in every line of Pawl's.

The scene finished. Julia sat staring mindlessly at other takes of *Warlords*. Spaceship mock-ups, static on set, or rocked by pulleys. Hawaii, but not Hawaii. A strange landscape with added CG-images transposed upon it.

Pawl fighting with the unfeasibly long, silver Dark Ages sword. It was a magic silver sword, which, of course, cast a containment field around the combatants so that they could not be just simply blown away with a ray gun. Pawl holding out a muscular arm, his hand open, into which his silver sword would fly out of a stone wall in a weird mix of Arthurian legend and *Star Wars*.

And there was Shoala being sacrificed for betraying Pawl. Julia thought her screaming on screen was a little shrill as she fell into the volcano. She felt irritated. It was always so difficult to scream really well on set. "I've had enough of this!" Julia shouted quite forcibly in Barb's ear.

Barb jumped, but agreed. "Yes. There's precious little actual human contact in this film. They're either shooting each other to bits in spaceships or acting to a blue wall which will turn out later to be a computer generated wobbly thing with less life in it than an ancient Egyptian mummy."

Barb paused. "That reminds me. Talking of wobbly things, the director has cut out most of the markeez stroke handmaidens. Perhaps it's all for the best. It was all getting far too much like *Carry On up the Khyber*. First rules of serious sci-fi are no smutty sex, no titty popping, no bawdy humour, no swearing. Apparently we are going to be so advanced in the future that we will all be quite unable to express ourselves in a vulgar way. We shall all be wearing little deodorising things stuck in our arseholes in case we fart, and…"

"Barb," Julia cut in, "I want to talk to you."

"Course darling. I was waiting for you to tell me in your own time, just how things stand between you and Ellis."

"There are no things standing between me and Ellis. We are finished. Finished Barb, because he still doesn't know what Bernard's planned. Because I can't explain to him how we are going to get out of this mess. Because I fudge the issue with him all the time. Because of you and Bernard and your well-meant but stupid interfering in my life!"

"Oo, oo, this sounds serious. We'd better go home so you can have a little lie-down. Must be your condition." Barb winked.

Julia felt a strong desire to hit Barb over the head with her handbag. Never before had she felt so out of tune and irritated by her outspoken friend.

Julia had calmed down a little by the time she entered Barb's large bedroom warmed by the endless sun outside the muslin-draped windows. "Don't you and Bernard sleep in the same room?" Julia eyed the beautiful, undoubtedly feminine, English country house style cum Gustavian bedroom a little jealously.

"Are you mad?" Barb laughed. "That's the quickest way to end a marriage. Well, my kind of marriage, anyway."

Julia let the remark pass. She sat in one of the pretty white chairs by the window, feeling scruffy in her jeans and shirt.

Barb settled back on her Cath Kidston cushions opposite.

"Do you mind if I smoke?"

"I never have before."

"Well, now it's different. You're expecting. Mercedes found the tester packet. Oh you may look. They're all trained to look in the bins. Most of the women in LA are trying to catch their husbands out. You know, nooky on the side. Divorce. Settlements. You couldn't get a housekeeper here who didn't ferret about for evidence."

"You're exaggerating, Barb. You're trying to wriggle out of being just sodding nosey."

Mercedes came in with the coffee and placed it on the pretty white Queen Anne table. Julia pointedly ignored the handsome Mexican woman that she had previously liked.

"And I don't want to talk about it, Barb, remember."

"OK. But you must just tell me, does Ellis know?"

"No. And you are not to tell him Barb. Anyway it's not certain. I haven't been to a doctor and I wish you would just shut up about it."

"I think I need that smoke now. Well, what do you want to talk about?"

"What do you think? What is Bernard doing? Why doesn't Ellis know about the plan?"

"Tonight. He's going to get the whole picture tonight. Tonight, you, me, Ellis and Bernard are going to sit down and thrash the whole thing out. Are you sure that you won't get back with Ellis? He really loved you."

"I'm sure. And am I likely to be, with you writing stupid things like 'clay' on his feet?"

Barb laughed. "That was just a joke. Seriously, how is he on set?"

"We have a good working arrangement."

"But you're not, sort of, gradually becoming closer...?"

"I told you – no." Trust Barb to put into words the tiny hope of reconciliation I'm allowing myself, Julia thought crossly.

"In spite of the...?" Barb broke off as Julia hit her on the head with one of her specially imported cushions.

Chapter Twenty-Five

Bernard looked at his watch for the sixth time and then at Barbara. "Call Ellis again."

"He won't answer darling, and his mobile's switched off. You will have to go and get him, Julia." Barb raised her eyebrows meaningfully at Julia over her last words. "He has to be briefed tonight and we start shooting in a few days."

Julia, already tense at the prospect of hearing Bernard's plan, pulled a sour face at Barb's dig. Reluctantly she agreed to fetch Ellis to Bernard's house.

Julia arrived at Ellis' door with feelings of excitement and dread, clashing horribly in her stomach. It was several minutes before Ellis opened the door.

He stared at her surprise for a second and then waved her in with the bottle he was holding in his hand

"You don't want to stay, I'm drunk," he said carefully. He moved slowly back to the sofa and sank down and picked up his glass of whiskey. "I've had too much Irish whiskey for you to stay here. So – what do you want?"

Julia looked round the over-ruched room and at Ellis on the sofa. The sofa where he had once asked her to marry him a few short months ago. Now, Ellis was drunk and obviously wishing that she would go away.

"What are you looking round for? Erica? You know, girls aren't too keen on keeping company with sexual pred... pred... weirdoes."

"Bernard wants to see you."

"Does he. He can go to hell."

"I think you should see him."

"Well, I don't want to see him. I'm not working tomorrow so I am going to drink Irish whiskey and sleep all day."

"I think you should come. I have a car waiting."

Ellis shook his head to clear it. "I'll come if you come here and give me a kiss. For old time's sake. Mmm, I like your dress. Turquoise. That's your colour Julia, turquoise."

Julia hesitated. Ellis was looking at her with unmistakable drunken passion. Her stomach knotted.

She sat next to him and he leaned over and planted a whiskey-fumed kiss on her cheek rather clumsily.

"Oops, missed." He put down his glass, moved closer and tried again. At first awkwardly. He rubbed his hand over his alcohol-numbed mouth irritably, pulled her even closer and kissed her again. She helped him with her own lips until the kiss became very deeply pleasant and satisfying for both. Rather sweet, like hot whiskey and honey, she thought when it ended.

"You're drunk and incapable," she whispered softly, making no attempt to move away from the circle of his arms.

He leaned back his head and his eyes gleamed with amusement. "You can arrest me – but only the first part of what you just said – is true."

Julia thought for a moment that if she stayed, if they made love perhaps...? No, she couldn't use her body to get him back. He wasn't sober. He wasn't quite himself. And Bernard was waiting impatiently. She sighed as Ellis began to kiss her neck, his free hand caressing her inner thigh.

"You've got to come and see Bernard, it's important."

"I never want to see that fat bastard again," he muttered.

"You promised to give him a chance."

Ellis growled as Julia pushed him gently away and stood up. She looked down at him in tender mockery as he glared back, his face a comical mixture of desire and latent anger.

Yes, she thought, they could make love, but he would still not be hers again when the sex was over and he was sober. "I have my principles," she said with playful severity. "I never seduce drunken men."

Julia made some coffee while Ellis was in the shower. He appeared in sweats looking rough but reasonably sober.

"What's so important that a man can't be left to drown his sorrows in peace?" he grumbled as he towelled his hair, which didn't take long as it was still short, but so much more attractive than a stubble head.

He stopped towelling and gave Julia a hard look. "I'm sorry I kissed you. I was drunk."

She took the insult coolly without flinching. She had been right. He was sorry he had kissed her and would have said the same even if they had just had the most sensational sex imaginable. She could cry later. "I told you, Bernard must see you."

The journey to Bernard's house passed in silence. Ellis' greeting was belligerent when he entered the sitting room where Bernard and Barbara were waiting. "Well, what do you want?" He threw himself in a chair and sat insultingly bored and off-hand. "What the hell do you want me for Bernard, that you have to send Julia to lure me over here?"

Bernard ignored Ellis' behaviour and handed him and Julia a script. "There's your lines," he said. "You have to learn them for the day after tomorrow, when we will shoot in one day, your parts in this film."

Ellis groaned. "I'm not interested in your lousy script Bernard." He threw the script on the floor.

There was a silence as Bernard, Barbara and Julia sat regarding Ellis.

Ellis' belligerence accelerated. "Look, what is this? Do you think that I am going to work again with you Bernard or you Barbara. people who filmed the most intimate... details of my private life, with the woman I loved, and then... were stupid enough to have it stolen and..."

"No, no, Bernard. If I could truly understand why you did it. But I don't. And telling me it was Peter and then it wasn't Peter, but you. All lies, lies, lies. From all three of you. Well, when I've finished this fucking sci-fi, I'm going to Mexico and you can all go to hell!"

Ellis sat back in his chair, closed his eyes and folded his arms stubbornly across his chest.

"It was bad for me too, Ellis. But I've forgiven Barbara, and Bernard, because it was done to help me."

Ellis opened his eyes and slowly turned to look at Julia. "Help you? How would it help you?" he asked in disbelief.

Barb got up. "Snacks. We must have snacks. You know Bernard. He'll fade away without snacks. There's enough food in that kitchen to feed an army. Come on Bernard."

Ellis gave Julia a considering look and picked up the script and began to leaf through it. His gaze focused on a particular bit and he threw the script down again angrily. He looked over at Julia and was obviously making an effort to be mellower. "OK, they've gone. Tell me. How would doing something as lousy as bugging you, help you? You've got to help me here, Julia."

"Barb was worried about me. She thought I might be – a bit mentally unbalanced. She thought, that if she recorded my conversations and played them to an English psychiatrist that she knows, that they would be able to help me. And it has helped, a little. Well, quite a bit actually."

"Conversations? With Peter? With yourself?"

"Telephone conversations with my mother."

"You told me that your mother had died last year."

Julia could see that he was thinking that here was another instance of her lying and secretive nature. She had to go on.

"Yes, she did. She couldn't hear what I said. You know, chats we should have had when there was still time, before it was too late. I was never there. I wasn't there when she died. She asked for me but... but I wasn't there."

Julia sniffed resolutely, keeping back the bad feelings. Now wasn't the time to cry. Now was the time to save herself and Ellis from ridicule and contempt.

"What did your therapist say?" Ellis' voice was gentle. His face softened with sympathy. This brought the time before their split painfully back for her. The time when he had loved her.

"I haven't got a therapist. I've never had a therapist. I just had a chat with this chap, Barb's friend, in a restaurant. He knows his stuff, I suppose. I was very rude to him. Basically, it's not a big deal to talk to a dead close relative as though they are still alive."

"No, no, I'm sure that's true, especially when a person is still grieving, as you are." Ellis relaxed a little. "I'm glad you've told me. It changes things. I shall have to think about it. But, there must be something else. You look as though there is something else. I can see it in your eyes, Julia. A deeper reason why Barbara did it. Because she loves you, I guess, but there must be more. As always there is something else that you are not telling me."

"As always? That's not fair. I told you I'm not the kind of person who tells, even the man they love, everything." Julia bit her lip. Here she was arguing with Ellis again about deceit. "The trouble is, you're damn well too perceptive."

"I'm sorry, I shouldn't have brought that little bit of bitterness into it."

"No you shouldn't. But you're right. There is something else. Something that Barbara was really worried about. I phoned my mother, yes, but sometimes, sometimes, particularly if I was daydreaming, I would – become my mother. I would speak as though I were my mother. Barb got worried, spooked, as I denied it. And Barb felt guilty because she wrote the play where I was my mother, my young mother, and she went just a little bit too far in picking my mother's brains. Way too far. You understand Ellis. You're an actor too."

"I think so. Don't all girls become their mothers, eventually? So they say. The dreaded mother-in-law."

Julia felt suddenly drained. Was Ellis trying a feeble joke because he was embarrassed. He thought she was devious. Now he would think she was potty too. And to be humoured. She sank back. This is all getting too much, she thought as she closed her eyes and pressed her fingers to her forehead.

Then Ellis' hands were gently pulling her up from the chair. He was pulling her to him. She laid her head at the base of his neck. Her arms stole round his back. She waited breathlessly. It was so nice to be held by him again. Sober, considerate, loving. A lover's embrace or a friend's embrace. Which was it?

"Hey, hey, it's OK. I understand. Now, I understand, a little. I've been thinking too much about myself and blaming you..."

"Ah, made up then. Good. We're running out of time. I'm on a tight schedule here trying to cram this film in. I've got you in it Ellis because you're a big name. Fortunately, the actor who was doing it, got a better part in another film. I had to pull a few strings there. Barbara's written some meaty lines and we're up and running." Bernard spoke with forced crispness, ignoring the fact that Ellis and Julia were in a close embrace.

Ellis did not turn to face Bernard. Slowly he partly released Julia. "Do you know what he's talking about?"

"I think so." Julia, conscious of the light pressure of his hands on her waist, began to lose herself in his intent blue gaze.

"So, I'm the only one here who doesn't know what he is talking about?"

"I think you've guessed," she whispered, still mesmerised.

"I'm the guy who – forces the maid in her bedroom?"

"Yes." Julia saw the fear creep into his eyes.

"I can't do it." His words were anguished and low. He still had his back to Bernard. He looked at Julia with dismay, his jaw and teeth clenched. He jerked her to him as though for comfort. "I cannot do it."

"You can do it. We were lying on a bed together only the other day. You can do it."

Slowly Ellis withdrew his gaze and went back to his chair. After a moment, he picked up the script from the floor, and began to read it.

Barbara brought in the snacks. They ate the snacks. They drank. Barb rather pointedly gave Julia orange juice.

"Right." Bernard wiped the crumbs from his mouth. "Ellis is the second husband. He's mean, he's violent, he's a womaniser, he's after his wife's money. She's crazy about him, he gets her onto drugs. He's unkind to the boy, his stepson.

"Julia is the au pair. I don't like that Barbara. Maid's better. She's young, beautiful, desirable. She's friendly with the black pool guy Peter, but in a platonic way. He later turns out to be her half-brother.

"Ellis has the hots for the maid, naturally, since he thinks he's God's gift to women. I don't like that either Barbara. Ellis thinks the black guy is screwing the maid. He bursts into the maid's bedroom sees the black guy, gets mad and forces himself upon the maid, at first anyway. But, she's an easy lay. She's a professional virgin.

"The wife's first husband finds out about Ellis' cruel treatment of the boy, encouraging the wife to take drugs, blah, blah, tries to get the boy back. Shoots Ellis. In the pool, it says here. Mmm, that was done in *The Great Gatsby*.

"Anyway, you get the picture. A few scenes, Ellis is dead. The maid and Peter are sacked. You're all out of it. The film moves onto the wife, the murdering husband, the boy, the court case. The husband coming out of jail and murdering her present husband. Ellis only appears in flashbacks, looking as charmingly dangerous as only he knows how."

Here we are, Julia thought, sitting in huge mock English Queen Anne armchairs in Bernard's huge living room in front of a false roaring fire, ruffling our scripts, and waiting for Ellis to say yes.

"Come on," Barb jumped up. "Bernard's done it. Show some appreciation here." She kissed Bernard. "You, are a genius darling. This is going to work."

Chapter Twenty-Six

"My agent will not like this." Ellis waved the script at Bernard. "I've just done a rapist and he will not want me to alienate my female fan club any more. I'm not sure I can do this."

"Well, you know as well as I do that a too large girlie fan club leads to a blind alley for a heart-throb like you. If you really want to regarded as a serious actor, that is. You could stick with the pussy hero roles, but what happens when you hit fifty? The days of Cary Grant have long gone."

"I'm not sure, Bernard," Ellis muttered.

"OK boys. Look Ellis." Barb stood, legs apart, hands spread out, within a foot of Ellis, her eyes fixed on him with intense concentration.

"You go to Peter's. You do the scene by the pool where you are being cruel to your wife and pushing drugs onto her. The boy comes out. He's scared of the water but you throw him in and laugh as he panics. Then you do the scene where you are shot. Bernard puts them on the Internet to confuse everyone.

"You do the scene with your wife in the bedroom at the studio where you are cruel to her and criticise her appearance. Then you do the crucial scene with Julia in the little blue bedroom at the studio where you copy the stolen film.

"You must wear the same suit and Julia must wear the same long blue vest. I will have several shirts fixed so that the buttons will come off. You must have your chest hair and other body hair and your hair exactly the same. You do the scene. Bernard puts in on the Internet. All that sodding hacker's got is a take from a pilot movie with you in a minor role. It's useless to him. He can't demand any more money. He can't sell his story to the press. We are home free. Reality turns into unreality. It's brilliant!"

"It's hopeless. People already know. They've seen it," Ellis was beginning to look a little strained.

"So what?" Barbara exploded. "It's just a pilot take like any other, to get the backing for the full film. You've got to do it for Julia's sake as well as your own. Come on Ellis! Stop being such a wimp. You're a bloody actor. Well act!"

Ellis relaxed. "It had better work. I wouldn't be able to take it if the wonderful feeling of relief I'm experiencing now is snatched away."

Barb took Ellis' face in her hands and kissed him soundly, full on the mouth. "It will," she promised.

Julia and Ellis met the next day after the big meeting at Bernard's house, over the bed of Gran.

"Oh lovely." Gran smiled weakly at Julia and Ellis and just touched their flowers before the nurse came to put them in water. "Oh you two both look happier than you did last time I saw you. I was sure that you had quarrelled. Now you're sitting together. You both look very happy."

"Yes, Gran we are happy," Julia said brightly.

Ellis' smile wasn't too obviously forced. "Of course we are, Gran."

Ellis did look less strained, Julia thought. Bernard's plan had taken some of the tension out of his body. She knew he was dreading their sex scene in the little mock-up blue room and so was she. She had never done such an explicit sex scene on camera before, well, not knowingly anyway. But she must put aside her own problems. Gran was looking noticeably weaker and it looked as though the end was very near.

Julia had put on her engagement ring for the visit. She was sitting next to Ellis by the bed when he suddenly took her hand, and his fingers located the ring.

Julia realised that Gran had asked to see the ring and Ellis had panicked at the thought that she might not be wearing it. Gran smiled over it and Ellis and Julia sighed inwardly with relief. Julia tried to force her mind to register the meaning of Gran's barely audible words. As always, Ellis' close proximity turned her brain to mush.

At the end of the visit, Gran made a surprising request. She asked if Ellis and Julia would come back to Hawaii with her.

"Will you come back with me?" she asked lovingly. "And stay at my beloved Hoonanea?"

They both hastened to reassure her that, of course, they would. Ellis' hand pressed Julia's comfortingly. They both knew what Gran was asking. They could not refuse.

"You know, I've seen a bootleg of this, I'm sure I have."

The young English director that Bernard had hired frowned at Julia and Ellis on the bed in the little blue mock-up room. "But it was much better than this. This is crap. And he comes across like a real wuss. Why don't you use the pilot tape and save us all the agony?"

Bernard hesitated. "Let's have a break. I'll have a word with them." Bernard carefully checked that no one could hear. "Well," he said. "You heard the man. Have we got to use the original pilot shoot?"

"You're a shit Bernard," Ellis growled pulling on his dressing gown. "A face-saving genius, but still a shit."

"I know. But think about it." Bernard went out.

Julia began to laugh. She had never seen Ellis so fumbling and sexless as he had been in the last take. "It's a bit funny, don't you think."

"Is it?"

"Oo you're so angry. You want to do this yet you don't want to do this. You've got to forget that we were once in love. I'm just an actress in the film. I'm the wanton maid and you are the lecherous master. Look." Julia pulled up her vest. "I've been waxed hairless and I'm wearing a flesh body stocking that wouldn't disgrace a Mormon. You're trussed up like a turkey. Nothing's going to happen is it?" Julia began to laugh again.

"I don't think this is funny."

"It is Ellis, believe me. Because you are going to go out there, put on your suit, pick up your briefcase. You come back, you rip off all your clothes and you bang me silly. And then we are free. We can forget this. If you don't, we're sunk. Remember, I'm a slut Ellis. I shall just have to kiss you."

Julia slid her leg over Ellis' as he sat next to her on the bed, facing him. She pressed herself against his naked chest between the dressing gown and kissed him sensuously, running her hands up his bare back. She broke away. "I shall keep on kissing you until your tapes pop," she threatened.

"OK, OK. I give in. Get off me. And stop laughing."

"Oh I needed that." Ellis groaned as he took a large gulp of scotch. "There's the end of *Tug of Love*. I'm dead and I have never felt better. I hope that film flops."

The last of the lighting rigs were being carried away from around Peter's pool, and the fake blood was being sucked out of the water.

"Yes," Julia agreed. "The less people who see it, the better. Though I…" She turned to Ellis on the sunbed next to her and grinned teasingly… "shall have a copy of *Tug of Love* especially for our last scene."

"I never thought that any of this was ever funny." Ellis gave Julia a half puzzled, half wondering look.

"It is now," Barb said. "You're like Bernard, Ellis. You're too serious. Let's drink to the failure of *Tug of Love*. Straight to DVD."

"I'll drink to that, though it was a nice little earner for me…" Peter sighed with satisfaction. "All I had to do was rake the pool, glower and lie on Julia's bed. And half the time I didn't even have to leave home. And you lot getting out of this mess, too, of course. Gerald is going to apologise to you Ellis. For attacking you. He really thinks he got it wrong. When he's finished his swim. He's still a bit suspicious though, and a bit hurt that we didn't tell him about this '*Tug of Love* thing. He thinks we're trying to cut him out."

Peter waved to Gerald in the pool. "Hi, Gerry mate. Bandits at six o'clock." he shouted. "That Jason's never going to get anywhere with our Gerald. I shall have to go and rescue him."

"Who's he going to rescue, Gerald or Jason?" Barb laughed.

"I'm going in. I feel like a frolic with some nice lean bodies. Makes a change."

"Barb, you will tell Bernard thank you, from me and Ellis, won't you?" Julia said anxiously, worried that Ellis was still a little sullen about Bernard.

"You can tell him yourself tonight at my party. You've got to give me at least four hours before you fly out to Hawaii."

There was a huge crowd at Bernard's house. Julia could see why Bernard had five huge fridges full of food and four dishwashers in his kitchen.

Julia soon picked out Ellis. He was dressed in a dark suit, like herself. They were flying out as part of a small funeral party. However, Julia was wearing a bright pink flower on her lapel.

Ellis came towards her. He smiled and touched her pink bloom, as he said hello. "Should we be here?" he asked uncertainly.

"Gran won't mind the flower or us being here." She hugged Ellis's arm. She wanted him to stay with her, but Erica Black, in bright shiny blue, was already bearing down upon them.

Erica took Ellis' other arm. She wanted to talk to him about *Warlords* she said. Julia had no further part in it, so Erica claimed full rights to Ellis' attention.

"When are you going back to England?" Erica asked sweetly. "I hear it's lovely there in the early summer. You don't want to miss it."

"Probably soon," Julia muttered looking down. She looked up as Ellis was being drawn into the mass of loud actors. He gave her a look which asked 'are you going back'. She turned away suddenly irritated. Her 'going back' was something that they simply were not discussing. Now the horror was over, could she and Ellis get back together again? Or was it too soon? Or had he meant it when he had said they were finished in such bitter tones that time by the coffee machine?

"Hi darling." Barb gave Julia a hug and kiss. "I see Queen Titania has carted Ellis off."

"Yes, but he looks more relaxed and he's got to mingle. He was telling me on the way here how relieved he felt to be going to a party where he no longer feared the whisperers. And if there are whispers, he can brazen it out. Yes he looks much better. Exhausted, but better. It's all thanks to Bernard. Your Bernard. I'm still not used to you being Mrs Bernard Donne and looking like Joan Collins in *Die-nasty*." Julia knew that her last remark would set Barb's back up.

"No I don't. I have to wear these clothes." Barb looked down at her cream silk dress. "In this town, where everyone's disappeared up their own arse, I have to. Come on, Bernard's waiting."

Julia simply gave Bernard a kiss, on the mouth. "Thanks."

Bernard was a little startled by the kiss. "I'm glad it's all over. But I had selfish reasons too as well as guilty ones. Barbara. I mostly did it for her. And I gained quite a lot of satisfaction from being so very clever, and fitting it all together like a jigsaw puzzle. But mostly Barbara. She is the love of my life. She wants you and Ellis to get married. Any chance?"

"Well, we're more friendly, but I don't know." So, Julia thought, Barb has to have everything she wants. Barb might think that her marriage was temporary but Bernard certainly did not.

"I know Ellis better than you two. He'll come round. He'll brood a bit. But I'd bet on you and he getting hitched sometime soon. A few months' time would be best."

"For your plan." Julia smiled thinly.

"A perfect plan needs a perfect ending." Unusually for him, Bernard smiled a genuine smile.

"I need you upstairs Julia," Barb urged.

"Of course, you've dragged me up here to your boudoir to ask me that." Julia set her mouth stubbornly.

"Well, I repeat. Are you going to tell him?"

"And I repeat. There is nothing to tell."

"You're bottling things up again Julia. Tell him. He will be delighted. He loves kids."

"Barbara please. You heard Bernard. A few months. I appreciate that you care for me. You want the happy ending now. But Ellis is complicated. When some people fall out of love, it's permanent. I feel that it might be permanent with Ellis. He believes that people in love should have no secrets from each other. I think I've lost him and I won't drag him to heel with the promise of a baby!" Tears sprang to Julia's eyes as she voiced the thoughts that had been running round and round in her head since the night on the beach when Gerald and Ellis had fought in the surf.

"Alright, I'm sorry. I won't tease you about it again, I promise. Well, I could say cheer up, but you have to go to that funeral."

"Oh, I'm going to cheer up, Barb, don't you worry. There's a party going on down there and I'm up for it. We can sing our song. Our David Soul song, *I'm Going in with my Thighs Open*. And *Lily the Pink*."

Barb giggled. "They won't like it."

"Have you got two red coats?"

"Well, I suppose most of them will be too drunk to notice."

"We don't care about them. We'll do it because I'm going to a funeral and that makes me feel wild. We'll do it for Gerald and Peter. We'll do it for ourselves. Because you're married. Because we're not young enough to do it anymore. And because I am so bloody glad that the nightmare is over."

"With apologies to lovely David for changing the words."

"As ever. Let's brush up *Lily* first. *We'll drink a drink a drink to Lily the Pink the Pink the Pink, the saviour of our human ra-a-ace. For she invented medicinal compound*."

Julia poised from her jigging and grasped Barb's arms. "I can't remember it all."

"It doesn't matter," Barb laughed. "They won't know what the hell we're on about."

Bernard appeared, his expression unreadable. Oh yes, Julia thought, annoyed by her jolt at his appearance, he does have every right to come into his wife's bedroom, after all. A piercing, nostalgic lance shot through her.

Chapter Twenty-Seven

"You look gorgeous sweetheart." Gerald nuzzled Julia's neck. "I'm glad you haven't got your hair all draped around in that horrible dolly fashion the way these Hollywood babes do it. And you can't have a decent laugh with them either, believe me I've tried. Do you know, when these bimbos laugh, it's about as real as their lips. And when I make love to them, I sometimes feel I'm fucking upholstered furniture, rather than a real live woman."

"Don't hold me so tightly, Gerald."

"You used to like it. Why, are you afraid your ex-boyfriend will see? I'm doing you a favour. He's looking a bit jealous, or is he just mad about something?"

"Just dance, Gerald." Out of the corner of her eye Julia saw Ellis talking animatedly to Zack and looking her way.

"I was surprised, you lot sneaking off to do that *Tug of Love* rubbish. Why didn't you tell me? Now that Ellis has given you the elbow, you need me. When we get back to England we can go down to the island and things will be back to normal."

Julia sighed. "I told you. It was something Bernard cooked up. He owed someone a favour. Anyway, you're always saying you only do acting for fun. Don't pressurize me Gerald. I'm going to a funeral and I'm feeling like nothing really matters any more. Life's not really all that long. Not as long as we think."

"That's precisely why you're coming back to the island, with me. Here comes Ellis. You are coming back with me?" Gerald still held her tight although the music had stopped.

Julia smiled up at him. He kept asking her the same question. She supposed that she had no choice but to go back. But she wasn't sure. That was what was making her so wild and restless.

Now Ellis was dancing with her. The band struck up *Strangers in the Night*. He wasn't holding her as tightly as Gerald. He wasn't holding as he had the last time they danced together.

They exchanged small talk about the party. The crowd of people. Big Hollywood names, like Ellis. Small Hollywood names, like herself. Some getting very drunk, some not.

Julia asked Ellis whether he had been offered any good parts, thinking wryly to herself that she had not received any offers at all. He described a few possibilities without much enthusiasm.

"You don't seem very excited about them," she said willing him to stop staring around and look at her.

He looked down with tender affection. "I'm all washed out."

"I know, I am too." She smiled back savouring the intimacy that had ignited between them, which was soon broken when a wet starlet cannoned into Ellis.

The dance floor had been invaded by wet beauties fresh from the pool. But it meant that he held her closer and the magic was still there.

The starlet apologised, sweeping a seductive glance at Ellis from above her augmented chest.

What better way to show off your new implants than leaping shrieking into the pool and rising up all wet and magnificent. But then, everyone here is selling themselves in some way or another, including myself, Julia thought.

Julia could see Barb fitting into it all. Barb was a fast and clever talker. She had organised the bash brilliantly. Hollywood stars singing and entertaining in side rooms, dancing to a real orchestra in the main room, frolics in the pool, mountains of food and flowers and, possibly, dangerous drugs.

"What a party. Bernard never threw any like this before he met Barbara." Ellis spoke with a mixture of appreciation and surprise. "How are the happy couple?"

"I think Barb likes all this. As you know, she has the gift of the gab, as they say in England, and Americans never stop talking once they get going. She told me once that she had given the Blarney stone a blow job. Do you know that you have to hang upside down to kiss it? And she's witty and clever. And she's married to Bernard who seems to dote on her. In fact, it seems that he does anything that she asks." Oh, Julia thought, I'm gabbling.

"She is very funny," Ellis conceded without much genuine warmth.

Julia began to feel happier. The intimacy between them was growing stronger. Suddenly, she felt worried about what Ellis had thought about her and Barb's rather rude song.

"I suppose Barb and I behaved a little crudely just now, doing that rude song. We haven't done it for years. We used to do it at the holiday camps. We didn't do our rude version for the campers, of course. Just for ourselves and friends, late at night. Barb and I got bored out of our skulls singing and dancing *The Birdy Song* and *Agadoo* many, many times every day."

"I enjoyed it. Really, I really did," Ellis protested. "I'm not such a stuffed shirt as Bernard. He smiled at Barbara but I could tell he wasn't very pleased. Anyway I spent most of the time looking at your legs. I didn't know you were a song and dance girl."

"Well, most girls have to do musicals when they start out. I think it was Barb and mine's swansong. We're older, she's married. In some way I've lost her. It's time I grew up."

"Yes, there's nothing like a funeral to make life seem more important and think about what you're doing with it." Ellis' hold tightened even more.

They were both drained by their recent filming. The band began to play *Smoke Gets in your Eyes*. Julia sighed. She wished the dance would go on for at least an hour. Close to Ellis and yet, not close.

"I think Barb's chosen all these old romantic songs on purpose." Daringly, Julia carried on. "You know, to bring us back together again. Now that it's over. The danger I mean."

"Oh, she thinks it's over, does she?"

Julia was startled by the suppressed anger in Ellis' voice and the way he abruptly widened the distance between them.

"Isn't it? You and I just have to keep... sort of... not together, for a couple of months," she floundered.

Ellis' face was grim. "You may have forgiven Barbara and Bernard, but I never will. They filmed us Julia. They filmed us making love. You may not be upset about that, but I am. I'm still having nightmares about it."

Julia began to falter in her steps and she felt a little giddy.

Ellis pulled her close again, but the hard, angry look was still there. She heard him sigh as he relaxed.

He blames me, she thought miserably. He blames me for not telling him straight away like a true love should. And he despises me for forgiving Barbara and Bernard. If I had run to him in hysterics and cried all over him, then he would have forgiven me.

Now the dance could not end quickly enough. Julia gave Ellis no chance to continue talking. She turned and Zack was quick to take Ellis' place.

"How's my little darling?" he said cheerily, twirling her forcefully around for a time.

When he at last slowed down, Julia stared at Zack's offensive lower lip fuzz, so close to her own mouth, for Zack was not much taller than herself.

"Oh, so you like me lip art and you're wondering why it's shaped like a heart?" Zack smiled his film star smile and his black eyes glittered as he widened the gap between them and ran his eyes appreciatively up and down her body, finally lingering on her cleavage and wisp of black lace, between the black lapels of her suit.

"Spare me the Irish charm," Julia snapped, realising that Zack was very sinewy and she had no chance of escaping him in a dignified way.

"Tell me, is your fanny shaved?"

Julia's mouth pursed in a cross between distaste and amusement.

"Oh I love it when you look like that. Ah well, 'cos if it's not, we could tidy it up and have a real heart to heart."

Zack pressed himself into Julia's pelvis and whirled her round the floor again. He stopped as he realised that she was shaking with laughter.

"Oh," Julia gasped as he released her slightly. "That must be one of the worse chat-up lines ever."

"As Miss Moneypenny said to James Bond…"

"We all know what she said Zack," Julia cut in. "And the answer is no."

"Ah, go on, go on, go on. You're afraid. You haven't got the guts to take me on board." Zack laughed. "Ah, but you're a real Irish beauty. Black brown hair, green eyes, pale skin with just a little pink blush on the cheeks. Ellis never says much about you, but I gathered he made your cheeks flush quite a bit when you were close. Well, you wouldn't be disappointed with me either."

"I suppose your Irish charm goes down very well over here." Julia realised that she was being steered into the more shady areas of Bernard's rooms, and tried to bring the dance to an end.

Zack continued to grip her firmly. "I'm Belfast, you know. A real Orange man. I don't tell this lot that, of course, and I've ditched my Ian Paisley accent. The soft southern goes down much better. But I can tell you. I can talk to you. Ah yes, the Americans like actors who are Irish, or the Scots, or the Australians, even the Welsh, when they know who they are; but the English well, they just want to be the English themselves, don't they? There's not much doing here for you Julia, unless you become an Americanised actress."

Julia had now given up trying to extricate herself from Zack's clutches. Besides he was quite an entertaining talker, when he wasn't thrusting himself upon her. "I suppose I have to agree with you."

"There you are. See how well we are getting on. Now that you've finished with Ellis, I really don't see why we can't have that little heart to heart we were talking about."

"In your dreams Zack."

"You're afraid. Afraid that you might like it too much."

"No Zack. There's animal instincts and there's self-respect. I'm not going to be added to your long list of Hollywood conquests."

"Well, if you ever decide to follow your instincts, let me know. I'm a six times a nighter, you know, with stupendous Jacobs Crackers."

"I know." Julia giggled. "I can feel them. But, seriously, I have to go to a funeral."

"All the more reason to be wild." Reluctantly he let her go.

"I just haven't got the time for six times, Zack. Sorry."

Julia walked away with relief. When she looked back, Zack was already pressing himself as close as possible to a double D beauty.

Julia wandered down to the pool looking for Ellis. Their promise to Gran must be kept. She saw Humphrey and tried not to catch his eye. She had never seen her agent in a party mood before. He was slumped in a wicker chair with two near naked blondes draped over him, and he was red-faced and drunk.

Just as Julia thought that she had made her escape, Humphrey's penetrating tones cut through the fug of chlorine, cigar smoke and grass that filled the air.

"Hey you little trollop, get over here."

"Yes Humphrey," Julia said resignedly, standing before him like a naughty schoolgirl, and thinking that the two blondes might be thinking that she really was playing the part of a naughty schoolgirl and was likely to whip up her short black skirt and assault Humphrey where it mattered most.

"Yes Humphrey. Yes Humphrey," he mimicked. "You come over here, do a small part in a dodgy science fiction, against my advice, and then do a cameo in a trashy weepy, without negotiating a proper fee, and now you calmly text me that you're going back to England."

"I told you, I've broken up with Ellis."

"Yes, so you have, but you've given no press interviews about that, have you? No publicity. No 'my life with the hottest man in Hollywood'." Humphrey was interrupted by one of his girlfriends falling onto his knee.

Julia edged away. Things were getting very rowdy round the pool and she was conscious that her conservative dress looked downright kinky. Several men were already eyeing her up and there was a danger that she might be thrown into the water.

"Well, go on then if you must." Humphrey was torn between stroking the lovely thigh lying across him and his annoyance with Julia. "Luckily, I've got you in on a new British-based film. *The Watsons* or is it *Sanditon*?"

Julia grimaced as she retreated. She was not too fond of costume dramas.

Julia trudged wearily up the mountainous staircase to the upper floor. Still no Ellis. Then she heard Zack's loud tones coming from one of the rooms and pushed open the door.

There were Ellis and Zack together with a crowd of noisy people, huddled around the inevitable glass coffee table.

Zack was too busy snorting his line of coke to look up, but Ellis did. He stood up immediately and hurried over. His body blocked out the room and Julia stepped back. He shut the door firmly behind him.

"Just saying goodbye to Zack." Ellis' clear gaze told her that was all he had been doing. "He's a bit of a wild man."

"I think the term is 'hellraiser'," Julia commented casually.

Ellis smiled and took her hand as they headed for the stairs. "He's not altogether... trustworthy... He does coke, as you saw. I think he sees himself as a kind of Errol Flynn, you know, live hard, die young."

"You mean he's as fake as his Irish accent."

Ellis stopped at the top of the stairs. "He is Irish," he said with a puzzled frown, and looking at her with suspicious amusement.

"You don't follow his philosophy," she stated, sidestepping Zack's secret.

Ellis shrugged and looked down at the wild crowd below. "Perhaps I did, once. I suppose I was one of the bad boys of Hollywood. I drank. I dabbled in drugs. I chased all kinds of women. I became a big disappointment to my folks. My father refused to speak to me and my mother cried when I called her.

One day Zack nearly killed us. He was high as usual, and smashed the car into a tree. Luckily we were able to walk away from it or both our careers could have ended then. I realised that I wanted different things from Zack. An honest woman I could love, a family, a decent life, in spite of my being an actor."

Julia stared up at him. Was he telling her that he had wanted these things with her and that she had let him down? Was he saying that he still wanted her, or expressing regret at losing her?

Suddenly, they were both conscious that Bernard was glowering upwards at them from the bottom of the stairs. They both knew that to keep to Bernard's plan, they could not be a couple again for at least two months and he was obviously cross that they were being lovey-dovey in full view of everyone.

"Oh sod Bernard," Julia hissed, suddenly feeling tremendously frustrated and over-tired. "He's like some fat spymaster. And what does it matter? Almost everyone here looks like they're likely to jump into each other's pants any moment soon anyway."

Ellis chuckled and took her hand, suddenly seeming more light-hearted as they descended the stairs. "That's partly the trouble. Bernard doesn't like these kind of parties and he hates it even more when he has to throw one. Come on, let's escape to Hawaii."

Chapter Twenty-Eight

They went to the airport as a couple. Ellis didn't have too much trouble with being recognised. There was just the odd garrulous fan to smile at. They got on the plane as a couple. But it wasn't the same as the first time they had flown to the Hawaii. Then, they had been a couple. Now, they were still estranged, in spite of the dance.

Julia was tired. Ellis had already closed his eyes. But sleep would not come easily for her. She had left her pills in her suitcase.

She knew that she had a weird split personality when it came to night and day. Awake at night, she became agitated, depressed and worried about whatever problems she had. And the more she worried, the more sleep she lost, and the more sleep she lost, the more she worried about the next day. The next day at dawn, a normal, more confident and often exuberant Julia emerged, to snatch a few hours of blissful oblivion.

She took sleeping pills. Too many probably. She made stupid little sleeping faces to calm her in the day. "They're not that stupid," she said to herself, feeling disloyal.

"What?" Ellis opened his eyes and turned towards her. He looked deliciously sleepy and relaxed.

"Oh I was just thinking how glad I am that the filming is over. It's whacked me out."

"I know. I'm the same. Shall we stay at 'Hoonanea'?" It was casually said, almost as an afterthought.

Julia's insides began to flutter. "Well, it is our holiday home."

"I can sleep in the attic." Ellis closed his eyes. "You should try to get some sleep."

In the attic. In the dormer bedroom. The room he had said would make a good child's room. Then she had felt a little rushed, now... Julia came back to Earth with a bump as though the plane really had begun to fall.

Her depression increased. The 'will he won't he' thing was really driving her up the wall. She was part way up the wall already. I really can't do this anymore, she thought. The plane droned on across the ocean.

Some imp of mischief prompted Julia. 'In the attic.' She would pay him back for that. It was fairly quiet on the plane, but there was always a fan or two of Ellis' lurking about.

She yawned and spoke loudly. "We must have had sex at least seven times Ellis. Or was it eight? Can you remember? I don't know how we survived it really, do you? I'm exhausted."

"Julia." Ellis leaned over and seized her hands. "We are members of a funeral party and people are sleeping." Amazingly he was trying not to laugh. "I'll get back at you for this," he whispered.

"Sorry old thing," Julia brayed. "Actually, funerals are supposed to increase libido, they say. How's yours doing?"

Ellis' answer was a kiss. Not too sexy. More of a warning to shut up. When he stopped his look was a mixture of embarrassment and amusement. "OK. Now. Stop it!"

Well, at least he's laughing and kissing me, Julia thought, now a little ashamed. But she was sure that Gran wouldn't mind.

It was dawn when they got to 'Hoonanea'. Everything looked just as wonderful as before, even more so. Julia showered and sat on the big white bed. She was bone weary. It was physically tiring when a man threw himself on top of you seven or eight times, even if it was simulated filming and that man was Ellis. She needed a few more hours' sleep before the funeral. She climbed into the bed.

She dozed a little and then realised that Ellis had come into the room. What did he want? He was supposed to be upstairs. She was tired of all this fannying around.

She sat up. "Are you coming to bed or not?" she said much more loudly and belligerently than she had really intended.

He smiled. "Is that an invitation or a threat?"

"Oh, damn you! Go away then."

"I came for a blanket."

"Right." Julia lay down, and pulled up the covers.

Ellis walked round to the side of the bed so that he could look at her face. "Men get headaches too, you know."

"Right." Julia turned the other way. Did he have to speak with such an attractive teasing look? She turned back. "Are you OK?"

He was nearly out of the door. "Yeah. When my head stops pounding." The door clicked.

Julia awoke feeling physically and mentally terrible. The door opened and Ellis came in. He was wearing black trousers and a white shirt.

"Oh the funeral," Julia moaned. "I hate funerals. I cry and get a headache. How's your head?"

"Better. I don't like funerals either." Ellis sat on the bed. "But we have to go. We promised."

"Yes, I know. How was the attic?"

"Are you annoyed with me for not sleeping with you?"

His eyes held hers. His had a hint of mischief. Hers were simply wide open.

Julia was stumped for an answer. She knew she was gawping. She threw herself back on the pillows in what she hoped gave a couldn't-care-less effect. "Well, it's always a shame when a gorgeous man, such as yourself, goes to waste."

"Is that a yes?"

"Yes! I'm bloody annoyed."

Ellis laughed smugly. Julia threw the pillow at him.

"And my back aches with that humping we did yesterday, or was it the day before?" She sat up and stretched.

"Come on, roll over." He paused with a wicked look. "I'll give you a massage."

Julia remembered the other massage Ellis had given her on the night that Barb and Bernard had told her about the 'problem'. He had loved her then. He was paying her back for the plane and teasing her now. Much as she wanted to feel his hands on her body, a mere friendly, bantering massage would be absolute cruelty.

Warm, loving, trusting Ellis had gone. There were just friendly echoes of him now. Everything about his attitude towards her had a 'for old times' sake' feel to it.

"It's OK," she said at last. "I'll have a hot shower."

That should be a cold shower, she thought.

Ellis shrugged and left. She couldn't tell if he was disappointed or not.

The funeral service was held in an Anglican church in Honolulu. The service was a very solemn affair. Julia felt quite at home in such surroundings but Ellis seemed a bit uneasy with the grandeur of it all. The church was full of mourners, mostly Hawaiian.

When they came out into the bright sunshine, Julia had already decided that she did not want to go to the graveside.

"I'm sorry Ellis. I'm a coward. I've never been to a funeral where the body is lowered into the ground."

Ellis hugged her affectionately to his side. "It's OK by me. We're both still tired. Hey." He wiped the trace of a tear from Julia's cheek. "Gran's smiling down. Anyway, your hat is too attractive for any graveyard."

Julia reached up to take it off. Perhaps a pillbox with a veil was a bit too dashing. But she had changed her black lace camisole for a white shirt, for that had been too much like hey look at me, you're dead and I'm alive with black lace over my cleavage.'

Ellis caught her hand. "Leave it on. I like you in it. I shouldn't say this, but you look…" He paused.

Julia could see the unmistakable desire in his eyes.

"You look very beautiful in black." He turned briskly away. "Come on, we'll watch Gran drive away and then go back for a sleep."

Julia took off her suit and the small black hat and pulled on a loose yellow dress. When she stepped onto the terrace, Ellis had made coffee and changed into jeans and a sexy blue shirt that matched his eyes.

"I can't believe that she's gone." Julia gestured to the sun flecked greenery below her. "Gran loved this view. A view that has been here for millions of years."

"We have to sleep this afternoon and fly out at four p.m. I have to be back on *Warlords* by tomorrow." Ellis' tone was brisk. He had his glasses on and he was reading a script.

Julia thought how she had once contemplated removing his glasses and enticing him into bed. That was unthinkable now. He was quite unapproachable.

Julia lingered by the rail looking out. Perhaps this is the last time I shall see this, she thought? She was going to have to ask Ellis about selling 'Hoonanea'. Perhaps to a young Hawaiian couple. Gran would like that. At a price that would cover their own expenses. Or donate any profit to some Hawaiian charity. She sat down and drank the coffee.

She had to face up to it. Although Ellis was sitting across from her with every appearance of normality, the ice shards had formed again. The contrast between his eager love and urgent desire to marry her when they had first come to 'Hoonanea', was almost unbearable.

She had given as much encouragement as her pride would allow. Invited into her bed, he had refused. Their love affair was over.

It would be wonderful to go back to the Big Island, to that romantic beach, she thought, feeling that she couldn't face up to a five hour flight to LA. She would be able to check up on Mrs Pussy. She was not sure that the cat was a stray, and as she would probably not return to Hawaii for many years, it would be nice to know if the cat had a good home.

"I'd like to see my Mrs Pussy again," she said, almost to herself.

Ellis dropped his pen and took off his glasses. "What? What did you say?" He stared at her across the table, half laughing.

Julia felt irritated. "I said," she answered emphatically, "that I would like to see Mrs Pussy again."

"Oh!" He was really trying hard not to laugh out loud. "You mean the cat."

"Of course I mean the cat!" she snapped.

Ellis ducked his head into his papers, still smirking.

Julia realised what Ellis had thought she had said. She spoke icily. "We don't call it pussy. We call it a fanny."

He looked up, falsely contrite and more than a little sexually aroused, she could tell. "I know. You wouldn't say that." His blue eyes were bright with suppressed amusement and desire.

Julia scowled. Oh yes, she could go and put on the little black suit, the black pillbox with the veil and the black stilettos, and nothing else but a waft of 'Amour Amour', and come out again and sit and cross her legs like Sharon Stone, and Ellis would be completely unable not to kiss her, or to stop kissing her, once he had begun.

But where would that get me, she thought? Oh yes, men say 'sorry, it's over darling', but they're not averse to a bit of reliable satisfactory nooky if it's available. After all, they can always say the next day, 'well, I did tell you it was over, dear'.

Julia realised that Ellis was speaking and that she had been staring at him.

"Are you alright, Julia? You look strained. A penny for your thoughts." He reached out his hand across the table and Julia took it. His touch ignited no response in her. Is this how love drains away, she thought?

"I would like to see Mrs Pussy again. I want to make sure that she's cared for."

Ellis' mouth began to twitch as they stared across the table at each other. A bolt of desire shot through her. How she longed to kiss him. So much for love draining away.

She withdrew her hand and began to laugh. She always giggled when she was nervous. "I suppose I shall have to call her something else. But I want to go and see her."

Ellis protested. Their flight was booked. They could not go.

"It only takes five hours to fly to Los Angeles," Julia insisted. "Please Ellis."

After giving several more reasons why it was not possible, Ellis agreed. He would call Bernard and say that they were delayed. They would spend the afternoon and evening on the Kohala Coast and fly back the next day.

"Perhaps it wasn't such a good idea to come here," Ellis muttered, as he surveyed the cabin by the beach and the long stretch of white sand, fringed with palm trees.

Julia silently agreed. They had made love in the bungalow when Ellis had produced the engagement ring. And they had last made love on the beach when everything had seemed so perfect. It all seemed a long time ago.

She decided to concentrate on the cat. It was just a question of wandering around until Mrs P turned up. She wondered if Ellis thought that she had enticed him here in order to reignite their romance. He probably did not understand that she could become quite anxious about abandoned cats. The semi-wild cats of Crete sometimes haunted her thoughts, particularly a ginger kitten she had been forced to leave mewing by the roadside.

Although they were not now lovers, walking on the beach was weaving its own particular magic. Ellis looked much more relaxed. "You know," he said longingly. "I really would like to live here and just go surfing every day."

As the moon came up they ate at a beachside cafe. Julia was not so worried now about mosquitos biting her or Black Widow spiders jumping up her skirt. She explained to Ellis that coming, as she did, from an island where only an occasional Dartmoor adder, Norfolk water spider bite and hornets sting might pose a slight risk, and where there were no dangerous animals or rabies, she was a real wuss when it came to foreign creepy crawlies and diseases.

"In England, Britain," she said, conscious that she was babbling on far too much, "people mostly don't like spiders, though none of them are dangerous, and it is considered bad luck to kill one. They are captured in glasses with a drink mat on top, and thrown out of the window. Personally, I like spiders, though I don't like them on me, especially those with the long legs that run very fast. The wolf spiders. Sorry I'm talking too much."

Ellis' answer was to move closer and lean slightly against her in easy companionship. "No, no, I like it." He sipped his beer contentedly. "I like the sound of your voice."

If he says we can still be friends, I shall scream, Julia thought. She looked down. There was Mrs Pussy, gazing up hopefully.

Chapter Twenty-Nine

Julia felt relief that the cat was safe, and picked her up. Mrs P felt light and also had an oil patch on her back from hiding under cars. She began to feed the cat fishy scraps from her meal.

"Well, what now?" Ellis asked, looking kindly on the cat between them and gently stroking it. "And don't pretend you haven't deliberately saved those large lumps of fish."

Julia looked at Ellis, narrowing her eyes so that he could not tell how heart-warmingly in love with him she was. He genuinely liked the cat. Gerald, and Barbara for that matter, would have been completely unsympathetic and irritated.

Julia dropped her gaze. She thought Ellis might see how much the boot was on the other foot now, if she kept on staring at him in such a besotted way. "Thanks for not telling me how silly I am. And for coming here."

He placed his arm over her shoulder, smiling in a relaxed and sleepy kind of way, which made her stomach flutter. "No, no. It's probably a maternal thing. You seem to have bonded with the animal."

She jumped slightly at the word maternal. "I've always been stupid like this about cats and dogs... birds, rabbits."

"Anyway," he said after a comfortable silence, looking down the beach. "I didn't want to come back here to where... you deserted me. But I'm glad I did."

She was too stunned to speak. Was that how she had really lost his love? After that vicious fight in the surf. Because she hadn't clung to him in hysterics over his injuries. Because she had gone with Peter. It had seemed the sensible thing to do at the time, especially as Zack had come along ready to mix it, and was able to help Ellis.

She tried to say something. At last she managed, "You never said." She added in a small voice. "Would you like to talk about it?"

"Not really your style is it, sharing secrets?" he replied coolly, tempering his unkind words with a small twisted smile.

Julia was glad that the light was now fading very fast. She didn't want to cry in from of him. Oh Ellis, you cold, blond ice-man, she thought. Never more sexually alluring than he was now. So masculinely hard and implacable.

She stood up hastily, clutching the cat to her. "Well," she said with as much sangfroid as she could muster, "a guy likes to know that he can rely on his gal, I guess. I'm taking Mrs P to bed. Don't worry, you don't have to think up an excuse tonight, another headache will do!"

They arrived back in Los Angeles, tired and dispirited. The newshounds were out in force and soon spotted Ellis. With only a brief brotherly parting peck he went off to film *Warlords* and Julia went to Barbara's.

"What?" Barb exploded. "You went to bed with a flea-ridden cat instead of Ellis?"

Julia was tired and irritated and not feeling in the mood for arguing. "Yes! I told you, my bites are from cat fleas. Now, will you let me sleep?"

"No, no." Barb pulled her chair closer to Julia's. "You are going to tell me everything. Bernard and I were quite sure that you and Ellis were staying longer on Hawaii because you were having the most shagtastic time in the world, and now you say you slept with a mangy stray cat."

Julia scowled, wishing that she could enjoy the tinkling fountain, the warm sun and the scent of flowers, in peace. "You've got an over-active imagination Barb."

"What happened?"

"Nothing happened."

"Except that you re-homed a cat with Gran's friend Ivy, and…?"

"Nothing."

Barb sat back, frowning. She lit a cigarette and sighed heavily. "And you didn't tell him about the baby. Under that romantic Hawaiian moon, and the smell of exotic flowers, and the waves caressing the beach. And you, all doe-eyed and languid, and him like some Greek god rising out of the water, you didn't tell him and you didn't shag him."

"That's right."

"Instead, you chased after some flea-bag old cat and spent hours re-homing it? Mmm, doesn't make a lot of sense. But as they say, truth is stranger than fiction."

At the mention of the word 'fiction', Julia sat upright and fixed her friend with a hard stare. "You wouldn't."

Barb laughed in a parody of evilness. "Oh wouldn't I? I liked the bit about Ellis and Gerald fighting in the surf too. And all the other ups and downs of your relationship with him would write up pretty good as well. I could be the next Jackie Collins. I'd make a fortune."

"I would kill you." Julia placed her hands around Barb's neck and squeezed playfully. "You wouldn't live to enjoy it. Anyway, you have all this. You've spent more on these two sun loungers we're sitting on than it would cost to furnish a whole house in the UK. And look at this patio and garden. And the house. We're surrounded by millions of dollars."

"That's true, but it's mostly Bernard's money. I had to sign a pre-nup. And Americans, you know, never seem to save up for a rainy day."

Julia lay back, resigned to being a little more open and honest. She could trust Barb, couldn't she. She felt Barb's fingers in hers and squeezed them back, pushing aside the thought that Barb had already loved her writing more than friendship. "Course, you wouldn't write it, I know that. The truth is, things between Ellis and I are delicate."

"Delicate?"

"Well, we get along quite well. The sexual attraction is still there, but there's a lack of trust on his side. He's going to Mexico to think things over, you know, stupid trial separation thing, which really means that it's over. And, he has to finish *Warlords*. He's worried that it might be an expensive flop."

Barb nodded. "I see all that. But I still think that I'm going to get my big Hollywood wedding soon."

Julia smiled falsely. If Barb wanted to believe in miracles, at least it would keep her quiet for a bit.

"And," Barb grinned mischievously, "*Warlords* is not going to be a disaster. I've altered some of it, which means that…"

"I'm going to have to do a little more in it," Julia finished dryly.

It was hot in LA. Julia went about being a minor Hollywood starlet with grim professionalism, all the time longing for the cool English sea breezes. She was desperate to return to the island. Ellis had not sought her out and she could not bring herself to try and attract him to her side, in spite of Barb's prompting.

So when they saw each other it was just a casual hello and the usual false Hollywood smiles. Julia's smile was mostly a little fixed, especially when she had Barb egging her on to spend more time with Ellis, and to his face too, like at an outdoor charity dance.

"Do you always do as Barbara wants?" Ellis said edgily, as they circled slowly on the windy terrace of yet another grand Hollywood mansion.

Julia laughed gaily. "Oh sorry. I know she's just practically pushed us into each other's arms. Never mind, Erica's coming this way with Zack and we can change partners."

Ellis shrugged. "If that's what you want."

Her false smile faded as she met his intense gaze. For a second it was as though they had never parted. "Well, no…"

He began to smile. "No?"

"Well, I wanted to remind you to arrange that money for the cat's maintenance."

Ellis' scowled in a mock kind of way. "That cat had fleas. Would you like to see my bites?"

She hurried on. "You know, for Ivy. Mrs P needs her teeth cleaning, de-fleaing and worming."

"I didn't forget it," he answered shortly.

"Well, I like to think of Mrs P sunning herself on our terrace. It almost makes up for us, me, not being there." Julia was floundering now. She wanted to ask him what they were going to do with the Hawaiian house. Perhaps he assumed that when their love had faded into a memory, they would be able to share it.

They stopped dancing. Julia's vivid blue dress fluttered and her hair was whipped up in a sudden wind storm. She thought that Ellis looked good enough to eat in his white suit. Unbidden visions of her eating strawberries and cream off his smooth golden chest made her blush. The flower tubs began to fall over as the wind became stronger. He put out his hands to steady her. The feel of them on her bare arms made her shiver. She hoped that he thought it was because of the wind. They took no notice of the other guests heading for the shelter of the house. For one moment she thought that he was going to kiss her.

Then he seemed to recover. "We ought to go in."

Julia, annoyed that she had been so completely captivated by him after only one small dance, managed to make her escape into the chattering crowd. She determined to avoid close contact with him in future. Later, she saw him leaning against the wall in that loose-limbed sexy way that he had, looking at her with a puzzled crease between his brows. They were both fighting to get over each other.

Julia tossed her head angrily and turned away. He was the one blocking their reunion.

In some ways it was nice to be back on the set of *Warlords* again and Julia was just as excited as everyone else that the film was finally going to make it into the can. And the vibes were not all bad. A science fiction film could always count on the nerdish buffs, but there were a vast number of older people, who had fallen in love with *Star Trek* in the sixties, who adored the genre. Barb had researched this. These older people, Barb said, wanted good old-fashioned drama, convincing performances and not too many wobbly CGI outlandish aliens. And while there was the odd distraught animator moaning at the loss of his six-legged fantastic creation, Barb got her way.

Thankfully, Julia's contact with Ellis did not involve any kissing, so she was able to add her extra bits without too much angst. The main problem was the ending of the film, where the lovers, Erica and Ellis, as the main characters, had to appear deeply in love. Barb sweated over Erica, whose real, rather shallow character came across on screen. So Ellis had to ratchet up his performance of overpowering love for Erica to bring out more animation from her.

"You were once real lovers," Barb screamed at them. "Come on, come on, you must have had something going."

Depak Choti took exception to this. "Excuse me Mrs Donne, but I am thinking that I am the director here."

"Of course you are Depak," Barbara gushed. "After all, I'm only a scriptwriter."

Depak preened, missing Barb's sarcasm, and her wink at Julia, and backing her up on the whole.

Julia was not sorry to be back in the chocolate creation. She knew that she looked good in it as it was so perfectly moulded to her figure. Ellis, sweating over his love scenes, often glanced at her and Julia hoped that he wished that he was making love to his ex-girlfriend instead of the wooden Erica.

"Perhaps I should have reminded him of your steamy affair," Barb quipped in Julia's ear.

"That would have caused too much trouble," Julia whispered. "You're a callous bitch Barb, dragging up old romances just to get a performance."

"Well, he looks as though he would rather be screwing you, to me."

"But Erica's the one he's going to Mexico with," Julia said glumly.

The giant finishing party was set to become a riot of over-indulgence and wild behaviour. It began quietly enough. Julia had no idea where she was. It was just another ostentatious Hollywood mansion and she had missed Barb and Bernard at the entrance. She saw Depak Choti looking her way. Depak had been more insistent in his pursuit of her now that she was no longer with Ellis. She had lost count of the number of times he had slipped his hand down her bum crack. Luckily, Gerald was on hand, and Peter was somewhere in the crowd. Julia had been warned by Gerald to only drink from a bottle, so she was not thinking of staying for very long.

She began to move towards Gerald across the multi-coloured marble floor. She was sure that he was behind one of the Grecian columns that flanked the room. Her Grecian-style silver dress, with one bare shoulder, was in response to the general theme of the party. She hoped that a Roman orgy wasn't on the cards too.

Gerald was wearing a preposterous gladiator-style helmet, but before Julia could reach him, Zack appeared, his toga barely covering his arse, and showing an expanse of black hairy chest, which he lost no time in pressing to her thinly protected one.

"Ah me darling. Here you are."

"You don't have to put on the Irish charm for me."

Zack sobered up, suddenly looking to Julia more handsome and attractive as his real self. His black hair was set in tight curls and his dark eyes glittered with sexual interest in her.

"No, for you, if I can remember me, I shall be myself, Robert Michaels."

"Well, you know why you can't remember who you are. And I wondered if Zack was your real name."

"You saw me snorting. I'm going to give it up. Ellis keeps trying to get me into re-hab."

Julia smiled. "You should let him help you."

"A little birdy told me that you're going back to the UK to do a film."

"Urrgh, it's a Regency period. I'm trying to get out of it."

"Oh, those Regency togs drive me wild. Do you know, they actually practically exposed their breasts at that time? Those little bodices, those high waistlines. When I see you popping out of your top, I shall be fair bursting out of my buckskins."

Julia stopped the shuffle that was all they could do in the crowd, "You're not in it?"

"I've wangled it."

"You're not Lord Osborne?"

"I am. The gauche lord. He's such a wimpy character, they need someone like me to rev up the sex appeal. Don't say you're disappointed. Don't say you won't be swooning over me tight trousers and frilly shirts."

Chapter Thirty

"Slashed to the waist, no doubt. But does a Jane Austen man wear tight trousers?"

"Trust me, he will." Zack grinned.

Julia had to laugh. It was impossible not to be amused by Zack. "We're going to look a right pair of prats. We won't be able to keep a straight face."

"No, no, it will be all very worthy and highbrow, apart from extracting every iota of sexuality out of the clothes. My agent insists that I do it. Do you know what my nickname is, here in Hollywood?"

Julia shrugged. "Casanova?"

"It's Bonobo bonker."

Vaguely Julia recalled the images, and David's dulcet tones describing a very naughty troupe of monkeys. "Ooh, that's a bit strong, but perhaps highly descriptive."

"Don't be cheeky. It's mostly the ex-pats who call me that. Luckily, most Americans think Bonobo is a place in Ireland. But my agent is windy, hence the very proper Jane Austin to the rescue."

Julia smiled, mentally deciding that she must get out of the heaving corsets drama toute suite, even if it meant doing a British comedy.

Zack was rugby tackled by Gerald, whose helmet lurched over his ear in, Julia thought, a rather endearing way.

"Zack," Gerald slurred. "Mate. Peter and I are going to do a song and we want you to join in, seeing as how it's about an Irish man."

"No Gerald. Not if it's Brian Barrue. You can't do it. This is America." Julia was half laughing, half aghast.

"You should talk," Gerald glared at Julia trying to look severe. "You did that rude thingy at Barbs."

"Well, I just hope that no one knows what you're talking about." Julia stopped abruptly. Ellis had appeared at her side.

"Is it so bad? This party is becoming more like a Roman orgy every minute." Ellis casually placed his arm around Julia's back.

Julia was pleased to see Ellis. He was reassuringly sober and his blue eyes were clear, if a little wary. Zack was notoriously wild and Gerald, determined to enjoy his last days in Hollywood, was rapidly losing his ability to stand up.

"Oh Ellis, I'm glad you're here. I think I should go home now. And I've missed Barb and Bernard."

"They asked me to find you."

"Oh." Julia felt a little deflated. "Thanks."

"But, we'll stay to hear this song, shall we?"

"Well, OK." Julia had to agree. Gerald was so drunk he would be unlikely to be able to sing it anyway, she hoped.

Ellis' fancy dress consisted of a long concealing toga, but the material was fairly thin and Julia could feel the muscles in his back as they clung together in the crush of bodies trying to slow dance.

Julia was still giggling about Gerald and Peter's song.

"Well?" Ellis looked down. "I'm mystified. What does 'hairy side outside tonight' mean?"

Julia began to laugh again. Zack belting out those words in his fake accent had been very funny.

"Oh I'm not a bloke Ellis. Girls aren't allowed in a rugby dressing room, unless they're smuggled in. How would I know?"

"You do know, obviously."

Julia sighed. "It's all quite innocent really. Now, what would you use for a condom in ancient Ireland?"

"I presume I wouldn't be wearing one."

"No, no, they were just as keen not to have too many kids. They weren't stupid, you know."

Julia savoured the feel of Ellis' body as he considered the options open to an ancient Irishman as regards condoms.

"Pig's bladder? Sheep's stomach?"

"Possible. But not very strong."

"Animal skins."

Julia smiled.

Ellis smiled back. "Furry animal skins. And a gentleman would naturally wear it hairy side out."

Julia grinned, suddenly all the tensions of their split slipping away. Oh what joy to gaze into Ellis' brilliant blue amused eyes as though they had never parted. "Yes, you are a hairy side outside kind of man."

Ellis was really laughing now. "But I would get the occasional hairy side inside tonight, if it was you."

"It's only an old rugby song from years back, all twisted and changed. Surely you sang rude songs at your frat house, or whatever?" Julia's heart had started to pound so much that she was breathless with excitement.

"Yes, though not quite the same. I am, and you sometimes make me feel like, a foreigner."

"Oh yes, but foreigners are always so much more interesting, don't you think?"

"All our shared language makes no difference. Your culture and attitude to life is different."

"But that's a plus Ellis, isn't it? It is a plus?"

Julia knew that a certain amount of pleading had crept into her voice.

Ellis' answer was to pull her close. Her chin found its usual place at the side of his neck. She felt his warm quickened breathing on her face. "Yes, one of many," he muttered as he kissed the curve of her cheek.

He pulled away. "Come on it's time to go." He held her hand and began to forge a path through the crowd.

Julia followed him breathlessly. Is this it, she thought? Have we made up at last? Ellis could drag her anywhere he wanted.

Julia's exultation was short lived. Ellis walked right into a fight. He went down in the melee and his hand slipped from hers. The next minute Gerald had grabbed her and was protecting her from the crush. Julia struggled to break free. She was not going to desert Ellis again when he had been attacked. But Gerald was very strong and determined. The bouncers herded them away and although she called his name, she found herself parted from Ellis, on unfamiliar ground and even without Gerald, who had been unable to resist throwing a punch himself.

Later, when Julia tried to recall subsequent events, her normal, excellent memory failed and she was left with only fleeting images of the end of the party for her.

She had found herself sitting in a crowd from the film set who were all saying how many gatecrashers there were. She had drunk from a Coke bottle. Depak Choti's hand had done its usual run down her back and she had fought to keep her one shoulder strap up. She had gone to the cloaks and begun to feel dizzy.

Returning from the cloaks she had begun to have difficulty remembering exactly what she was doing and only the bare bones of what she had just done. Alarm bells had begun to ring in her head. She couldn't be drugged could she? The light had been dim. She had nearly fallen over an entwined couple on the floor. She had seen no one that she knew. She had realised that whoever had spiked her bottle would be coming back for the kill. The strange whining music had begun to bounce around in her skull. What was she to do in situation like this? Think, think. What had she done before? She had seen the sofa against the wall. If the back was curved she could crawl behind it. Like a silver snake she had sunk into the plush carpet and squeezed into the gap. She had relaxed but still fought to keep her mind sharp. Anger. That was it. She had been very angry.

Julia tried to wake up. She was pinned between two forces. They were crushing her. She was dreaming. She endured the period of being mentally awake but physically paralysed. Wake up, wake up, her mind screamed! As always, only sound would release her from her prison.

That sound was a snore. Julia gasped as though new born, and opened her eyes. The room ceiling looked familiar but she had never seen it from this angle. It was ruched with hideous taupe material which flowed across to the half-tester bed and windows, where festoons cascaded wastefully downwards. She was in the bed and jammed against a bolster. She was lying partly on her left side and, as she turned her head, there was Ellis fast asleep beside her.

She was filled with a mixture of pleasure and doubt. So they had made it back to his hotel room, she thought, shifting slightly so as to feel the length of him between the sheets.

But what about the night of passion? Why couldn't she remember a night of sex with Ellis. She realised that she was still wearing her dress, knickers and tights. One silver high-heel shoe was perched on the bedspread. So, no night of love then. Her head began to throb and she moaned. She could not remember what had happened the night before.

She began to drift off to sleep again. When Ellis wakes up, I shall tease him about his snoring, she thought. Or is this all a dream?

Depak's blunt brown hand was doing a bouncing bomb run down her spine. Julia jerked awake again to a loud snore. It was lighter. She turned, Ellis was looking at her with tenderness. She moved instinctively into him. "Oh I love you, Ellis."

He kissed her lightly on the mouth and stroked her hair from her eyes. She lay back. She wanted him to kiss her again.

Instead he propped himself up on his elbow. "Are you OK? Do you feel alright?"

"Just a headache. But I can't remember what happened after you were punched. Oh, not again." She ran her fingers tenderly over his bruised lower mouth and raised her lips to kiss away the spot of dried blood on his chin. The delicious, tender kiss that followed tasted sweetly of blood too. She prised his mouth open with her fingers which he nibbled. "Not your teeth this time?"

He shook his head. "It's not your fault. You don't remember what happened after we parted?"

"No." Kiss me again, she thought. Kiss me again. What are we waiting for? But Ellis, although they were in bed together, although they were kissing, although he was looking at her with tender concern, although she had just said that she loved him, was not sexually aroused. She realised that he was still wearing his tunic and underpants. Short of throwing herself on top of him and raping him, her longed for reunion was not going to happen. Still they could cuddle. It was so nice to slip her arms around his body.

Then she looked up into his relaxed and avuncular face.

"All I remember is that we were dancing. We were kissing. We were leaving. I thought that we were heading here to…"

"We were. But you don't remember being behind the couch. You don't remember kicking me in the groin when I pulled you out?"

It was several seconds before his word's made sense. "I kicked you in the…? I was behind a sofa? Oh no, no, that can't be true. I don't remember. Oh Ellis." Julia threw herself upon him, kissing his mouth, and face and nose. Finally she stopped. "Can I kiss it better?"

"It wouldn't make it better, Julia. Besides we have company."

The crease was forming on her brow, the puzzled questions were taking shape in her mind when another loud snore shattered the moment.

Julia realised that the bolster behind her was alive, and snoring. She whipped back the sheet and there was Zack, out like a light, his head burrowed into the pillow.

Sleepily Zack opened his eyes and gazed up at Julia. "Oh hello. This is what I call a good dream." He raised his head and his eyes widened even more when he saw Ellis. "Oh a threesome. Just like the old days."

Ellis frowned. "Not a threesome Zacko," he warned.

Zack appeared not to hear him. His eyes drooped and he yawned. "Let me know when it's my turn," he slurred before passing out.

Ellis shook his head in annoyance. "We never did any threesomes Julia. Well… not exactly."

Julia smiled at Ellis' embarrassment, pleased that he was embarrassed.

At that precise moment, there was a knock on the door and the maid entered. "Do you require any more towels," she said flatly.

Julia shrank back and Ellis, hiding a smile at Julia's expression, and seemingly unfazed by the maid's question, very calmly ordered more towels for his guests.

As the po-faced maid unhurriedly departed, Barb exploded into the room. "Ah, there you are. Ellis rang me last night and said he had got you. Have you still got your Marks and Sparks on?"

Dumbly Julia nodded.

"That's fine then. No harm done. God, I need a fag."

Chapter Thirty-One

Barb sat on the bed and puffed heavily. "Looks like an orgy in here. That maid's on the blower to some hack as I speak. What's Zack doing in your bed? Julia doesn't usually do musical beds. Don't tell me you had to rescue him as well, Ellis?"

Julia now felt that with her head pounding like a drum, that all she could do was just give up and sit back limply. "This is like a scene from a French farce."

"Without the sex," Ellis agreed softly, sitting up slowly.

"And it's getting even better," Barb laughed, as Gerald, followed by Peter, lurched groggily into the room and collapsed on the end of the bed. Peter was much more interested in sitting next to Zack.

"Hands off Peter," Barb playfully.

"Mmm he is rather gorgeous isn't he?" Peter gave one of his wide, white-teethed, blue-eyed grins and stroked Zack's curly black hair. "And I rather liked his arse-flashing outfit. Is he still wearing it?"

Zack awoke with a final snore as Peter lifted the blanket. He did a double take at the sight of Peter's grinning face.

"God Almighty!" Zack croaked. "It's the Devil himself." He shot up in the bed quickly, took in the amused faces around him, and flopped back again, holding his head in agony.

"Ah, shall I kiss it better?" Peter teased Zack. Then he leant over him and kissed Julia. "Hi, princess. I tell you, it was like a cavalry charge rescuing you from Depak."

Julia smiled at Peter and then turned to Ellis. She hugged his muscular arm tightly, wishing that everyone would go away and leave them in peace. "Thanks Ellis." Ellis smiled his lazy affectionate smile. She turned away quickly, fighting a desire to squeeze him tight unmercifully. "Thanks, everyone."

Gerald had just about managed to get his eyes to focus. He looked at Julia accusingly. "You caused to lot of trouble last night."

"I don't remember. I don't remember anything after the fight started."

"Well, you didn't take my advice about only drinking from bottles, did you?"

"No, no, it's not her fault," Barb cut in. "Bernard says they were playing Russian roulette with them, and pouncing on the girls who fell over. What you should have told her is to only drink from a sealed bottle, like I said."

Gerald's tone softened. "Sorry Jules. The sooner we leave this hell-hole of a place the better. Anyway, I think I deserve a kiss for rescuing you." He lurched up the bed and kissed the helpless Julia lingeringly. She felt Ellis tense beside her. Finally Gerald stopped. He looked at Ellis and his wicked smile was a mixture of delight and compassion. "To be fair, you deserve to kiss her more than me. Although I'm the one who saw the silver drape behind the sofa, you're the one she kicked in the nuts."

"She didn't!" Barb was now up the bed laughing. "Oh that's from our days at the holiday camps. It was the only way to stop a drunk, holidaying Scot dead in his tracks."

Ellis surveyed the grinning faces sourly. "Yes, I'm sure it's all very funny. I'm surrounded by mad Englanders."

"I'm not English," Zack muttered wincing in pain as he moved his head.

"Well, as good as. You're a Proddy. Proddy by name and proddy by nature." Barb laughed at her own wit, and hitched up her tight suit skirt to sit more comfortably on the heaps of bodies on the bed. She lit another fag. "Oh I'm enjoying this. Just think Jules, you have four knights to the rescue here. The white knight – Ellis, the black knight – Peter, the Irish knight – Zack and, of course, the noble knight – Gerald.

"Noble my ass," Ellis muttered under his breath.

Barb heard him. "Of course he is. Didn't you know? Gerald is set to become a peer of the realm. We shall have to call him milord one day and tug our forelocks."

Ellis' face held a slight sneer for a moment. "I didn't know that."

"Oh yes. He'll be a belted earl." Barb grinned mischievously at Ellis' puzzled look. "As opposed to an earl whose trousers are falling down." Barb laughed out loud, bouncing about on the bed in a way that made everyone else groan.

"Barb's joking. Gerald will be a knight, not an earl. A real knight." Julia smiled at Ellis' puzzled look. "It's no big deal nowadays." She wondered if Ellis was jealous.

Surely he did not think that she would be better off choosing a title over him? She longed to say that she adored him. That she wanted him. But they were in a rumpled, ruched, half-tester bed surrounded by crazy, hung-over, half-drugged people, and Zack had begun to snore again.

Suddenly Julia saw Bernard was standing on the shag pile carpet in front of the bed, dourly surveying them all from behind his thick glasses. Peter was draped over Zack. Barb had begun to hit Gerald with a pillow and she and Ellis were sitting, heads together, both looking as though they wished they were somewhere else.

Bernard calmly selected a chair and placed it into the bedroom doorknob.

Barb shook her head at him. "What's the matter, dear? Are you afraid the bell-hop's going to come in and take a photo?"

Bernard puffed heavily back to the bedside. "It's only hearsay now," he said sourly. "I don't want my wife splashed all over the gossip papers."

"Oh, don't be so stuffy, Bernard," Barb, teased throwing a pillow at him. "If you weren't so big I'd pull you up on this bed right now."

A small smile of pleasure crept over Bernard's features as he looked at his wife.

He really does love her, Julia thought, sighing. She felt suddenly washed out. She could no longer cope with Ellis' warm body lying beside her. And the unpleasant feeling of jealously rising in her breast must be shaken off. She was jealous of Barb because she was married and Bernard was not afraid to show that he loved his wife.

Ellis, if indeed he did still love her, showed his affection by accident. And yet, it was Barb's fault that the Julia and Ellis romance and marriage had foundered. Julia's head began to pound even harder.

Julia had barely recovered from being drugged when she told Barb that she was anxious to get back to the UK.

"Why the rush?" Barb moaned. "You could come down to southern California with me and Bernard, see the sights, while we film on location. Ellis will be there. He has only to do a few more outdoor scenes and he's free."

"Barbara, I have told you, Ellis and I are finished, and I do not want to talk about it. I'm going for a swim."

It was easier to cry in the pool. It was not so noticeable. And she had to cry just a little. She and Ellis had made such plans for the future when they were married. The tar pit fossil dinosaurs and then on to Yellowstone, where Julia had hoped to see a golden eagle, were just some of them. Happy plans that it now seemed would never happen.

Julia looked up to see Barb hovering over the pool. "Perhaps she thinks I'm going to do myself in," she muttered to herself. She wished Barb would stop following her around. Something about the look on her friend's face made her agree with Barb's waving and shouting about a brew-up, and follow her into the garden. Hugging her robe aggressively around her, Julia stalked bad-temperedly out into the sun-drenched garden.

"Oh look at you. Little Miss grumpy knickers. And you could so easily get Ellis back inside them. You're going to miss this paradise and all this lovely blue sky and sun if you go back."

"When I go back," Julia said heavily, trying hard not to let her friend needle her. "And it isn't so long ago that you thought the South Hams was paradise."

Barb shifted uneasily. "So they are."

Barb paused over the tea trolley, her dark eyes raking over Julia. "You should let me get the doctor. Those drugs could have harmed the baby."

"Will you shut up about it!" Julia snapped.

Barb sniffed. "Well, seeing as we are already quarrelling, I may as well tell you that I'm having my nose fixed."

After a stunned pause, Julia recovered enough to say faintly. "After all you've said about plastic surgery."

"It's only the tip. People keep saying I should get fixed. It's no fun looking like the wicked witch of the west."

"People, people keep saying. You mean LA people. Film people."

"They're still people, Jules, even if they live here. You'll hardly notice."

"You won't be the same."

"Of course I'll be the same."

"You won't be my Barb."

"Oh yes, you'd like to keep it as you as Cinderella and me as the ugly sister..."

Gerald buckled up his seat belt. "You know, I'm glad to be going back, aren't you?"

"I suppose so. I'm always glad to go back home." Julia struggled with her clasp.

Gerald leaned over to help. "You see, you do need a big strong man like me to fly back with. Pa can't understand what I'm doing over here. He wants me back."

"You never do what your father wants."

"Well, I would be if you married me."

"You've never asked me to marry you."

"Ah, come on Jules. You know that was going to happen. Wouldn't you like to be Lady Alltonthorpe?"

"Is that the line you used when you pulled your Hollywood conquests? Erica Black for one."

"Well, it helped. Actually I didn't do all that much screwing around. Not any more than you did anyway."

"I was not screwing around," Julia said angrily and then was annoyed with herself for rising to Gerald's bait.

"Oh sorry. Was it lurv?"

"Anyway, aren't I a little bit too common for your father?"

"He doesn't care if I want you. He just wants healthy heirs."

Julia turned away her head. Not a Yankee by-blow, she thought cynically. Poor Gerald didn't know that his case was hopeless.

The plane roared up and up. The G-force kicked in. When they were cruising, Gerald said casually. "Talking about Ellis, I saw him at the airport before we left."

Julia who was preparing to doze, was jolted into instant blood surging consciousness. "Where? Where did you see him?"

"At the airport. He was just below us. I think he waved."

"And you didn't say anything?"

"We'd gone through the barriers Jules. If he had come to see you, he was too late."

"You could have said." Julia tried to relax. It was pointless to be annoyed with Gerald. Had Ellis really come to say goodbye? Or was he just there, seeing someone else off? What would he have said? Now she had to fly all the way to London before she could ask Barb.

Perhaps a little ashamed of not pointing out Ellis, Gerald exerted himself to be charming and helpful all the way on the long tiring journey to London. He carried the luggage when they changed planes, he bought her coffee and magazines. He amused her with light chatter.

All in all, Julia was quite in charity with him by the time they were cruising over the Atlantic. He could not help being in love with her. It was not his fault that she had broken up with Ellis.

He was not as bumptious and belligerent as he had been in the US. He explained it quite entertainingly. "You know Jules, when I was over there, I really felt that those Yanks were trying to emasculate me. I really did. Especially when they found out that I would one day be Sir Gerald Alltonthorpe.

"How could I possibly be a regular guy with a handle like that? I must be effete, or queer. And they never let us appear in their films as real sexy guys, with the exception of James Bond perhaps, and they couldn't really wriggle out of that one. But they'll have an American James Bond, one day, you see. Oh yes. Want a queer, a pervert, a smarmy villain, a mad child killing bastard, a paedophile – send for a Brit actor."

"I don't think the Americans realise what utter shits you ex-public schoolboys are. That you actually go to a public school to become utter shits."

Gerald laughed. "If you take me on, you'll have an utter shit who adores you and can fight off the world."

Julia smiled and turned her head to look closely at Gerald. It was impossible not to like him. "You seem more like the old Gerald now that we're approaching Blighty."

"Oh Julia, when you smile at me like that I could just fuck you right now."

Seeing as how they were lying on first-class loungers, this was quite possible, Julia thought. She knew that the have-it-all-now rich passengers sometimes got quite frisky on the loungers and in the loos. She took Gerald's hand. "I am fond of you, Gerald. But we are not going to the toilet. Being a member of the mile-high club only proves that you're good at gymnastics."

"Do you remember how we first met?" Gerald grinned. "In that bird hide. You were looking at the birds and I was looking at you."

"I was quite an innocent bird watcher. I didn't realise what sinks of depravity bird hides were. I was never sure that you were ever really interested in birds of the feathered kind." Julia began to prepare herself for an onslaught of memories and pressure from Gerald. They were heading back to his London flat where they had lived together, and he seemed determined to get her back.

Chapter Thirty-Two

Julia drowsed in the planes' hum and began to mentally chastise herself. She had been too weak to insist on ordinary tickets. Too weak to resist going to the London flat. Too weak, too depressed, too shattered. And now she had to be nice to Gerald, because he loved her. Because he was showering her with the luxury that his money could buy. And he had asked her to marry him. She decided to talk him to sleep. He was a sucker for that.

"Then we went down to Torbay," she said softly. "A place that does not exist." Julia allowed Gerald to place his cheek next to hers. "They had to change the motorway signs from Torbay to Torquay, because people thought Torbay was a place. "We went down to Start Point. It was winter. That was the day the arctic terns went over. On the ground, their long wings fold up. When they fly it's in a low looping, twisting way. Slice one way, slice the other way. Cutting through the air like a hot knife through butter in an almost unreal way. Utter determination to get down south before they became too exhausted.

"And the light was going. And then the stragglers, struggling, the wing-cutting motion through the air not quite so smooth. Probably youngsters, thinking where the bloody hell are we going. And a few leaders seeming to encourage them on. To where? Slapton Sands? The Teign? Thatcher's Rock? Remember, I shouted, 'Stay here, it's warmer now'. Would they go on the Spain and leave safe old England? Then another wave of seasoned flyers, two hundred maybe, going so fast and cutting so effortlessly through the air, that one blink and they've gone. And then the stragglers. And then it's over, in ten minutes, and it's dark and it seemed that only you and I had seen them."

Gerald was half asleep. "And after, we had the most fantastic sex."

Too late, Julia remembered that bird migration was quite an aphrodisiac. She hoped that Gerald, who had now fallen soundly asleep, would not recall her words and think that she was coming on to him.

In a way Julia was almost happy when eventually they got to the flat in London. First came the smell of England, so fresh and rain-washed, then the busy streets and familiar skylines, and lastly the flat. Smelling a bit of what. Gerald had switched off the fridge but forgotten the Stilton was still inside it.

She had done a lot of suitcase hopping over the last few months so it was nice to be back to something familiar. She had lived with Gerald in the flat for a fair time after all. The lovely view of the Thames was just the same.

Gerald appeared, quite starkers. "I don't think it's appropriate that you go around naked when we are estranged," Julia said in what she knew was a prim manner.

"Just showing what you're missing," Gerald said airily with one of his trademark cheeky grins which said go on you're gagging for it.

Gerald soon reappeared decently clad in a fetching bath robe and flopped down next to Julia. "Why aren't you phoning Barb?" he asked, towelling his hair. "God, I feel like shit. I don't know whether to eat breakfast or lunch. You know the best thing for jet lag is don't you? Bed and sex. It's dark in America. Ellis is probably giving some starlet a good seeing too this very minute."

Julia registered Gerald's clumsy posturing with weary patience. It was time to sleep and get over the journey. Time to get ready to see the doctor. She had decided not to phone Barb. Her recovery from Ellis would not advance by scratching at old wounds.

"Thought you would be anxious to find out why lover-boy was at the airport." Gerald waited for a response. "Come on, you didn't really love him, did you? You said yourself that he was a typical American addicted to shooting helpless little furry animals. Write him off as a holiday romance."

"You ride to hounds," Julia said dully.

"Yes, but that's different."

"How exactly?"

"Well, it's more sexy, for one thing. I remember you being quite turned on by me in my hunting togs. Very turned on. Davy Crockett's hardly got the edge on me." Gerald shot Julia a glance full of longing and desire.

"I was bitterly ashamed afterwards."

Gerald threw back his head and laughed. "That's the trouble with you plebs, you're full of hang-ups. But that's why I love you. You're my real girl, my lady, my only love."

Julia struggled to avoid eye contact with Gerald and inched away from him. "Do you know what Barb said about the fox hunting?" She said, 'Look at all those breeches and boots. Sexy eh? But the same as sleeping with the enemy and having it away with a Nazi SS officer'.

"She would say that. But, why aren't you on the phone to her?"

"We've quarrelled. She's going to have a nose job."

"No more beaky nose."

"She wants a nose like mine."

"Can't blame her. Yours is adorable." Gerald kissed Julia's nose lightly, pausing for permission to continue, his eyes bright with ardour.

Julia ignored him. "But she won't be the same Barb. She said that I was just miffed because beautiful girls like me can't compete any more when every girl can be a beautiful girl. And if I get famous, girls will get my nose, whether I like it or not. And when I'm forty and past it, some starlet will have a whole face exactly like mine and I won't be able to do anything about it. And that rich men won't be trading their wives in for a new model but for a new, old model so that they can pretend that they're still thirty years old. And she went on and on and most of the things she said will probably come true. And that I was frightened that she might become better looking than me. And that I was too used to being the pretty one. That I thought of it as my right because I had been born beautiful. Of course, I asked her what Bernard was going to do when he couldn't find any natural middle-aged women for his films. And she just laughed and said make-up, of course, or airbrushing to make people look older. But I think you can always tell…"

"Oh baby. Sod Barb." Gerald put his arms around Julia comfortingly. "She's really ripped into you. She's a witch, you know, except that she won't look like one anymore. Perhaps she never liked us calling her a witch."

Exhausted Julia let Gerald cuddle her. It was true that the bitter and slightly twisted things that Barb had said had upset her. And it was true as Barb said, and as Julia knew very well, that natural beauties do have in-built feelings of superiority that comes from looking in the mirror every day, deny it if they will. Though she was used to Barb sounding off outrageously on every subject under the sun, still their quarrel had been vicious like never before. And then, there had been the covert filming, still there, still rankling, that had caused her to lose Ellis.

As if reading her thoughts, Gerald began to caress her washed hair and smell it. "I never understood that odd little film you were all involved in. Where you were the maid and Ellis the errant husband. That got jacked onto the Internet. I thought Ellis had filmed you both, or worse, when I saw it. I felt such a prat afterwards. You have forgiven me for breaking his teeth, haven't you?"

Julia nodded. It was comforting being held by Gerald. If only he wouldn't get too sexy.

"It seems to me that you fell out seriously with Barb then, over something. And I wasn't told anything. It really hurt to be left out, you know. After all the pact is supposed to tell each other everything."

Gerald was now very close. Julia could smell Imperial Leather and feel the heat coming from his warm body through her silk dressing gown. He kissed her throat. It would be so easy to give in. Make him a substitute for Ellis. The river flowed by the window mesmerisingly. She would live in a large Georgian manor like Elizabeth Bennet. She would watch *Desperate Housewives* and have housewifely Bree attacks. Have children who would never have to worry about money.

Roam wild Yorkshire and holiday in south Devon and the Med.

"I'll buy you a house in the Vale of Beaver," Gerald whispered, and kissed her.

For a moment Julia did not resist. Then the Imperial Leather reminded her of sex with Ellis. Gerald had a lot going for him. For one thing, he was a gung-ho lover who never got headaches. Was it wise, really, to hanker after a foreign lover who did? But then again, was it wise to marry Gerald and still be able to think lucidly whilst he was kissing her?

The next day Julia felt better and determined to get on with her life. Secretly she planned to drag her old Clio out of the basement, where it was parked next to Gerald's Range Rover, and scuttle down to Devon without Gerald. But firstly, she had to see the doctor, secondly, contact her agent about fittings for the new Jane Austen film, and thirdly, get rid of Gerald.

Getting rid of Gerald was easy. He just had to go and see Pa, he said. He could not get out of it. He kissed her forcefully before he left. She had to listen to a bit of twaddle about how he knew she would come back to him and that was why he had kept her bottle of Body Shop shampoo. The smell of lemons in her hair was driving him wild. And she could see them both reflected in the tall windows. Him dressed to impress his folks and show off his tan, in a blue polo shirt, and her dressed to impress her agent in a favourite sea-green dress with a nipped in waist, shampoo advert hair rippling. And she looked tanned which made her turquoise green eyes more blue. In America she had been pale. Here she was positively sun-kissed and different, thinner, unreal.

Julia's knew her GP quite well, so it was not so much of an ordeal to see him. But it was still an ordeal. The trouble with doctors was that you never knew what they were going to say. And very often quite nasty and unexpected surprises would come up. Julia avoided doctors whenever possible. It was not possible now.

"Pregnant?" He was pleased. Julia thought he was going to say *About time* since he was of the old school who thought that woman should start producing before they were twenty-five.

After he had examined her, he became paternally severe. She was too thin. No doubt she had been dieting. He didn't hold with dieting. It was not good for the young breeding woman. He took a blood sample, and frowned when she stepped on the scales.

"Hollywood!" he sniffed. "No doubt you're thinking of having breast implants as well as starving yourself to death." Julia said little. She just fought to relax more while she waited to see whether he would say that she was pregnant or not.

Finally it was the doctor's view that she was not pregnant. Foreign travel, a starvation diet, stomach bugs, change of climate, tension, depression, all these things pointed that way.

Julia thought that he looked more disappointed than herself. But then, she didn't know how to feel. In one way it was good news and in another way it was regretful that there was to be no Ellis' baby.

The doctor said dismissively, which was shorthand for times up, that there were more deserving patients to see, that he would let her know the conclusive results and advised her to go away and fatten up before she had a complete breakdown.

The M5 was, as usual, very busy. In summer, the holiday makers roared down the road to the West Country undeterred by the bands of heavy rain sweeping up from the Atlantic. Julia's heart lifted as it always did. The M5 gateway to the romantic and beautiful west.

It was so great to be back on familiar territory, driving her own Clio on the right side of the road, which was the left side of the road. Passing the Wellington Monument and the Wicker Man. Must remember the new slip road to Okehampton and get in the right lane. Plymouth lot going off. Hit Newton Abbot. She debated whether to go and see Dad. He might be out.

Crawl along the road to Torquay. The third busiest road in Devon. Up the ring road. Turn right for Totnes. Crawl over Brutus Bridge. And then time to relax a bit. To look at the trees hanging over the road and the wild flowers along the hedgerow. Then on up into the South Hams and her first glimpse the sea, the rolling landscape and the island.

She was free. Free from America and Ellis and all the quite amazing things that had happened to her. Free of the baby. Though that was regrettable. Anyway, she wasn't quite ready yet to be a mother. Her career would nose-dive for one thing. It was time to start again and what better place than her destination – the most beautiful place on earth?

Chapter Thirty-Three

"To the most beautiful place on earth." Gerald raised his glass. "Come on, come on, drink up. I hereby call the pact to rally and order everyone to drink."

"Barb's not here, you twat. Come on dance with me. It's the divine Howard Brown from the Halifax." Julia began to sway to the music.

Gerald, though a little unsteady on his feet, obliged, scowling when Julia sang to him "my first, my last, my everything".

"Oh smoochy, smoochy," Julia said, kissing Gerald.

Gerald wasn't pleased. He knew a fake kiss when he felt one. "What's so divine about Howard anyway?"

Julia, who had the song on a loop, waited for her favourite bit then answered with exaggerated dreaminess. "Oh, well, it's the way he moves. Very important, the way a man moves. Some men can move and some men can't. Most men can't. And then the voice, very important, the voice. Deep and warm and cheerful. And then the little boy goggle glasses and big brown eyes. Irresistible. And the smile, with that sexy slight gap in the front teeth."

Gerald threw back his head and gave Julia such a searing look of desire and despair that, she had to acknowledge, would have sent most women wild.

"I don't know why you fancied Ellis then, with his perfect gnashers," he said carelessly at last, lowering his gaze.

"It is true, Gerald, that I do prefer your teeth to Ellis'. I like your teeth." Julia giggled, glad that she was tipsy.

"Do you remember Gnasher from the comic? Who…"

"Look Julia," Gerald said heavily. "Am I to carry on getting legless, or are you going to put me out of my misery and tell me straight that I have no chance with you?"

Julia stopped laughing. She thought of saying that she did not feel like talking seriously. She had known when Gerald had arrived from London a week after her, that something had happened to him. For one thing, his physical pursuit of herself had stopped, dead. Barely able to wriggle out of his embrace in London, in Devon he just gazed at her broodingly. Eventually he had confessed that his tryst in the crypt had born fruit. The girl was expecting his baby.

"When I first told you it was over, I meant it, truly," Julia said softly, for an exasperated Peter had turned off the music.

Gerald nodded and they danced close together sadly.

"Are you two back together?" Peter asked. His words were so slurred that he tried again. "I said, are you two back together?"

"No. She's still moping for that Hollywood stud Ellis McCready. When it's in all the mags that he's dating Carmella, queen of the catwalk. And Erica Black's always hanging on his arm as well. Mind you, I've had her. Pants a lot, but I'd give her eight out of ten."

"Don't talk about other women when you're dancing with me." Julia admonished playfully. She knew that Gerald was baiting her, but she had seen the mags too, and it hurt.

"Oh, what a mess." Gerald was getting to that stage in his drinking when he got morose.

Peter was at the stage when he was just about to pass out.

"If you two are sick, I am not cleaning it up," Julia warned. She went outside and sat in the wild garden, looking at the sea and the island. She had been at the bungalow at Bigbury for four weeks. Long enough to get over all of her problems and get on with her acting career. Her agent was not a sympathetic man. Humphrey expected her back in London in two weeks or else.

She wanted to go back to work. She had enjoyed her time of recuperation here by the sea. Walking on the cliffs, swimming in the sea, reading on the beach. Wading over to the island. Gerald often took her to dinner in the hotel on the island when she would get all glammed up. She knew that he had little hope now of getting her back.

Julia gazed affectionately at the bungalow. It was a bit of a mess inside and not really a bungalow any more. In the beginning, Gerald had found it just a little too cosy. He hadn't actually said that he wasn't used to slumming it, but he had made it into five bedrooms with two dormers upstairs.

They had always treated it as a holiday home which meant that it did not get the attention that it deserved. It was built of stone with a slate roof, which had originally been made of thatch. Gerald said he was going to put the thatched roof back on, but he never did. Slowly Julia wandered back into the house.

"To the pact," Gerald was saying again. "Julia and I were the breeding pair, you know, since you," he poked Peter in the chest, "are a damned fairy and Barb swore that she would never have any brats. All pacts have got to breed. Can't have all this sea and beach without a couple of kids to play in it. Well, it seems that I'm doing the breeding on my own, doesn't it?"

Barb flew in. "Not like a witch anymore," Peter said quietly to Julia.

"You didn't think I would miss all this," Barb stretched out her arms over the seascape below their house. "I've been dying for this. I can't tell you how glad I am to get away from that place. That place LA. Another month and I would have been in a straitjacket."

"You don't mean that Barb," Julia said.

"Of course I do. I would rather be here. But then if I lived here all the time I wouldn't appreciate it would I?"

Julia screwed up her face at typical Barb double-speak.

"What's the matter?" Barb raised her hand to the pink shield that covered her new nose. "Has it slipped?"

"No, it looks… straight. Are you pleased with it?"

"Well, it's about time you mentioned it," Barb said tartly. "I was beginning to think that I was going to have to put up with your surly silence on the subject all the time I'm here."

Julia gulped. Barb had never accused her of being surly before. A black cloud of depression settled over her. She had lost Ellis, she had lost his baby, she had lost Gerald, she was losing Barb and her career was on the skids. "I shouldn't have said… I shouldn't have complained about you not being my Barb if you had a nose-job. It was selfish of me. I'm sorry." Julia knew that she sounded awkward, and she felt awkward too. Why shouldn't her friend be all glamorous and Hollywood shiny from top to toe. If she herself was happy to be sitting around in scruffy jeans and T-shirt, with wind-blown hair and a bad tan, why should she resent Barb not being the same.

Barb smiled warmly for the first time since their meeting. "That's my girl," she said. "Sorry I'm tetchy. It's a hell of a long tiring slog to get here, but it's worth it."

The next day, Julia was glad that she felt more comfortable with Barb. Down to the beach was the only plan that the pact had. For September, the weather was brilliant with a hot mellow sun shining relentlessly down. They all did a bit of bonding in the surf. They all linked at the shoulders and did a little jig until Julia fell in. Then they all went in. The weather was fine. The sun was shining all day. The kids were back at school so it was not too crowded.

"Oh I love, I love it. Let me just lie down here and soak it all up," Barb yelled.

They all seemed to be doing a lot of yelling. Like children. Or was it because they were all approaching thirty, Julia wondered, with one of them about to become a parent, another married to a jealous man and in the first throes of plastic surgery, and herself and Peter floating aimlessly around in the romantic stakes?

When they were all lying relaxed on the warm sand, Gerald told Barb about the baby.

"A baby," Barb was surprised. "A baby for Gerald. A baby for our Gerald. I can't believe it." After she had kissed him Barb sat back on her heels. "What's her name the girlfriend?"

"Samantha. I'm not sure that it's really mine." Gerald looked a bit gloomy. "Or whether I like her enough to marry her. I don't know what happened, except it was a bit awkward down in the crypt. The thrill was that someone might come down the steps at any moment. But that means that I must have been careless and here I am lumbered with a baby to maintain.

Pa will be furious. He will want me to marry her, especially if it's a boy."

They all laughed. "Oh come on Gerald you've got so much money that you could keep a dozen kids," Peter said.

"Well," Julia was determined not to let the baby spoil anything. "We don't want to think of our troubles when we are down here, do we? This is our special time together."

Gerald and Peter went off for a swim.

Barb spread out her sarong on the sand and looked around. The tides were coming in. "Do you remember when we were kids how fabulous we thought it was when the island became cut off. It was like a fairy story. And the only way to get to the island to rescue the princess was by sea dragon, or sea tractor? And when we were older we swore that we would come and live here and we have, sort of."

Barb rolled on her stomach, and gave Julia a long Irish look as she lay on the sand next to her. She said with obvious casualness, "What's Humphrey got for you?"

"Oh Brit film. You know, a comedy, perhaps."

Barb sucked air through her teeth. "Sss could be dodgy."

"Or a Regency. *The Watsons*."

"Oh you're much too tall for Emma. Jane Austen has been done to death."

"Not quite, apparently. Zack's in it. He's Lord Osborne. He's already threatened me with his tight trousers."

For the first time since Barb had returned, she let rip with real, genuine laughter. "Omigod," she gasped at last as the tears ran down her face, "not the usual type Jane Austen then? You'll have to get it in your contract that wardrobe sews up all your split-leg combinations."

Julia gave in to fit of the giggles, transported back twenty years in time, as she and Barb rolled helplessly in the sand. Julia could forget that Barb had a pink shield on her nose, for her fine dark eyes still shone with mischief and affection. "Come on." Julia dragged her towel to the middle of the sandy causeway and Barb instinctively followed. They would lie midway between the tides until they came in as they had always done.

As they lay back to back waiting, mesmerised by the incoming seas, Barb spoke quietly. "So you got rid of it then."

Julia felt a rush of annoyance. "Rid of what? The only thing I've get rid of is several pounds of excess fat." This was not the way to treat Barb, Julia knew that, but she had to be just a little spiteful.

Barb turned. "Of course, you look fab. Better than ever. How have you been, since, you know, since the Ellis thing?"

"Oh Barb, I miss him. I want him. But apart from that OK."

"He's in Mexico. But I saw him the other month. We had a little chat. I got the impression that he might come over and see you."

Julia sat up. "Why? He made it very clear that we were finished. We are to be just friends in the future."

"Well, I don't really think that you gave him enough time to get over it, you know. It was a terrible blow for him. In some ways he's more straitlaced than you are. He would never have dared to show his face in Vermont again if it hadn't all been pasted over so satisfactorily. The trouble with you Julia is that you are so cagey."

"You mean I'm not feminine enough for a man like Ellis."

"Well, if you really wanted him you'd go after him."

"How?"

"You know how."

"I've never been the hysterical type, Barb."

Barb frowned. "I was sure that Ellis would fly over to see you when you were in London. I was sure he would, before…"

Julia began to feel alarmed. "What have you been up to Barb. "Have you been interfering in my life again?"

"No. Yes. I think Ellis must have gone back to Mexico for something important. If he didn't see you in London. Something to do with Erica. Some crisis or something. Now, Erica does get hysterical. She probably got bitten by a crab. I don't know. I think he will come here to see you sometime soon. I haven't been able to contact him lately.

"Well, perhaps it's all for the best. I think Ellis still loves you. He missed you at the airport, you know. The LA traffic.

An accident, as usual. I know he wanted to tell you something. He told me. But he didn't tell me what it was."

"Oh don't worry Barb. I shall get over him. He must have stayed in Mexico with Erica. Come on, you've got to enjoy your time here. The tides are nearly up..."

Peter came over and put an end to more conversation about Ellis. Julia wasn't sorry. She felt better not knowing about Ellis whilst they were supposed to be having fun on the beach, and she had an ominous feeling that Barb had betrayed her again.

Peter sat between Julia and Barb as they relocated to the rocks and gave each a big kiss, and put his arms round them. "Just to disturb the locals," he grinned. "I must be the only black man here, and I am obviously banging the two most beautiful girls on the beach. The locals see Julia living with two men, and they can't work out which is her partner."

"Well, as I'm an actress, I think they think I'm sleeping with both of you." Julia laughed. And if Ellis does turn up, that will make three, Julia thought to herself. But why was he coming?

Later, Julia tackled Barb in the garden. "You've told him, haven't you?" she said without preamble.

Barb's silence said it all.

"You have told Ellis about the baby."

"Believe me, I wish I hadn't... now."

"And Ellis is flying all the way here from Mexico to see me because he thinks that I am having his baby?"

"I shouldn't have said anything," Barb said miserably. "I just wanted to get you two back together."

"This wasn't the way, Barb. I think you should leave here tomorrow." And that's it, Julia thought. Barb and I sitting on a wall in a Devon garden looking at a glorious sunset and as far apart as the Atlantic that will soon divide us.

After a few days, life without Barb returned to normal, Peter and Gerald had sensed the bad atmosphere between the girls and were not surprised when Barb left. They were all conscious that the pact had been dented. Then Gerald announced that he had invited Samantha to visit.

Samantha turned out to be a tall, dark-haired girl. That was the type Gerald favoured. He always went for the tall brunettes. It was quite obvious that she was about four or five months pregnant. But she looked pleasant and anxious to please.

Gerald had always wanted the pact to consist of just the four of them, which he said was perfect. A bisexual but mostly gay Peter Martin, a man-hating Barb Bark, a straight Julia Slater and himself, Gerald Atherton, the breeding pair. It was well-balanced. They would come together at Bigbury whenever they needed help. Divorce, death of a relative, disease, disfigurement, murder, crime, imprisonment, penury, old age – anything – they would be there for each other.

And when their careers had finished with them or they had finished with their careers, there was always Bigbury. They used to joke about them all being very old and sitting outside eating rusks. As long as they could still see that view, life would still be worth living.

The pleasant days passed. On rainy days they read books or went to Plymouth or Exeter. On good days they lived on the beach. English summers did not last very long. Julia loved the cliffs with the wild flowers and wheeling birds. She had once hoped to study the wildlife of Hawaii, but that all seemed like a dream now. She tried not to think about Ellis, but she often dreamt about him.

Samantha was easy to get on with. She spent a lot of time with Gerald, talking earnestly about their future. At first she hadn't slept with Gerald, but now they were a couple.

"I see you are sleeping with Samantha," Julia said to Gerald one evening when they were alone. "Is that wise?"

Gerald shrugged. "Well, what difference does it make? You are obviously never going to take me back."

"Do you wish that Sam had had an abortion?"

Gerald looked affronted. "No, Jules. What are you saying? Sam phoned me as soon as she knew I was back. I didn't tell anyone because I thought I might still have a chance with you. She said she wasn't having an abortion and I agreed with her. She was straightforward and honest about it and I admire her for that."

"Yes, of course you do. Men like those kind of qualities in a woman, don't they? Anyway, I think most men would rather the child be born than not, especially as they don't have to give birth to it themselves." Julia's laughter was a little forced.

"I think I would have felt a bit gutted if she had had an abortion without telling me." Gerald brightened up. "What's a little sprog anyway? Liven the place up a bit."

Chapter Thirty-Four

Julia began to feel that living with Gerald and Samantha was somehow not quite how paradise should be. She was used to having Gerald all to herself and though it was silly that she should resent that he had obviously found a new romantic interest, still Samantha's presence began to jar. For one thing, Samantha was rich, well connected and had been to a private school and university. In short, she was all the things that Julia was not. But these things did not matter, Julia knew, as much as the fact that as Gerald had said that Samantha was straightforward and honest. Things that Julia was not, either.

It was a blow to Julia when Peter said he was flying back to LA to do a film. Julia knew that Peter had been keeping things from her. He had been going around with a preoccupied look for a few days and had received a lot of mail from LA. Eventually he began to drop hints that the house that he leased there had been sold out from under his feet. He clasped Julia's hand in his big warm one, and steered her towards the big shabby sofa. "That bastard Ellis has bought my house, Princess."

Julia, who had been worrying that Peter had caught Aids, cheered up immediately. It was only a house, after all. But it was a bit strange that Ellis would buy it.

"Apparently," Peter was saying. "Ellis is going to knock it down and completely re-built it. He's written me a note apologising and saying that I can stay there any time. Should I believe him?"

"You're asking me if we are going to get back together." Julia tried to sound offhand.

"I saw your face when I called him a bastard. Anyway he's coming over. Why, if not for you?"

"I'm not sitting around here waiting for him if that's what you think," Julia snapped.

Peter laughed. "You are. You are."

Julia seethed quietly on the sofa. I am, I am, she admitted to herself. God, how she hated this man must chase and woman must wait thing. It was hardly modern and she was going to make Ellis pay.

Julia was left like a gooseberry with Gerald and Sam. Still it meant that she could sit and brood undisturbed on the beach, watching Gerald and Sam walking along the shore. Yes, they definitely looked like a pair, Julia thought. Sam's bump seemed bigger and she carried it well.

Julia regretted parting from Barb in a miff but it was so annoying that Barb had told Ellis about a baby that never was.

Barb had smoothed things over a bit by saying that she had to go to Harley Street to have her nose checked. "I'm sure I've been over-retroussed," she had moaned in a tragicomic way, that had caused Julia to put a little more warmth into her parting hugs and kisses.

Julia shook thoughts of Barb off. What was Ellis going to ask her at airport? Why had he gone to Mexico to see Erica instead of coming to London? Were Barb and Peter right when they said that he would come to Bigbury on Sea? Would he be able to find Bigbury, for that matter?"

Julia stood up. She needed a dip in the cold ocean. The day was getting blustery and black storm clouds were gathering in the west. She turned and looked right, towards the island. All the questions that she had just been asking could now be answered. Ellis was standing on the other side of the River Avon that ran down to the sea.

They were right. He had come! Julia stood on tiptoe and waved excitedly. "Oh no!" she cursed under her breath. Here she was on Bamtham sands and there he was on the other side of the narrow, treacherous river. Then she became worried. Did Ellis know that he couldn't cross the dangerous river? Had he seen the sign? "Hi Ellis. Ellis!" She waved again.

"I have to come round," she shouted. She pointed up to the road above the beach. "Round by the roads."

Ellis was standing indecisively by the shoreline. He was wearing jeans and a blue shirt.

Indecisive. Why was he indecisive, Julia wondered? It reminded her of the first time she had seen him. Why fly the Atlantic to look indecisive? Was it just the river?

He had started to wave. Now he stood, seemingly turned to stone. He jammed his hands in his pockets, and stared at her. His hair was longer. It was ruffling in the breeze. He looked very American and heart-stoppingly desirable. She wanted him so much.

Then he turned and began to walk back towards the island. He had seen the sign, yes, but why had he turned so abruptly away with barely a wave and no smile?

Julia dressed hurriedly, waved to Gerald and Sam, and ran up to the road where the Clio was parked. She had to go up to the main road and back down another road to Bigbury on Sea.

It would take her a good half-hour. As she drove along the narrow lanes, never had she sworn so much as she was forced to reverse into a passing place several times. She slithered down the sandy path onto the beach, breathless, expecting to find Ellis waiting.

Julia paused to get her breath back. Where was Ellis? Surely he had waited for her. It was evening. The black clouds were getting closer. The crowds had gone, but still she could not see him.

Then she saw him. Somewhere that she had not expected to see him. He was walking up the path to the hotel on the island.

Julia froze. Why had he flown across America and the Atlantic to see her, and then just turned away? She walked numbly up and down the beach puzzling it out. Slowly she realised why.

She began to walk towards the island, not thinking about the tides. She was some way across when she realised that people were shouting at her. She looked down. The water was up to her jeans' pockets

She hurried on as well as she could through where the two tides met. If she lost her balance and fell into the water it could be dangerous. The tides swirled round the island in a fierce fashion.

Julia was helped up the last few metres onto the path by two fishermen. She was told how foolish she had been. She felt embarrassed and muttered her thanks and walked off. "Stupid bloody grockles," she heard them say. She squelched up the path to the hotel, cold with fright, and cold from the sea.

It was only because some of the staff knew her, and she said that she had an urgent message for Mr McCready, a guest, that Julia, in her wet and bedraggled state, was allowed into the hotel. She sat behind a small table, trying the hide her wet jeans. Her hair was a windswept mess and she had left her bag on the beach. She held her arms across her chest, acutely aware that she looked like an entrant in a wet T-shirt contest and that her jeans were making a damp patch on the upholstery.

She felt awkward, embarrassed and awful, for her puzzling over Ellis' behaviour had already crystallised into hard facts.

Ellis came into the room. He was wearing a suit and obviously going in for dinner. It was so good to see him, that Julia momentarily forgot everything.

He stood awkwardly for a moment. Then his eyes softened and he crossed the room quickly to sit beside her. "Hi Julia."

Julia managed to say, "Hi." She found that she could hardly speak.

They stared at each other. Ellis opened his mouth to say something and then noticed that she was soaked. "Are you OK? Have you fallen in the sea?"

"I waded across."

"Wasn't that a bit dangerous?"

Julia stared at him sulkily. "No."

"I don't think…" Ellis paused. He had obviously decided not to comment on her appearance any more, and ordered two coffees. "You look like you need a hot drink." He took her hands and warmed them with his own.

"I saw you on the beach," she said accusingly. "I went round by the road, but you weren't there. You weren't waiting for me."

"I'm sorry. I should have waited for you. I did for quite a time. Have you come straight here? Why has it taken you so long?"

"Oh it takes ages to get round." Julia smiled wanly. She could not expect Ellis to know the geography of the area.

"Aw come on honey. Come up to my room. Let's get you warmed up." Ellis' spoke in a tender lover's way. He held her hands tighter and moved closer to her, his face expressing his desire to hold her.

Julia thought that he might pick her up and whisk her upstairs. He didn't seem to care that people were watching.

Resolutely she swallowed the lump in her throat, and although he was ready to let love and physical contact work their magic, she was not.

"You're short-sighted. You thought I was Sam."

"Sam?"

"Gerald's pregnant girlfriend."

"Yes. The girl with Gerald. I thought it was you. I thought… for a moment, that it was you. And although you were with Gerald, I felt that you still loved me." Ellis' body stiffened and he moved away a little. "I'm sorry." His eyes became wary and anxious. "I'm sorry that it's turned out this way."

Oh yes, you're sorry, Julia thought. You're sorry for what you think you have lost. All the questions that she had wanted to ask him, now choked in her throat.

Ellis had thought for a moment that she had been the pregnant Sam. Then, he had seen her, waving, slender and the same as he had last seen her. He had thought, in that moment of time, that she had aborted his baby. "Damn, damn, damn Barb! She told you!"

Ellis released a long held breath. "Yes. Perhaps it would have been better if Barbara had said nothing at all." He chafed Julia's hands. "You feel cold. I'll get you booked in."

Julia felt herself unable to move. A wave of intense irritation washed over her. She had often imagined that Ellis might come to the island. They would meet romantically on the beach at sunset. She would fly into his arms and they would kiss as the avocets flew above them. He would take her to his hotel and… "She told you."

Julia realised that she had spoken the words aloud. Ellis was holding her hands and putting on a brave face that there was no baby. That the baby had been discarded as inconvenient. Julia's feelings choked her and gathered like a black cloud. If only she had confided in Barb. If only she had confided in Ellis. She wouldn't be sitting, wet and numb, with a disappointed Ellis who still loved her enough to try to comfort her.

"I don't blame you Julia. I understand. You're an actress. You have to work." Ellis' voice was kind but regretful.

Julia snatched her hands away. "Of course you do. I know you do. This shouldn't have happened."

Julia jumped up. "I have to go. I have to get the tractor before it's too late." She blundered into the coffee table. It fell over and the coffee spilled onto the floor. The other guests began to stare.

Julia ran. Shoes squelching, wet jeans flapping. Ellis was left tangled in the coffee table. He could not catch her. She did not know why she was running, only that Ellis had come for her at last and because of Barb's' loose lips her longed for reunion with him had turned to ashes because she didn't know whether he had come for her or the baby. She made the sea tractor just as it was about to go. She didn't look back. She heard someone say, "It's that damn silly girl again. At least she got the tractor this time."

By the time Julia got back to the house, the light was fading. The black storm was still heading in from the west. The tide was fully up and a stiff breeze was blowing. Unless Ellis choppered over, she was safe from him until the next day. She turned off her mobile and took the phone off the hook and prepared to steal away in the night back to London.

Gerald had left a note. He had seen Ellis on the beach and knew where she had gone. He and Sam had left for Yorkshire. The note ended with 'Good Luck'.

Julia huddled on the shabby sofa as the thunderstorm finally broke over the house. She and Ellis seemed a little short on luck. If only Barb wasn't so nosey. If only Barb didn't feel so guilty about causing the break-up between Ellis and herself. And now, by trying to get them back together, Barb had pushed them further apart.

Julia knew that although she blamed Barb, and Ellis, she herself was in the wrong. Why did she not go to bed with Ellis in the hotel? Tell him everything. Let him take off her wet clothes. Fuck his brains out. Cry on his shoulder. Why, why, not? Stupid pride. Nothing was her fault. It was not her fault! These were the kind of feelings that got people hung for murders they didn't commit. Deigning to explain.

Julia shut up the house and took one last look at the island in the moonlight. Go over there tomorrow, her inner voice said. He's over there on the island. He still loves you.

Julia drove through the night to Gerald's flat in London. She arrived in a state of exhaustion. Again she switched off all the phones. She raged up and down in front of the calm Father Thames.

How had she got herself into such a mess? If only Ellis had managed to speak to her at the airport. If only he had come over to England earlier like he had planned. If only he had come over not knowing that there might be a baby. No, no, Barb would have said that there was a baby, because she, she, stupid, stupid Julia, had not told Barb that there wasn't.

Eventually, Julia realised that she was being way too melodramatic, that she was an actress with a career to make, and reached for the sleeping pills.

By the next afternoon Julia signed up to do the Brit film. The film seemed to be slanted towards comedy. Julia prayed that she would be feeling more cheerful when the time came to film it. She was too tall for the part of Emma Watson, of course, but she would wear flats and Zack, as Lord Osborne, would wear heels in their romantic scenes. Zack would have a blond wig and his tight trousers and frilly shirts. Julia thought that it would be hard to imagine the worldly Zack as the awkward lord, but that was showbiz. It was rumoured that Zack was holed up in a Mexican clinic being purified. But Julia was not sorry not to see him.

Barb phoned from LA. Reluctantly Julia took the call. Julia must come over. Ellis was in LA and he wanted to see her. He had bought the house that Peter had leased in LA Ellis now owned the small blue bedroom that had caused so much trouble.

Julia hesitated. She had to go to LA to face Barb and Ellis. She was on the high moral ground. She had never done anything that she was ashamed of. Barb and her well-meaning antics had wreaked the havoc.

The trouble with the high moral ground was that it was lonely looking down. Anyway she had already decided that she would go over there and have it out with them both once and for all. She ignored the little voice that whispered inside her head, 'He still loves you'.

Chapter Thirty-Five

Julia pleaded jet lag when she got to Barb's and went straight to bed. She needed all her strength to deal with Barb and possibly Ellis. She rose at noon and headed down to the pool. It was not long before Barb tracked her down.

"Oh Jules, you look terrible."

"Thanks, Barb. Still wearing the nose shield then?"

"I'm glad you've come down at last. Ellis is on his way over here right about now."

"Why exactly?"

"To see you, of course. He wants to see you. Don't be perverse."

"Look Barb, I don't know what you've been telling Ellis, whatever your suspicions have been, but from now on, just keep the hell out of my life."

Barb sniffed. "You don't mean that."

"Just watch me."

"Yes watch you being a stubborn fool. The man flew thousands of miles to see you and you had not the grace to give him a meeting."

Julia stared at Barb feeling unable to explain about the pain she had suffered when Ellis had thought for a few seconds that Sam was a pregnant Julia. "You don't know anything about anything," she spat at last.

Barb pulled a face and checked that her nose-wrinkling had not dislodged the shield. "Oh yes, give me your green-eyed she-devil look. I'm trying to help you."

"Barb, let's just get this clear shall we? I don't want you to help me, ever again."

Julia sank gratefully into Bernard's large indoor pool. She swam a few lengths and began to feel better physically, but the injustices she had been subjected to still welled up in her heart and brain.

Above the shimmering water, she could see Barb sitting by the pool. A tall figure appeared. Julia shot up to the surface.

She heard a splash and knew that Ellis was in the water. Julia ignored him. She lay floating gently, at the side of the pool.

Ellis sidled up beside her. His eyes were as blue as the water, his mouth was just as well-cut and kissable as she remembered. His chin was as firm, his cheek bones as well defined but his hair was no longer spiky. The expression on his face was open and affectionate. "Hi Julia." His voice was warm.

Julia recoiled. She didn't want him close until her tightly controlled anger had exploded. "What do you want?"

"I went to your house at Bigbury and you had gone."

"What did you expect? You walked away from me."

"I did. I'm sorry. I was… disappointed."

"You came for the baby, not me."

"I came for both of you."

"There's only me."

"Yes."

"There's only ever been me."

Julia turned away and got out of the water. She walked towards her chair, gave Barbara a scathing look and put on her wrap.

Julia went quickly towards the door as Ellis began to walk towards her. She turned. "There never was a baby," she shouted. "Go on Barbara, explain to him how you poked about in the trash and put two and two together and made two." Her words echoed round the pool harsh and hysterical. "I didn't have a termination. I was not pregnant!"

Barb's mouth fell open and Ellis stopped walking.

"I thought there might be but there wasn't. And I didn't tell Ellis because he didn't love me anymore and I didn't tell you Barbara, because it was none of your bloody business. But mostly, I didn't tell either of you because I just didn't want to. Get it!"

"Oh yes, we get it! You're shouting loud enough to tell all of LA." Barb turned and spoke to Ellis as he grabbed a towel. "She's such a secretive little bitch!"

Ellis suddenly seemed more relaxed. He smiled nodding his head "But kinda cute." Hurriedly he began to towel himself.

"And such a white bra and pants girl." Barb knew that Julia could hear her.

Julia caught a slight smile of amusement on Ellis' face. He had his hands folded aggressively across his chest in a way that said to Julia that she was his. That all barriers were down.

Julia turned and ran out and down the corridor towards her room straight into Bernard.

"What's all the shouting about?" He steadied her gently.

Julia clung to Bernard's large comforting chest for a moment. Then she broke away.

"Your wife's ruined my life. That's what it's about. Your wife is a bloody nosey cow, Bernard, and you can tell her from me to keep her bloody nose out of my affairs."

"She loves you," Bernard said softly, holding Julia's arm so that she could not move. "She'd do anything for you. She even married me."

Julia's head snapped back in annoyance. "Oh yes, lay your bloody monkey on me, why don't you? Well, she wouldn't stay with you now, would she, if she didn't want to, since we're not friends anymore?"

In the silence as Bernard considered her words, Julia slumped slightly. "She told me once that she thought that you would be someone special, Bernard."

Bernard smiled but it was difficult to tell whether he believed her, Julia thought, but then he relaxed and nodded as though in agreement.

Julia packed quickly. Thank God Peter was back in LA even if he was living in Ellis' house. She took a deep breath. She felt better. She had lost her temper and it felt good. She prepared to steal out of Barb's house like a thief.

"What have you been saying to Bernard?" Barb burst into the room at the very moment Julia was at the door with her case.

Julia sighed and dropped the case on the floor with a thump. "I merely told him that you loved him."

"Mmmm," Barb almost snarled. She sat on the bed and lit up. "So you're running away… again. Ellis won't hang around for you for ever, you know."

"Ellis isn't my problem Barb… you are."

Barb spread out her hands imploringly. "I know I shouldn't have told him you were preggers but you should…"

"It isn't just that." Julia flung out of the door and ran down to Barb's office. Barb followed. Julia startled Barb's prized secretary by seizing a pile of paper on her desk and throwing them into the air.

"Mrs Donne!" The secretary tried to recover the papers.

"It's alright Louise." Barb signalled for the secretary to leave and shut the door behind her with a bang.

Julia squatted on the floor and began to read the pages out loud. "Torin was walking out of the sea towards Rosita, his golden torso gloriously bathed in the warm radiance of the setting sun, when Ricky suddenly appeared from nowhere and hit him smack on the jaw." Julia sat back on her heels.

"Well? Interesting poolside reading isn't it?"

Barb sucked air through her teeth defensively. "It's only romantic toshery. Louise shouldn't have left it lying around."

"So you weren't even going to tell me about it." Again Julia read aloud, "Rosita, seeing the blood pouring from her lover's mouth, screamed, *Torin, oh Torin!* As Torin and Ricky began to fight with bestial savagery, the black eunuch prevented Rosita from throwing herself upon them, by picking her up and carrying her screaming up the beach. Rosita was soon to find that the black eunuch Caspar was, in fact, not a eunuch at all."

Julia scrabbled in the paper. "Romantic toshery eh? You're doing this for some publication called *The Red Hot Flame of Love*."

"Well exactly, no one will ever think that it's you."

"No, not a white bra and pants girl like me. You called me that in front of Ellis."

"I'm sorry. Look, Jules…"

"Don't call me that."

"Look Julia, you can read the book when it's finished. Hot sex is very popular. I have to break in somewhere. I can't rely on Bernard to give me work for ever."

Julia threw down the papers and stood up. She walked menacingly over to Barb. "I told you I would strangle you if you wrote about my personal life again. It was your fault that I ever went potty over my mother. Why I had to phone her up every night because her life story was on telly every week. When she was alive nobody cared and when she was dead nobody cared either. And you wrote it and I acted in it." She placed her hands around Barb's throat and regarded her with mock anger and a small smile of affection. "You need strangling. But I could just settle for removing this." Julia's fingers moved to the pink nose shield.

Barb stiffened. "It's not… I'm not…"

"You don't have to wear it when I'm around, Barb."

"I'm not sure that I like it." Barb looked suddenly insecure.

"Does Bernard like it?"

"This sort of thing is more normal for him. I don't think his nose is his own." Barb raised her hands and carefully peeled off the shield.

"You look like Joan Collins… a younger Joan Collins."

Barb pulled Julia's hands to her waist. "I'm still Barb. Even with a new nose. Tell me I'm still Barb."

Julia could see a faint scar at the tip of Barb's nose. If she really wanted to be nasty she could mention it. "Your eyes are still the same, so I guess you are," she said reluctantly.

"I can hear Bernard coming. Julia, for all our sakes, marry Ellis and tell me that one day we'll meet at the island and be friends again."

"Only if you swear that that there are no double anuses in your book."

Barb laughed. "I swear, but I think you mean double anals. And another thing. I only found out today. Unlike you, I tell my friends things straight away. I'm having a baby."

Julia felt a queer mix of emotions as Barb's disclosure. Some of it was jealousy, some of it was resignation and some of it was sheer annoyance that her friend had again stolen something from her. Barb had stolen her mother. She had stolen Ellis' love. She had stolen her marriage to Ellis. She had stolen the idea of a baby. She was writing about her life. Hell, she had even stolen her nose. Suddenly Julia realised that the only way to stop all the bad feelings was to cut Barb out of her life. For at least a year anyway. There was still that stupid pact.

Julia shook herself and smiled falsely. "Congratulations," she cooed with all her skill as an actress that she could muster. But still there was a gleam in Barb's eye that said that she knew. As they embraced Bernard's face appeared owl-like round the door.

Chapter Thirty-Six

Julia awoke in the small blue bedroom at Peter's. For a moment she didn't know where she was. Oh dear. What did I do yesterday at Barb's, she thought? That wasn't handled very well.

She felt jet-lagged and lazy, but better, definitely better than she had felt for – it seemed like a long time.

She knew why that was. She had a strong feeling that Ellis had emerged out of the doomy quagmire of their failed relationship. The interest, love and desire was back in his eyes again. He had looked positively wolfish.

There was a quick tap on the door. "Good morning princess. Tea up. Lover boy's waiting outside. What are you going to do about him? Jack him in, or not?"

Julia sat up. "He's here? Already? Oh Peter, I'm not prepared." She sighed unconvincingly. "I would forget him if I could."

"Well, he's not a bad chap, for an American. And if you've got to have him, you've got to have him."

Julia lay back feeling drained. "When does he get this house? It's a shame you haven't bought it."

"I couldn't afford it. But then, when you two are married, I'll come here anyway."

"Now we are jumping forward just a little too much."

"You haven't seen him yet. He's holding a red rose and froggy has definitely come a courting. Oops there he is at the door. Can't wait. Is he to come in?"

"No. I have to get dressed…"

The door opened. The red rose appeared first and then Ellis. "Hi Julia." He stood smiling as though not quite sure of a warm welcome. But that was a sham, Julia thought. He knows it's all systems go.

Her feelings were a queer mixture of elation and annoyance. "I'm not up yet."

Ellis took Peter's place by the bed as Peter departed with a thumbs up, and a cheeky grin.

"I don't mind." His eyes had an intense expression and he kissed her lightly on the mouth.

Julia took the rose. "Thank you." She looked at Ellis over the top of it. She was no longer annoyed. "I have to go to the bathroom."

He sat on the bed. "I'll wait."

When she came out, she was glad she was wearing her old orange 'ELLE' vest which was long and looked like a dress. She got back into the bed, smoothed the sheet, and then because she couldn't help it, turned to him for a healing kiss.

The kiss was rather like their first kisses in his trailer, sweet and electrifying.

"What do we do now Ellis?"

"We don't have to do anything, except stay together."

"Is it as simple as that, really?"

"Why not? I've worked through the bad times. I've tried to get over you, but it was impossible. I love you. I love you Julia. Nothing else matters."

His kisses were no longer sweet, but demanding and she responded. He stopped suddenly, and lay back recovering his breath. "I don't like this room. I'm going to knock down all the walls and nothing but nothing is going to be painted blue."

She laughed gently. "Exorcise the demons." She ran her hand over his shirt buttons.

"So, we fly out tonight to Hawaii." Ellis disentangled himself and stood up.

She wailed. "But I'm already jet-lagged."

"Well, it doesn't matter. You can stay in bed when we get there." The old teasing look was back in his eyes again.

"I don't know whether I'm ready... whether we should... start a serious sexual relationship again until we have matters straight between us."

"Give me a break! You were ready just now."

"That would have been just a fling."

Julia laughed at Ellis' stupefied face.

"I don't understand." Then he sat down again. "OK," he said slowly. "I'll make a start at getting things straight between us. I'm sorry about the mix-up. On the beach. Thinking that I was going to be a father.

"I like kids. You know that. I was attracted to you from the beginning because…" He caressed her hair gently. "You often look kinda wild and unpolished. You looked like a girl who wouldn't mind having kids. Wouldn't mind chipping your nails changing diapers. Wouldn't mind having a baby and all that it would mean to you physically, and to your career too, of course."

She listened to his apology knowing that she was grinning like an idiot. He was being so endearingly serious. But it was wonderful.

"I know," she said. "I've read about it. Men get broody. But I'm not sure about the part where I'm always looking a mess."

Ellis laughed. "That's not what I meant and you know it." His expression changed. "I love you."

"I'm sorry. I know you're being serious. I only get serious when I'm angry. But I think you are wonderful to try to explain your feelings honestly to me."

"I'm not so wonderful." He took her head in both of his hands so that she could not look away. "I wasn't so wonderful the last time we were in this bed."

"Oh that is forgotten."

"No it's not. You'll be getting yourself an insanely jealous, broody man, you know that Julia, don't you? A man who all but raped you. An actor who gets too immersed in his parts."

"It was consensual rape."

He did a double-take and dropped his hands. "There's no such thing."

"Yes, there is. Of course there is. I could rape you now. You would have to give in."

"OK, I'm giving up being serious now." He kissed her lightly on the lips. "We've made up?"

"We've made up."

Julia was feeling more refreshed and in control of her feelings when she met Ellis on the patio. Well, she was trying to be more in control, but she had that little skippetty-skip beat going on inside her which said 'I'm back with him'.

Ellis was sitting with Peter, drinking coffee. He turned and saw Julia's bags and smiled with relief.

Peter got up. "Well, I see that all is sweetness and light." He kissed Julia goodbye. "Good luck, princess."

"Gerald wished me luck too."

"Good for old Gerry."

Julia sat down feeling that a new life was beginning. "We have to talk."

"Oh no. You don't like to talk. I've accepted that."

Julia stared at him. "When did I ever not talk?" She paused. "Alright, you mean serious stuff. But you want to know if I would have got rid of our baby, if there had been a baby."

"Do I?"

"Well, I wouldn't have. Mostly because I would spend the rest of my life wondering what it would have been like."

"I believe you. That sounds like you."

"Even though you think that I'm not a very open and honest kind of person."

"I never thought that you were an outright liar Julia. And I'm OK with you not always telling me the serious stuff. Well I have to be OK since I can't live without you."

"I'm starting to get annoyed. I'm making an effort to tell you things. We can't just spend our time having sex and not talking."

"Sounds good to me."

Julia laughed. "Alright, I give in. We'll do the sex bit first. When I went to see the doctor in England, he said I should go on the pill, just to regulate my periods. He thought they had been upset by a change of country or… shock. So, you are happy with that then?"

"Judging by past experience, I think I will be more than happy with that." Ellis failed to keep his face straight any longer.

"Don't laugh, Ellis. This is serious stuff. I messed up the pregnancy test as well. I'd never done one before."

Ellis reached across the table for her hand. "I'm sorry. I never really gave enough thought to your shock on finding out that Barbara's stupid idea of bugging you had backfired so spectacularly."

"It was worse for you."

"And then you had to go all through the worry of being pregnant on your own."

"Well, I should have come to you... even though you were..."

"Being an absolute shit!" Ellis said bitterly.

"So now we agree that neither of us can do without the other and fly to Hawaii for two weeks of mad, passionate nooky."

"If nooky means sex, then yes. We both have two precious weeks before you film in London and I fly to Paris."

"Paris?"

"Yep, it's the nearest film deal I could get to you. And it's also something I want to do. It's a thriller about a hunt for Nazi gold."

"You're not going to be wearing a Nazi uniform are you?"

"Only as a disguise."

"I can live with that. But that's my mother talking."

They arrived at 'Hoonanea' at dawn. The unknown birds were singing and squawking. Julia had brought her binnies and was looking forward to finding out their names. Well, if she had any time left from kissing Ellis.

They walked up to the door, hand in hand, pulse to pulse. As if by magic, Mrs P suddenly appeared from the bushes. "Oh she remembers me," Julia crowed, as she stooped to stroke the cat's arched back.

They put down their cases in the musty smelling living room and kissed, not passionately, that was to come.

"It's good to be back." Ellis looked round.

"I was going to ask you about selling up. Not for a profit, but to some young, in love, Hawaiian couple."

"Are you nuts?"

"I thought you really didn't love me anymore."

"The last time we were here I was going crazy for you, especially when you wore that little black hat with the veil."

"I thought that was just the funeral. But why didn't you say?"

"I don't know. I just had to be sure that the bugging thing had been completely cleared up first."

"It was always much worse for you."

Now, the first time we came here, I think we started in the shower." Ellis began to take off his clothes.

"Oh, I need a drink and I'm doubly jet-lagged."

"Well, I need you in the shower."

"I need tea first. And I must feed Mrs P."

"Alright, but no chat. It's sex first and talking after. You don't know how I've longed for you."

"You had Erica and Carmella." Julia began to familiarise herself with the kitchen.

"I did not," Ellis shouted from the bedroom. He came into the kitchen and caught her round her back. He kissed her neck. "I did not."

"Was Erica ill when you had to go to Mexico to see her?" Julia was beginning to lose track of all the things she wanted to ask him, for his bare arms were caressing her.

Ellis sighed. He sat down and leaned his golden muscular arms on the table. Julia regretted the removal of them from her body and wished she hadn't asked about Erica.

"She had a lump. She thought she had breast cancer. I was once sort of in love with her but I didn't know what love really was until I met you." He took her hand and kissed it. "Sounds corny, but it's true."

"Anyway, I flew down to Mexico to see her. She had all the treatment done and everything was fine. Now, I know it's sacrilege to tear an English person away from their tea, but I am running out of patience."

"Poor Erica. I hope her Borg mesh survived."

"Her what? Well she's OK now. So hurry up. I'm running the shower any minute now." Ellis stood up and began kissing her neck.

"And you got Zack into rehab?"

His head was still bent over her neck. "If you don't hurry up I will carry you into the bedroom." The warmth and feel of his body was suddenly withdrawn, and she could hear the shower running.

Julia gave up on the tea. The kettle was taking far too long to boil and Mrs P was busy with the tinned fish.

Anyway, she desperately wanted Ellis close again.

Ellis was far too eager and sexually frustrated to control himself for very long. Julia took the precaution of removing her clothes before she was anywhere near the shower. Jumping in the shower with your clothes on was not something English people did. Their first two couplings were quick, once in the shower and once in the bed. Only then was he able to relax and apologise.

"Ah Julia, I am such a jerk." He was still lying over her with his face on her neck.

"What were you going to say to me at the airport when I left LA?"

"Shut up," Ellis groaned. He kissed her for a very long time.

"What were you going to say?" she whispered after a time.

"You didn't see me. Your boyfriend did. And well-meaning, but deadly, Barbara told you I wanted to speak to you. I was going to say that I would never ask you to marry me again." He lifted his head and kissed her on the nose. "But you would have to ask me."

"Does that still stand?"

"No. I'm going to keep asking you until you do."

"So you still loved me?"

"I'm beginning to feel that I have to keep answering your questions before you will fuck me again. I could just stop now, you know. I am tired."

"No, Ellis, that was just the hors d'oeuvres. No more questions, I promise."

"I could stop." He began to kiss her lightly on the face and breasts. He looked down at her. "But then again…"

Julia pulled him down to her and pressed herself to him. It was so nice, so very nice to have him back in her bed again. They began to make love. Julia's head had been so full of questions that she was not really fully aroused. There was something else right at the back of her mind. She stopped.

Ellis stopped. "What's the matter?"

"There's something else." Julia stroked her hand gently over his appendix scar. "Who's Penny?"

Ellis began to look quite cross. "She was a bitch. A dog. She saved my life, going back for help when I collapsed with my appendix in the woods. I was sixteen."

"There's no need to get cross."

"I'm sorry." Ellis threw himself onto his back.

Julia climbed on him. "I'm all done now. You were sixteen. I wish I'd known you when you were sixteen."

"I was… an…. arrogant brat." He ran his hands down her body. "Julia please, no more talking."

Julia trembled in response to him. It was so good to have him close to her again. So very close.